T0072567

ESSENTIAL
STORIES

V. S. PRITCHETT

ESSENTIAL

STORIES

Selected and with an
Introduction by Jeremy Treglown

THE MODERN LIBRARY

NEW YORK

LIBRARY OF CONGRESS CATALOGING-IN-PUBLICATION DATA
Pritchett, V. S. (Victor Sawdon)
[Short stories. Selections]
Essential stories / V. S. Pritchett; selected and with an introduction by Jeremy Treglown.
p. cm.
ISBN 978-0-8129-7294-8 (trade pbk.)
I. Treglown, Jeremy.   II. Title.

PR6031.R7A6 2005
823'.912—dc22   2004054682

Modern Library website address: www.modernlibrary.com

146028962

V. S. PRITCHETT

Victor Sawdon Pritchett, the extraordinarily prolific and versatile man of letters widely regarded as one of the greatest stylists in the English language, was born in Ipswich, Suffolk, on December 16, 1900. His father, whom he recalled in the enchanting memoir *A Cab at the Door* (1968), was a boundlessly optimistic but chronically unsuccessful businessman whose series of failed ventures necessitated frequent moves to elude creditors. These uprootings interrupted Pritchett's formal education, yet he was a voracious reader from an early age. Apprenticed in the London leather trade at fifteen, Pritchett alleviated the boredom of a menial clerical job by delving into the classics. At twenty he left for Paris, vowing to become a writer. He later reflected on his experiences there in *Midnight Oil* (1971), a second volume of autobiography that endures as an intimate and precise record of an artist's self-discovery.

Pritchett began his writing career as a contributor to *The Christian Science Monitor,* which, in addition to sending him on assignments in the United States and Canada, employed him as a foreign correspondent in civil-war Ireland and then Spain. *Marching Spain* (1928), his first book, recounts impressions of a country that held a lifelong fascination for Pritchett. His other travel writing includes *The Spanish Temper* (1954), *The Offensive Traveller* (1964; published in the U.K. as *Foreign Faces*), and *At Home and Abroad* (1989). In addition, he collaborated with photographer Evelyn Hofer on three acclaimed metropolitan profiles: *London Perceived* (1962), *New York Proclaimed* (1964), and *Dublin: A Portrait* (1967).

While continuing a part-time career as a roving journalist, Pritchett increasingly focused on writing fiction, living with his Anglo-Irish first wife in Dublin, and then in the bohemian London of the mid to late 1920s. *Clare Drummer* (1929), the first of his five novels, draws on his experiences in Ireland, while *Elopement into Exile* (1932; published in the U.K. as *Shirley Sanz*) again reflects his enthrallment with Spain. He also wrote *Nothing Like Leather* (1935), a compelling saga about the rise and fall of an English businessman, and *Dead Man Leading* (1937), an allegorical tale of a journey into darkness that is reminiscent of Conrad. Pritchett's best-known novel, *Mr. Beluncle* (1951), is a work of Dickensian scope featuring an endearing scoundrel-hero modeled after his own father.

Yet it is widely acknowledged that Pritchett's genius as a storyteller came to full fruition in the short fictions which he began to publish in his early twenties and continued to write up to his nineties. "Pritchett's literary achievement is enormous, but his short stories are his greatest triumph," said Paul Theroux. From *The Spanish Virgin and Other Stories* (1930) right up through *Complete Collected Stories* (1991), Pritchett published fourteen volumes filled with masterful tales that chronicle the lives of ordinary people through a flood of details and humorous, kindhearted observations. His other collections, all of them published during his long second marriage to Dorothy—a working partner as well as an adored wife—include: *You Make Your Own Life* (1938), *It May Never Happen* (1945), *The Sailor, Sense of Humor, and Other Stories* (1956), *When My Girl Comes Home* (1961), *The Key to My Heart* (1964), *Blind Love* (1970), *The Camberwell Beauty* (1974), *Selected Stories* (1978), *On the Edge of the Cliff* (1980), *Collected Stories* (1982), *More Collected Stories* (1983), and *A Careless Widow* (1989).

"We read Pritchett's stories, comic or tragic, with an elation that stems from their intensity," observed Eudora Welty. "Life goes on in them without flagging. The characters that fill them—erratic, unsure, unsafe, devious, stubborn, restless and desirous, absurd and passionate, all peculiar unto themselves—hold a claim on us that is not to be denied. They demand and get our rapt attention, for in their revelation of their lives, the secrets of our own lives come into view." And

Reynolds Price noted: "An extended view of his short fiction reveals a chameleonic power of invention, sympathy and selfless transformation that sends one back as far as Chekhov for a near-parallel."

The acclaim lavished on Pritchett for his short stories has been matched by that accorded his literary criticism. "Pritchett is not only our best short story writer but also our best literary critic," stated Anthony Burgess. *In My Good Books* (1942), *The Living Novel* (1946), *Books in General* (1953), and *The Working Novelist* (1965) contain essays written during his long association with the *New Statesman* and also, after the Second World War, *The New Yorker* and *The New York Times Book Review.* Pritchett continued his exploration of world literature in *George Meredith and English Comedy* (1970), *The Myth Makers* (1979), *The Tale Bearers* (1980), *A Man of Letters* (1985), and *Lasting Impressions* (1990). His magnum opus of literary criticism, *Complete Collected Essays*—which reflects, too, his central association with *The New York Review of Books,* from the journal's earliest days—was issued in 1992. In addition he produced three masterful works that artfully meld criticism with biography: *Balzac* (1974), *The Gentle Barbarian: The Life and Work of Turgenev* (1977), and *Chekhov: A Spirit Set Free* (1988).

"Pritchett is the supreme contemporary virtuoso of the short literature essay," said *The New York Times Book Review.* As Gore Vidal, who deemed him "our greatest English-language critic," put it: "At work on a text, Pritchett is rather like one of those amorphic sea-creatures who float from bright complicated shell to shell. Once at home within the shell he is able to describe for us in precise detail the secrets of the shell's interior; and he is able to show us, from the maker's own angle, the world the maker saw." "It would be very nice for literature," Vidal added, "if Sir Victor lived forever."

From the 1950s on, Pritchett was increasingly in demand as a distinguished visiting professor at American universities, from Princeton to Berkeley, Smith to Vanderbilt. But in spirit he always remained a freelance writer. "If, as they say, I am a Man of Letters I come, like my fellows, at the tail-end of a long and once esteemed tradition in English and American writing," Pritchett once said. "We have no captive audience. . . . We write to be readable and to engage the interest of what Virginia Woolf called 'the common reader.' We do not lay down the law, but we do make a stand for the reflective values of a humane culture. We care for the printed word in a world that nowadays is dominated by the camera and by scientific, technological, sociological doctrine. . . . I found myself less a critic than an imaginative traveller or explorer . . . I was travelling in literature."

Knighted in 1975 for his services to literature and made a Companion of Honour in 1993, Sir Victor Pritchett died in London on March 20, 1997. As novelist Margaret Drabble noted before his death: "Pritchett has lived as a man of letters must, by his pen, and he has done it with a freshness of interest and an infectious curiosity that have never waned."

CONTENTS

INTRODUCTION

Jeremy Treglown

V. S. Pritchett's stories leave you with unforgettable glimpses of movement: Charlie, in "The Two Brothers," running his hands over his
dog, "feeling the strange life ripple under the hair and obtaining a
curious strength from the tumult"; or the sailor in the story named
for him, on a wet day in a busy London street, "lifting his knees
high and putting his hand up . . . as if, crossing the road through that
stinging rain, he were breaking through the bead curtain of a Pernambuco bar." It's no accident that Pritchett's letters and notebooks were
filled with cartoons. These are intensely visual stories: verbal anima-
tions.

Then again, they leave you with haunting echoes of talk: Spanish
men arguing over where to sit in a restaurant, contradicting themselves and each other and forgetting to order their meal in an amiable
fury of anecdotes; or the aging parents in "The Lion's Den," nervously
competing for the attention of their visiting grown-up son:

> "Oh, there you are, that's it, dear," said the mother, timidly clawing her
> son out of the darkness of the doorway and kissing him. "You got here
> all right. . . . Have you had your tea? Have a cup of tea?"
> "Well, let's see the boy," said the father. "Come in here to the light."
> "I've had tea, thanks," Teddy said.

"Have another cup. It won't take a tick. I'll pop the kettle on . . ."

"Leave the boy alone, old dear," the father said. "He's had his tea. . . . Now—. . . . Would you like to wash your hands, old chap? . . ."

"Yes, go on," said the mother, "wash your hands. They did the water yesterday."

Pritchett grew up in a singing family, and his ear was alert to the idiosyncratic rhythms and theme tunes of his characters. Their clichés, too, which so often gave him his titles: "A Serious Question," "Just a Little More." These are intensely aural, and oral, fictions.

Another of their lasting traces is an indelible impression of the fantasy life of the most ordinary people. The mother in "When My Girl Comes Home" has convinced herself and her neighbors that her daughter has been interned in wartime in Japan, when in fact—that is, so far as there are any facts in this tale of self-deception and role-playing—the girl self-preservingly married a Japanese man. The bombastic father in "The Lion's Den" turns out to have a room full of aspirational possessions—riding boots (though "He's never ridden in his life"), redundant silverware—the props, theatrical as well as supportive, of his mythomania. Fictions of self, Pritchett knew, are among the defining activities of being human. In the phrase of the anecdotal barber which gives another story its title, "You make your own life." He partly means, you make it up. Among other things, these are stories about the importance of stories.

The visual, the aural, the fictive: all are anticipated in one of Pritchett's earliest published works, "The Sack of Lights." It appeared in the magazine *Outlook*, in 1928, when the author was twenty-seven, and again, a couple of years later, in his first collection, *The Spanish Virgin and Other Stories*. Yet in common with everything else in that book, he later suppressed it. Pritchett was among other things a great literary critic, but he was much less generous to his own work than to others'. Forgotten for three quarters of a century, "The Sack of Lights" poignantly encodes the artist himself in the character of a deluded and—except by the story—neglected vagrant Cockney woman, with her song of another world, "Valencia, land of oranges," her mysterious mission to "git me [get my] lights," and her mad yarn of rockets and a general:

No one else could hear what her mind heard. No one else could see what her eyes saw. Alight with it, she walked from her room at the back of Euston to Piccadilly Circus with a sack on her back—the sack which she always carried in case there was anything worth having in the gutters—and "Valencia, land of oranges . . ." twiddling like a ballroom of dancers in her head.

No one noticed her as she stood on the curb of Piccadilly Circus, nor guessed that at that moment she could have died of laughter, she was so happy. She wanted to shout to see what would happen, but she laughed instead. A miraculous place as high and polished as a ball-room. The façades of the buildings were tall mirrors framed in gold, speeding lights. "Chucking it about," she cried out. The crowds did not even hear her in the roar.

Pritchett had the tenderness for eccentricity that has characterized so many of the greatest English writers. In his daily walks through London, he watched and listened to people as a naturalist observes wild creatures and birds. He knew that oddity is the norm, not the exception. The man who likes to show off his stage fall, in the story ambiguously titled "The Fall," is based on an actual encounter of Pritchett's at a party. James Wood has argued that his attention to such "little billowings of pride and egotism" influenced Harold Pinter, William Trevor, Alice Munro, J. F. Powers.[1] Martin Amis, who worked with Pritchett on the *New Statesman* toward the end of his fifty-year association with the magazine, saw it as an investigative process, and also a profoundly egalitarian one. Pritchett "went into ordinary peo-ple," Amis said, "and showed us that they weren't ordinary. . . . [He] came away with their genius in all senses. . . . Almost frighteningly in-timate, he possesses his characters, he knows almost everything about them in a way that startles me when I look at him."[2] You have only to read "The Wheelbarrow" to see what he meant. Pritchett understands so much about the two people on whom he intensely focuses: the fact that in clearing out the house of her recently dead aunt, Miss Fresh-water's niece has to face something about losses in her own life; and that in employing an opportunistic Welsh taxi driver and part-time evangelist to help her, she is risking an intimacy all the more powerful for being temporary; and that the man's very Welshness involves a colonial element, and with it a resistance to colonization; and that if he has designs on his new employer, he has equally strong designs on her wheelbarrow ... the list could go on. By not straying too far, Pritchett's imagination goes very deep. He always worked exceptionally hard, writing draft after draft, distilling his material—sometimes initially of novelistic dimensions—until it combined astonishing density with superficial lightness. As Thoreau pointed out, a good story needn't be long, "but it will take a long while to make it short."[3]

Pritchett's habits of imaginative recording began in his childhood. Many of his stories fictionalize a "real" early experience. "The Lion's Den" is almost straight autobiography: Pritchett's own father was a fantasist like the one in the story, and the son returned to him often for fictional copy, most ambitiously in his 1951 novel, *Mr. Beluncle,* and later, with a more forgiving poignancy, in his cameo of a recent widower, "Just a Little More."

Pritchett Senior was a Christian Scientist. While the vagrant woman in "The Sack of Lights" embodies both the liberating irresponsibility of the imagination and its consoling privacy, in "The Saint" V. S. Pritchett takes a simultaneously sterner and funnier line on self-delusion through the character of Hubert Timberlake, the self-important leader of a fictional sect very like Christian Science. Mr. Timberlake's belief that he knows how to manage a punt has to contend with the empirical reality of a low branch:

... he put out a hand to lift it. It is not easy to lift a willow branch and Mr. Timberlake was surprised. He stepped back as it gently and firmly leaned against him. He leaned back and pushed from his feet. And he pushed too far. The boat went on, I saw Mr. Timberlake's boots leave the stern as he took an unthoughtful step backwards. He made a last minute grasp at a stronger and higher branch, and then, there he hung....

... I prayed with all my will that Mr. Timberlake would not walk upon the water. It was my prayer ... that was answered.

I saw the shoes dip, the water rise above his ankles and up his socks. He tried to move his grip now to a yet higher branch—he did not succeed—and in making this effort his coat and waistcoat rose and parted from his trousers. One seam of shirt with its pant-loops and brace-tabs broke like a crack across the middle of Mr. Timberlake. It was like a fatal flaw in a statue....

The comedy is partly a matter of observation, and partly, too, of sheer clowning: a bumptious man is separated from his trousers and gets drenched. But it's also verbal: that "unthoughtful" step backward is perfectly judged, as is the parenthetical "he did not succeed"—one of those comic moments that depend precisely on being superfluous. As a musician of language, Pritchett had perfect pitch. Another of his editors, *The New Yorker*'s Roger Angell, was to exclaim, "he could *write*. Again and again, he is capable of the acute perception, the absolutely convincing illumination of thought, that can transform the eye's journey down the page into a sensual and startling experience."[4]

You can't, in fact, say much about writing as good as this without quoting, and as soon as you start it's hard to stop: What about the next sentence? the whole paragraph? Why not the whole story? Pritchett's friend Eudora Welty wrote with an insider's knowledge about the flaring self-completeness of each of his works: "any Pritchett story is all of it alight. . . . Wasteless and at the same time well fed, it shoots up in flame from its own spark like a poem or a magic trick . . . with nothing left over."[5] (The comparison with a poem is one Pritchett himself often made. The story writer's art, he said, "calls for a mingling of the skills of the rapid reporter or traveller with an eye for incident and an ear for real speech, the instincts of the poet and the ballad-maker, and the sonnet writer's concealed discipline of form."[6]) So, in "Sense of Humour," every detail, however accidental-seeming, has its place. One of the main characters, Muriel, tells her new boyfriend, Arthur, that her father used to work "on the railway." The glib Arthur responds with a music-hall couplet: "The engine gave a squeal. . . . The driver took out his pocket-knife and scraped him off the wheel." We half remember that squeal when Arthur's obsessive rival in love, Colin, drives his red motorbike under a bus. The story's title itself runs throughout like something between a refrain and a commentary: an ironic one, because a sense of humor is something the main characters lack—in Colin's case, fatally. Stories like this don't end with the sharp click of an O. Henry tale, but—as Welty implies—with a quieter sense that everything has been made use of. The seemingly random pile of materials which is all most of us can make of what we find around us in life has, by Pritchett's conjuring, been turned into something beautifully coherent.

Given Welty's description, you might expect his work to feel like a set of closed systems, yet miraculously it doesn't. On the contrary, most of Pritchett's stories fit his own description of Maupassant's, which he contrasts with those of more "artificial" writers. By "artificial," Pritchett meant something you could test on the final page: "Do you, at the end of a story, feel that the lives of the people have ended with the drama of their situation? Do you feel that their lives were, in fact, not lives, but an idea?" He conceded that all short-story writers (including himself) produce some stories of this sort, because, "like the sonnet, the short story is liable to become a brilliant conceit." But more often than not, he argued, Maupassant's tales—like Pritchett's own—operate differently. As Pritchett puts it, "The characters go on living. They are beginning to live their way into a new situation."[7]

Edmund Wilson didn't get the hang of Pritchett's fictions when he first encountered them. (From 1949, they more often than not appeared first in *The New Yorker*.) "They don't have the kind of ending one expects . . . ," he wrote to his friend, in later self-extenuation: "the point is that in your masterly use of detail, you so exactly hit the nail on the head that the reader expects a more usual kind of point at the end, & I haven't always grasped that the final details, though they may seem . . . random . . . are equally significant in their accuracy."[8] Wilson might have been writing about "A Serious Question" but he wasn't, because this, like "The Sack of Lights," is among the early stories that Pritchett suppressed—though for a different reason. It is a delicate and loaded exploration of a failing, childless marriage: in essence, Pritchett's own first marriage, to which he hardly ever alluded once it was over. The bitter divorce came four years after "A Serious Question" was published in the *Fortnightly Review*. Robert Louis Stevenson famously prescribed that "The ideal story is that of two people who go into love step by step, with a fluttered consciousness, like a pair of children venturing together into a dark room."[9] Lost to readers since 1931, "A Serious Question" puts Stevenson's formula into tragic reverse.

There are other sadnesses among these fictions, very funny though they generally are, and despite Pritchett's rare knack (for example, in "The Evils of Spain") for communicating happiness. "The Two Brothers," with its powerful firsthand sense of the fate of early-twentieth-century Ireland—where, as in Spain, he worked as a reporter for *The*

Christian Science Monitor; or "The Upright Man," about a rigid-minded office clerk who is maimed in the First World War; or, much later, "On the Edge of the Cliff," partly based on the wayward last years of Pritchett's closest friend, the writer Gerald Brenan—they can make you cry. But such reactions are never simple. "Our Oldest Friend" is an anatomy of what it means to be rejected: the title, once again, turns out to be powerfully ironic. But, as the story unfolds, the narrator is revealed to have been partly complicit in the rejections of his friend, ever since the two men were at school together. By being made, first, to laugh at the victim, we find ourselves taking the side of his tormentors:

> "Look out!" someone said. "Here comes Saxon."
> It was too late. Moving off the dance floor and pausing at the door with the blatant long sight of the stalker, Saxon saw us all in our quiet corner of the lounge and came over. He stopped and stood with his hands on his hips and his legs apart, like a goalkeeper. Then he came forward.
> "Ah! This *is* nice!" he crowed, in the cockerel voice that took us back to the Oxford years. He pulled up a chair and placed it so that none of us could easily get out. . . .
> "How awfully nice." For niceness was everything for him. "Everyone is here," he said. . . .

From this comic start, the unfolding of something more serious forces the reader—more, if anything, than the narrator—into a self-examining kind of sympathy. One recalls Chekhov's requirements of short-story writing, as Pritchett listed them in an essay:[10]

1. absence of lengthy verbiage of political-social-economic nature.
2. total objectivity.
3. truthful descriptions of persons and objects.
4. extreme brevity.
5. audacity and originality: avoid the stereotype.
6. compassion.

Each of these qualities is found in V. S. Pritchett, but none more than the last.

JEREMY TREGLOWN is the author of *V. S. Pritchett: A Working Life*. A former editor of *The Times Literary Supplement*, he is professor of English at the University of Warwick and has recently been Margaret and Herman Sokol Fellow of the Cullman Center for Writers and Scholars at the New York Public Library. His previous books include *Roald Dahl: A Biography* and *Romancing: The Life and Work of Henry Green*, which won the Dictionary of Literary Biography Award. He lives in England.

NOTES

1. "An English Chekhov," *The Times Literary Supplement*, January 4, 2002.
2. *V.S.P.*, BBC Radio 3, December 14, 1997.
3. Henry David Thoreau, letter to Harrison Blake, November 16, 1857, published in Thoreau, *Correspondence*, ed. Walter Harding and Carl Bode, 1958.
4. *The New Yorker*, December 22–29, 1997.
5. "A Family of Emotions," *The New York Times Book Review*, June 25, 1978.
6. Introduction to *The Oxford Book of Short Stories*, 1981.
7. V. S. Pritchett, *Complete Collected Essays*, "Maupassant," p. 435.
8. Edmund Wilson, letter to VSP, March 17, 1970, published in Wilson, *Letters in Literature and Politics*, ed. Elena Wilson, 1977.
9. "On Falling in Love," in *Virginibus Puerisque*, 1881: *The Works of Robert Louis Stevenson*, Vailima Edition, 1922, vol. ii, p. 43.
10. *Complete Collected Essays*, "A Doctor," p. 793.

ESSENTIAL

STORIES

THE SACK OF LIGHTS

She was an old charwoman whose eyes stared like two bits of tin and whose lips were twisted like rope round three protruding teeth. All day long she was down on her knees scrubbing flights of stone stairs, cleaning out evil passages, emptying oozy pails down the drain with the soapsuds frilled about it, and listening to its dirty little voice gulping out of the street. All day long she chattered to herself and sang "Valencia, land of oranges . . ." and broke out into laughter so loud at some fantastic recollection that it sounded as though she had kicked her pail downstairs.

One evening, after a week's absence from her work, she said mysteriously, as she left the house, "I'm going to do it again. I'm going orf to git me lights."

"Lights?"

"Yes, 'e stopped me 'e did. 'Better practise it at 'ome,' 'e said. So I took the lot. I took the train, an' rockets, an' that wicked ol' General with the monercle, oh, I took 'im. I took 'em all 'ome. O, 'e warn't 'arf a wicked ol' dear." She laughed, and her teeth seemed to skip up and down like three acrobats with the rope lips twirling round them. "Yer know what 'e called me, the ol' monercle? 'Lor,' says 'e, peeping through the winder, 'ain't she a proper beauty!' That's what 'e called me. We didn't 'arf dance."

"Trains! Rockets? Generals? Dance?" The people of the house

touched their sound foreheads. "Gone, oh quite gone," said the people of the house. "Haven't you noticed, the last few days? Away a week and comes back singing and talking about dances and Generals worse than ever."

Before there was time to say any more she was off again down the road singing "Valencia, land of oranges . . ." and gutter children calling after her.

No one else could hear what her mind heard. No one else could see what her eyes saw. Alight with it, she walked from her room at the back of Euston to Piccadilly Circus with a sack on her back—the sack which she always carried in case there was anything worth having in the gutters—and "Valencia, land of oranges . . ." twiddling like a ball-room of dancers in her head.

No one noticed her as she stood on the curb of Piccadilly Circus, nor guessed that at that moment she could have died of laughter, she was so happy. She wanted to shout to see what would happen, but she laughed instead. A miraculous place as high and polished as a ball-room. The façades of the buildings were tall mirrors framed in gold, speeding lights. "Chucking it about," she cried out. The crowds did not even hear her in the roar. If she jumped, could she see herself in the mirrors? She jumped, but not high enough. She laughed. Rockets shot up in numbered showers and exploded noiselessly into brief diagrams of green stars. A tilted bottle dripped beads of wine as red as rail-way signals into a glass and there was the General—Smoke the Army Smoke—standing on a house-top, with a white-hot monocle in his eye, and his cigarette pricking red. Diamonds and pearls and rubies were streamers flying into the Circus and flashed so that people's faces bobbed up and down like Chinese lanterns.

But below the streaming lights everything was dancing. That was what she noticed. Below it was "Valencia, land of oranges . . ." She sang it out and waved to the cars as they passed. "Valencia . . ." The dark couples of taxis waltzed down dipping to the roll of the tune, and the big dowager cars slipped by, their jewelled bosoms beaming. The young sparking cars darted like dragon-flies—those were the ones she liked, the noisy, erratic ones. The perfume of the dance rose among them. Low horns breathed out flights of warning. The saxophone horns wailed, the jazz engines drummed—how her heart was dancing—and under all was the everlasting undertone, the deep 'cello vibration of the wheels. The 'cello, the voice of movement being born, the voice of the soul. That sound caught her by the waist like a lover. "Valencia . . ." She ran out into the traffic, not to cross the road, but to dance in it!

In a second she was carried away by the traffic, and it waltzed graciously, understandingly about her. She felt its rhythm. Dancing a grotesque step she let herself drift on a river of circling moody joy as though she were another Ophelia floating with flowers about her.

She was dancing in a land of oranges, and she saw women as beautiful as orchids gliding high beside her in their dowager saloons. She chased them as you chase butterflies, but she could not keep up with them. The chauffeurs were at their wits' ends, swerving to avoid her, as something too awful even to run over. Then as she gambolled the cars began to slow down; she saw the spaces narrowing, the floor of the Circus disappearing under thickening wheels. The traffic crowded, breathing and swearing about her. To her surprise she saw it had stopped. A policeman was coming for her. She wanted to throw her arms round his neck and kiss him, but he gripped one arm and led her away.

" 'Ere, Lizzy," he said. "You'd better practise it at home a bit before you try it on 'ere."

"Yer right. In course y'are," she shouted at him. "But I must get me lights. Can't do it without me lights." And with her free hand she held the sack open like a pail she was filling to wash down flights and flights of stairs with, but in poured the lights instead: all the signs and diagrams and patterns, the bottle that poured endless wine, the engine wheels that never stopped, all the jerks and clicks of brilliance. The last to go was the General, monocle and all.

"Garn, yer wicked ol' dear," she laughed, giving him a kick. The following crowd laughed to see her give the policeman one like that.

"Lor, it's ol' Bertha," voices shouted. "Drunk and disorderly, got it bad. Ya! Gor!"

She was in a cold cell, but she was far too excited to know that. As soon as they left her she carefully took her sack and shook it upside down. The warder was watching her through the grille. The tune began turning again in her head. "Valencia . . ." she jumped to her feet. Out of the sack the lights sprang like so many eels and serpents. The wine poured, the engine wheels whizzed, the yellow rockets broke upwards, and the General—he skipped out like a harlequin.

"Gawd! Ain't she a proper beauty!" said a voice from the grille of the cell.

"Lor, General!" she retorted. "I'm surprised at a man of your age." She danced up to him and tried to pull the monocle out of his eye. He dodged her. She danced up to him and away from him, leading him on while the lights rained their brilliance upon her. Big cars swayed by as she pirouetted, and there hummed in her ear the buzzing undertone of wheels, like the voice of a lover. She jumped sky high to see herself in the tall gilt mirrors that went up out of sight among the stars. She jumped, but not high enough. She laughed. The rockets clicked and spilled and glittered in tune like an orchestra playing. The railway engines running on catherine-wheels rushed on and on, into infinity. Words hopped off into space. The messages of the electric signs stepped away as daintily as a ballet into nothing.

A Serious Question

That night, when it was time to go to bed, James Harkaway kissed his wife, went to his room and she to hers which was next door, and there they lay like two children talking guiltily through the wall to each other. But talking like adults, long-married and never saying what they meant, keeping it all on the surface and only letting glints of real intent and buried brooding appear. You can lead a very tolerable life if you play at everything. Harkaway was irritated by this fact. The one thing he could not stand was playing, for he was a small, trim man with a wide patient chest, blue eyes that looked slightly upwards as if to penetrate what was a long way ahead, and a sandy moustache as neat as a little arithmetic. He did not wish to play. He did not wish to be a child, though he desired children as a bill desires its receipt. That was the trouble: he was, as it were, a payment going begging, a man with a fanciful desire to be suspected of passion, to be known for his dangerousness and to father progeny. His difficulty was his fatal unobtrusiveness, his resignation. Once a rent collector always a rent collector, he argued, once on the earth and of it always on the earth and of it. And this is where he and Mrs. Harkaway differed. She was not the kind of woman to commit herself or resign herself to anything; to regard herself as the vehicle of nature, the tool of a fate, or the wedded wife of James Harkaway. She would not admit it. This was the reason why they had no children and talked through the wall; why she was most affectionate when Harkaway kept on the other side of it. She was a perverse woman, small, young and dainty, with a voice like the playing of a musical box, and a will of iron.

The questions she had to ask when she got into bed! How agitated her head and her wide open eyes were, that lay quite still like indoor flowers in the dark. She stared at the ceiling wondering if there were any spiders on it. "Did you lock the back door?" she said. "Did you let the cat in? Did you leave me my matches? What was that? It must have been that mouse. Do you think it was really only him? What a noise those apples make when they fall off the trees. Why don't they gather those apples instead of letting them waste? Did you put the guard round the fire? Did you shut the gate?"

Ah, that was a *serious* question, thought Harkaway leaning on his elbow and looking out towards the window. Did he shut the gate? He was a man of habit and he always shut the gate, but this night had he or hadn't he? He strained his eyes and could see nothing but the hairy darkness of the trees and the brow of pale sky above the hedge.

And then a breeze of reckless greatness inspired him, who was rarely reckless and never great except on the day he proposed to Mrs. Harkaway, and then he was not thinking.

"Yes. I shut the gate," he called.

But in between their talk that white gate seemed every now and then to rush down the full length of the garden, wide-open and accusing into his mind.

Then Mrs. Harkaway's mind was easy and she laughed, given freedom by the dark. She mocked. She thought her warm bed was a boat that floated free of everything towards delightful dangers; and she laughed more to make it rock merrily on the ripples. And then she tried something sharper than laughter. Something more dangerous. But Harkaway's bed was a bed, nothing more, straight, still, and serious, and with brass knobs on the end of it. It was meant to be slept in, Harkaway perceived and prepared to sleep. Mrs. Harkaway had no notion of sleeping.

"I feel very talkative," she said.

"Well I don't," said Harkaway.

"You never do," said she.

There was no reply.

"Talk to me," she pleaded. "Say something to me."

"Oh dear," sighed Harkaway, "What shall I tell you?"

"Tell me what you think."

"Oh, my God!" thought Harkaway, as though his soul were slipping out of his body. Then aloud, "I don't think anything."

There was a long silence and Harkaway was nearly dozing when his wife began again: "Did you see Mrs. Feathers this morning?"

Harkaway grunted. He couldn't remember. What was the importance of Mrs. Feathers? Sleep was the most important thing. And "What did old Mr. Dukes say?"

"Oh nothing. Only about his dogs," grunted Harkaway.

"Lovely boys. I wish we had a dog," persisted Mrs. Harkaway. "And Mr. Radfield," she went on, "has he paid his rent yet?"

That touched John Harkaway on a serious matter. He opened his eyes.

"No," he said. "It's a bad look out for him. He hasn't."

"Poor man," she said.

"Poor man!" exclaimed Harkaway slightly annoyed. "I like that. He'll be poor if we sell him up." To call dogs "lovely boys," and an old scoundrel like Radfield "a poor man"!

"You're not going to do that?" exclaimed Mrs. Harkaway rebelliously. "He can't help it. It isn't a crime."

"I'm not so sure," returned Harkaway loftily, putting his chin over the top of the sheet. For, to a rent collector, it is a crime not to pay your rent. It is a blow at the roots of society. "I say I'm not so sure. It's stealing, when you think it out. It's taking what isn't yours."

"How can you say so," exclaimed Mrs. Harkaway, hot in the defence, for she knew that Harkaway rebuked her in a general way when rebuking others in a particular one.

"Supposing I took all my takings every month," he said derisively at the ceiling, but intending it for her.

"Well," she tossed out the word. "Suppose you did."

For lying in the dark with the wall between them and the door pleasantly open every mocking sentence was like a dip of the paddle which shot her boat wildly forward, more sharply every time into the mists and uncertainties of a quarrel which could, after all, be stopped in a moment.

"And land me in gaol and you in the workhouse," he said. "A fine lookout."

"Well," she said giving a final reckless push to the argument. "What of it? What about it? We're not like that poor Mrs. Radfield. We haven't any children."

That was the sore point and yet she played like this with it.

"No, thank God," said Harkaway with painful bitterness, but he did not mean that at all. At the word "children," his thoughts froze him and then his heart galloped like horses, his blood rushed back in a swirl as though his limbs were filled with the roll of drums, rousing him and waking him to pain. There was a fiery anvil in his breast. No children. This perversity and playfulness in his house, but no children! Why did he live adding little bits of charm and persuasiveness to his manners; "Good morning to you, Mrs. Feathers," and "A very good day to you, Mr. Radfield," only to have Radfield slamming the door in his face and others treating him like a licensed burglar. Was there nothing serious, understanding and purposeful in the world? Was he wasting the pride of his strength as he sang down the hills on his bicycle with his bowler hat over his eyes; and was there no reward for the sense of moral endeavour which filled him as he got off his machine and, with greater pride because it was difficult, pushed it slowly up the steeper hills? And all the time, when he knocked at a door, schooling himself to pretend that the last thing he had in him was a packet of virgin receipt forms.

Now Mrs. Harkaway knew she had said the word which ought not to have been said. She had said something real to him by accident, when the only way she could be happy with him was by inventing a fairyland of pretence. Their talk became painful, bitter, and spasmodic.

"I ought not to have married you," she said in a small high voice. She had often said that in the middle of the night, from the safety of her room and the darkness.

The ripe September cold came in at the window blowing the smell of fallen apples with it and the dampness of the fields. She sighed and he dramatically groaned. She sighed again and beat the sheets with wafts of desolation. He muttered aloud. In a moment they were playing at sighing and being unhappy, until at last startled by the distance to which they had mysteriously slipped, he said.

"What is it, dear?"

She would not answer.

"What is it darling? . . . Oh well, if you won't speak . . ."

He sighed miserably and she relenting said, "Darling."

This was his turn to enjoy silence.

"Oh dear, what has happened!" she said.

A devilish joy gurgled inside him where the bitterness had been. He unclenched his fists and smiled and stretched himself spaciously. Lord, but bicycling didn't half play up the calves of your legs! There was no way out of it. Once a rent collector always a rent collector. Once a husband always a husband. So on it went day after day, night after night, he yawned. World without end, he went on yawning. Now and ever shall be, he punched the pillow and sank from depth to depth into sleep.

But Mrs. Harkaway troubled by her pillow, wondering if she were going to be warm enough, if there were any spiders on the ceiling, sitting up to listen for the watch, wondering if that mouse was going to nibble at the wainscot again—in short, refusing to be resigned to anything and determined to do the opposite of all the sleeping people in the world, Mrs. Harkaway lay awake as long as she could. There were always noises; the apples falling off the trees, the creeper rustling, the chickens fluttering in the barn, the sound of the cat padding in the room. Now he was asleep, she thought, she could passionately love her husband. Tears were in her eyes.

She slept at last with a pretty, defiant heaviness and her head became alive with dreams that burned as clearly as the scenes of a lighted stage. One after another, hour after hour, through the night the caravans passed. She listened astonished to her secret thoughts. She heard herself say in fright "What's that noise?" Saw herself sit up in bed, saw herself see a man with hob-nailed boots on climb in at the window, and walk through the room; the tall, dark man whom you see when a fortune teller, noting you have no wedding ring, encourages your hopes. But he was a burglar. She heard herself scream. Harkaway said when she screamed: "It's only a burglar."

Wasn't it like him to be still and doing nothing! Then several men came in and she lay deathly still, stiffening gradually from the toes and keeping herself rigid and holding her breath. She lay so a long time until she woke up gasping as though she had put her head in a bucket of cold water. The eyes of sky between the branches of the trees were looking in at the window. It was morning already and there *were* noises. She was not dreaming. In the garden. Men walking in the garden. She screamed out:

"Darling, there are men in the garden. Quick."

Harkaway sat up in bed dazed. The elms were full and clear, and the sky under the branches was cold and white. The ragged hedge stood up like hair on end. He listened and also heard the sounds. Men in the garden! And then he saw a smooth and silvery shadow pass by the sill. He jumped out of bed, his heart pumping loudly.

"All right," he said, trembling, glad she was next door, the wild one. As he fumbled for his slippers he heard an unmistakable stamping of feet, a crunching, ripping noise, a heavy groping breathing as though some huge man were leaning and groaning against the house, and straining to push it over. There was an eerie snorting and hissing under the window. Some creature fantastic, malevolent and supernatural, was in the garden. And now he knew that stumbling, that snorting, puffing, tearing, crunching. The white gate, wide open and startling, seemed to whistle like a ghostly wind down the garden into his conscience; horses had got into the garden. Herds of horses trampling through the flower beds, kicking up his lawn.

"It's horses," he said, in consternation, for he was afraid of their jaws and legs, being a man for wheels, a bicycling man himself.

"In the garden," exclaimed his wife. There was a scuffle of clothes, and a thump like the fall of one of those apples as she jumped out of bed. She met him at the door in her night-dress, her hair was bushy and her eyes were wide open and eager to get to the battle.

"The naughty boys!" she cried, as he pulled the door open. "Look at them."

And with her behind him he picked up a twig and advanced upon them. He did not mind, he was indeed glad that she had called them boys.

In the cold air they stood, not a herd but three great farm horses, two roans and a grey, standing still and staring at him in his pyjamas. The creatures stopped like gawky louts who had been caught robbing an orchard. Sardonic in their nakedness, swishing their tails, and the smell of hide, manure and bruised grass steaming on them. While he had been sleeping they had been out all night, mysteriously arched, and munching through the darkness. The stars had shone upon them, the darkness coated them. Three grotesque gods, he thought they were, naked between wild mane and bearded fetlock, with fine feathery hair on their bellies; three gods sniffing raw morning at their nostrils, the rime of the morning on their backs, and amazed grins gone askew on their slobbering mouths.

Harkaway squared his shoulders and delivered them a final notice in his professional way.

"Go on. Get out of this. Gee up," he shouted. They lowered and stretched their long necks, so weirdly long, to the grass, and casually, prosaically ate their way through the clover to the gate, turning to eye him as they went. He watched their great casual gait with awe as they swaggered through his Michaelmas daisies, snapped his sunflowers, slithered against the flints in his rows of potatoes, and shot up their shining hooves as they sprang, amid a shower of dew, through the bushes. He advanced upon them at a discreet distance, with dignity.

"Go along, you naughty boys. I will tell your master. They know they've done wrong," cried Mrs. Harkaway. Harkaway emboldened, shouted louder:

"Get out of my garden. Gee up. Go on now!" And two of them trotted out with a ringing clatter. But the third, the grey, took fright and plunged at the wire in panic, wheeling round at every gap and throwing himself against it, broke into a brief clumsy gallop to the end of the garden, almost as far as the house, and then up again. Harkaway kept clear.

"Don't frighten him," commanded Mrs. Harkaway. How great Harkaway felt at the idea of his frightening anything. Down went the grey again and, at last, with an unearthly neigh as though he were laughing at Harkaway, he broke through the sunflowers, slithered on the gravel and went blindly at the gate, not stopping until he was on the road with the others, who were taking bites at the hedge in impudent farewell. At the grey's arrival they swung their heads, neighed, and broke into a jog trot down the road with a confused gobbling of hooves.

"Well I'll be danged!" said Harkaway and turned to look at his wife, grateful for the excitement. The air was like a cold pond put in a swirl. It reeked of the animals, the smell of leaves and of grass from which the dew had been dashed. His ankles and shoes were soaked and his pyjamas' legs were wet, too. She, fey and war-like, was waving her twig.

The dashing gods had gone. And now, as the ring of the hooves on the road grew fainter, Mr. and Mrs. Harkaway stood alone on top of the silence which spread like a dew on the earth. The broad aspect of the country was weird with melting capes of mist. The new day shapes were not yet born and as yet there was an unearthly configuration on the land. The hills and their woods had capsized and disintegrated and in the valleys below the Harkaway's cottage the lower vapours poured into milky lagoons that smoked and foamed, and the higher ones grew out of the earth in melting smoke through which the woods could be seen fragmentarily in violet immaterial palisades. Appearing above the highest branches of the mist, like a gaudy parrot in a forest, was the glow of the unseen sun. Harkaway in his pyjamas and his wife in her night-dress seemed to be the only living and breathing creatures in the world, for there was no sound, not even singing, and they stood in awe like two travellers who in a dream had come upon the beginning of a world before anyone was born in it and unshaped spirits kneeled in the final vigils of their ritual, entranced. Harkaway, feeling his moustache, thought in his professional way of all the people he would call upon after the sun had long risen that day. They were all asleep. Even Radfield in his farm that was sunk in mist—asleep, and their houses dead. He thought, supposing they were not there. Supposing there were nothing. No more rents to collect. He marvelled. If at any time in his life he had felt magnified and immortal it was at that moment. Jupiter, the great progenitor. He thought he shone like the god upon his wife with sudden love.

She laughed at him.

"You have a spider web in your hair," she said. But that did not dash him. He flung the mockery aside and suddenly picked her up in his arms and ran stumbling into the house. He laid her down upon her bed, with all the morning winding in his blood and his heart beating like the hooves of the horses. He was like them, godlike and great and ruinous, a communicant with darkness and mystery. But as she lay there quickly curled up like a feather, looking at him with a kind of fear, he suddenly became timid, tender, pitiful, apologetic. Alas! he sneezed and the god vanished.

"You will catch cold," she said, "if you stand there."

And at this, misery stamped out his fire and almost with tears of desolation he kissed her and went to his own room and the tepidity of his bed. She called to him through the wall:

"You did leave the gate open. That is how they got in, the cheeky boys."

That serious question of the open gate came rushing into his mind to add to his perplexities. When he was calm the daylight became cold and golden and the new sun was born. The vigilant hills had got their day but, his children, they had vanished.

SENSE OF HUMOUR

It started one Saturday. I was working new ground and I decided I'd stay at the hotel the weekend and put in an appearance at church.

"All alone?" asked the girl in the cash desk.

It had been raining since ten o'clock.

"Mr. Good has gone," she said. "And Mr. Straker. He usually stays with us. But he's gone."

"That's where they make their mistake," I said. "They think they know everything because they've been on the road all their lives."

"You're a stranger here, aren't you?" she said.

"I am," I said. "And so are you."

"How do you know that?"

"Obvious," I said. "Way you speak."

"Let's have a light," she said.

"So's I can see you," I said.

That was how it started. The rain was pouring down on to the glass roof of the office.

She'd a cup of tea steaming on the register. I said I'd have one, too. What's it going to be and I'll tell them, she said, but I said just a cup of tea.

"I'm TT," I said. "Too many soakers on the road as it is."

I was staying there the weekend so as to be sharp on the job on Monday morning. What's more it pays in these small towns to turn up at church on Sundays, Presbyterians in the morning, Methodists in the evening. Say "Good morning" and "Good evening" to them. "Ah!" they say. "Church-goer! Pleased to see that! TT, too." Makes them have a second look at your lines in the morning. "Did you like our service, Mister—er—er?" "Humphrey's my name." "Mr. Humphrey." See? It pays.

"Come into the office, Mr. Humphrey," she said, bringing me a cup. "Listen to that rain."

I went inside.

"Sugar?" she said.

"Three," I said. We settled to a very pleasant chat. She told me all about herself, and we got on next to families.

"My father was on the railway," she said.

" 'The engine gave a squeal,' " I said. " 'The driver took out his pocket-knife and scraped him off the wheel.' "

"That's it," she said. "And what is your father's business? You said he had a business."

"Undertaker," I said.

"Undertaker?" she said.

"Why not?" I said. "Good business. Seasonable like everything else. High class undertaker," I said.

She was looking at me all the time wondering what to say and suddenly she went into fits of laughter.

"Undertaker," she said, covering her face with her hands and went on laughing.

"Here," I said. "What's up?"

"Undertaker!" she laughed and laughed. Struck me as being a pretty thin joke.

"Don't mind me," she said. "I'm Irish."

"Oh, I see," I said. "That's it, is it? Got a sense of humour."

Then the bell rang and a woman called out "Muriel! Muriel!" and there was a motor bike making a row at the front door.

"All right," the girl called out. "Excuse me a moment, Mr. Humphrey," she said. "Don't think me rude. That's my boy friend. He wants the bird turning up like this."

She went out but there was her boy friend looking over the window ledge into the office. He had come in. He had a cape on, soaked with rain and the rain was in beads in his hair. It was fair hair. It stood up on end. He'd been economising on the brilliantine. He didn't wear a hat. He gave me a look and I gave him a look. I didn't like the look of him. And he didn't like the look of me. A smell of oil and petrol and rain and mackintosh came off him. He had a big mouth with thick lips. They were very red. I recognised him at once as the son of the man who ran the Kounty Garage. I saw this chap when I put my car away. The firm's car. A lock-up, because of the samples. Took me ten minutes to ram the idea into his head. He looked as though he'd never heard of samples. Slow,—you know the way they are in the provinces. Slow on the job.

"Oh Colin," says she. "What do you want?"

"Nothing," the chap said. "I came in to see you."

"To see me?"

"Just to see you."

"You came in this morning."

"That's right," he said. He went red. "You was busy," he said.

"Well, I'm busy now," she said.

He bit his tongue, and licked his big lips over and took a look at me. Then he started grinning.

"I got the new bike, Muriel," he said. "I've got it outside."

"It's just come down from the works," he said.

"The laddie wants you to look at his bike," I said. So she went out and had a look at it.

When she came back she had got rid of him.

"Listen to that rain," she said.

"Lord, I'm fed up with this line," she said.

"What line?" I said. "The hotel line?"

"Yes," she said. "I'm fed right up to the back teeth with it."

"And you've got good teeth," I said.

"There's not the class of person there used to be in it," she said. "All our family have got good teeth."

"Not the class?"

"I've been in it five years and there's not the same class at all. You never meet any fellows."

"Well," said I. "If they're like that half-wit at the garage, they're nothing to be stuck on. And you've met me."

I said it to her like that.

"Oh," says she. "It isn't as bad as that yet."

It was cold in the office. She used to sit all day in her overcoat. She was a smart girl with a big friendly chin and a second one coming and her forehead and nose were covered with freckles. She had copper-coloured hair too. She got her shoes through the trade from Duke's traveller and her clothes, too, off the Hollenborough mantle man. I told her I could do her better stockings than the ones she'd got on. She got a good reduction on everything. Twenty-five or thirty-three and a third. She had her expenses cut right back. I took her to the pictures that night in the car. I made Colin get the car out for me.

"That boy wanted me to go on the back of his bike. On a night like this," she said.

"Oh," she said, when we got to the pictures. "Two shillings's too much. Let's go into the one-and-sixes at the side and we can nip across into the two-shillings when the lights go down."

"Fancy your father being an undertaker," she said in the middle of the show. And she started laughing as she had laughed before.

She had her head screwed on all right. She said:

"Some girls have no pride once the lights go down."

Every time I went to that town I took a box of something. Samples, mostly, they didn't cost me anything.

"Don't thank me," I said. "Thank the firm."

Every time I took her out I pulled the blinds in the back seat of the car to hide the samples. That chap Colin used to give us oil and petrol. He used to give me a funny look. Fishy sort of small eyes he'd got. Always looking miserable. Then we would go off. Sunday was her free day. Not that driving's any holiday for me. And, of course, the firm paid. She used to take me down to see her family for the day. Start in the morning, and taking it you had dinner and tea there, a day's outing cost us nothing. Her father was something on the railway, retired. He had a long stocking, somewhere, but her sister, the one that was married, had had her share already.

He had a tumour after his wife died and they just played upon the old man's feelings. It wasn't right. She wouldn't go near her sister and I don't blame her, taking the money like that. Just played upon the old man's feelings.

Every time I was up there Colin used to come in looking for her.

"Oh Colin," I used to say. "Done my car yet?" He knew where he got off with me.

"No, now, I can't Colin. I tell you I'm going out with Mr. Humphrey," she used to say to him. I heard her.

"He keeps on badgering me," she said to me.

"You leave him to me," I said.

"No, he's all right," she said.

"You let me know if there's any trouble with Colin," I said. "Seems to be a harum-scarum sort of half-wit to me," I said.

"And he spends every penny he makes," she said.

Well, we know that sort of thing is all right while it lasts, I told her, but the trouble is that it doesn't last.

We were always meeting Colin on the road. I took no notice of it first of all and then I grew suspicious and awkward at always meeting him. He had a new motor bicycle. It was an Indian, a scarlet thing that he used to fly over the moor with, flat out. Muriel and I used to go out over the moor to Ingley Wood in the firm's Morris—I had a customer out that way.

"May as well do a bit of business while you're about it," I said.

"About what?" she said.

"Ah ha!" I said.

"That's what Colin wants to know," I said.

Sure enough, coming back we'd hear him popping and backfiring close behind us, and I put out my hand to stop him and keep him following us, biting our dirt.

"I see his little game," I said. "Following us."

So I saw to it that he did follow. We could hear him banging away behind us and the traffic is thick on the Ingley road in the afternoon.

"Oh let him pass," Muriel said. "I can't stand those dirty things banging in my ears."

I waved him on and past he flew with his scarf flying out, blazing red into the traffic. "We're doing 58 ourselves," she said, leaning across to look.

"Powerful buses those," I said. "Any fool can do it if he's got the power. Watch me step on it."

But we did not catch Colin. Half an hour later he passed us coming back. Cut right in between us and a lorry—I had to brake hard. I damn nearly killed him. His ears were red with the wind. He didn't wear a hat. I got after him as soon as I could but I couldn't touch him.

Nearly every weekend I was in that town seeing my girl, that fellow was hanging around. He came into the bar on Saturday nights, he poked his head into the office on Sunday mornings. It was a sure bet that if we went out in the car he would pass us on the road. Every time we would hear that scarlet thing roar by like a horse-stinger. It didn't matter where we were. He passed us on the main road, he met us down the side roads. There was a little cliff under oak trees at May Ponds, she said, where the view was pretty. And there, soon after we got there, was Colin on the other side of the water, watching us. Once we found him sitting on his bike, just as though he were waiting for us.

"You been here in a car?" I said.

"No, motor bike," she said and blushed. "Cars can't follow in these tracks."

She knew a lot of places in that country. Some of the roads weren't roads at all and were bad for tyres and I didn't want the firm's car scratched by bushes, but you would have thought Colin could read what was in her mind. For nine times out of ten he was there. It got on my nerves. It was a red, roaring, powerful thing and he opened it full out.

"I'm going to speak to Colin," I said. "I won't have him annoying you."

"He's not annoying me," she said. "I've got a sense of humour."

"Here Colin," I said one evening when I put the car away. "What's the idea?"

He was taking off his overalls. He pretended he did not know what I was talking about. He had a way of rolling his eyeballs, as if they had got wet and loose in his head, while he was speaking to me and you never knew if it was sweat or oil on his face. It was always pale with high colour on his cheeks and very red lips.

"Miss MacFarlane doesn't like being followed," I said.

He dropped his jaw and gaped at me. I could not tell whether he was being very surprised or very sly. I used to call him "Marbles" because when he spoke he seemed to have a lot of marbles in his mouth.

Then he said he never went to the places we went to, except by accident. He wasn't following us, he said, but we were following him. We never let him alone, he said. Everywhere he went, he said, we were there. Take last Saturday, he said, we were following him for miles down the by-pass, he said. But you passed us first and then sat down in front, I said. I went to Ingley Wood, he said. And you followed me there. No, we didn't, I said, Miss MacFarlane decided to go there.

He said he did not want to complain but fair was fair. I suppose you know, he said, that you have taken my girl off me. Well, you can leave *me* alone, can't you?

"Here," I said. "One minute! Not so fast! You said I've taken Miss MacFarlane from you. Well, she was never your girl. She only knew you in a friendly way."

"She was my girl," was all he said.

He was pouring oil into my engine. He had some cotton wool in one hand and the can in the other. He wiped up the green oil that had overflowed, screwed on the cap, pulled down the bonnet and whistled to himself.

I went back to Muriel and told her what Colin had said.

"I don't like trouble," I said.

"Don't you worry," she said. "I had to have someone to go to all these places with before you came. Couldn't stick in here all day Sunday."

"Ah," I said. "That's it, is it? You've been to all these places with him?"

"Yes," she said. "And he keeps on going to them. He's sloppy about me."

"Good God," I said. "Sentimental memories."

I felt sorry for that fellow. He knew it was hopeless, but he loved her. I suppose he couldn't help himself. Well, it takes all sorts to make a world, as my old mother used to say. If we were all alike it wouldn't do. Some men can't save money. It just runs through their fingers. He couldn't save money so he lost her. I suppose all he thought of was love.

I could have been friends with that fellow. As it was I put a lot of business his way. I didn't want him to get the wrong idea about me. We're all human after all.

We didn't have any more trouble with Colin after this until Bank Holiday. I was going to take her down to see my family. The old man's getting a bit past it now and has given up living over the shop. He's living out on the Barnum Road, beyond the tram stop. We were going down in the firm's car, as per usual, but something went wrong with the mag. and Colin had not got it right for the holiday. I was wild about this. What's the use of a garage who can't do a rush job for the holidays! What's the use of being an old customer if they're going to let you down! I went for Colin bald-headed.

"You knew I wanted it," I said. "It's no use trying to put me off with a tale about the stuff not coming down from the works. I've heard that one before."

I told him he'd got to let me have another car, because he'd let me down. I told him I wouldn't pay his account. I said I'd take my business away from him. But there wasn't a car to be had in the town because of the holiday. I could have knocked the fellow down. After the way I'd sent business to him.

Then I saw through his little game. He knew Muriel and I were going to my people and he had done this to stop it. The moment I saw this I let him know that it would take more than him to stop me doing what I wanted.

I said:

"Right. I shall take the amount of Miss MacFarlane's train fare and my own from the account at the end of the month."

I said:

"You may run a garage, but you don't run the railway service."

I was damned angry going by train. I felt quite lost on the rail-way after having a car. It was crowded with trippers too. It was slow—stopping at all the stations. The people come in, they tread all over your feet, they make you squeeze up till you're crammed against the window, and the women stick out their elbows and fidget. And then the expense! A return for two runs you into just over a couple of quid. I could have murdered Colin.

We got there at last. We walked up from the tram stop. Mother was at the window and let us in.

"This is Miss MacFarlane," I said.

And mother said:

"Oh, pleased to meet you. We've heard a lot about you."

"Oh," mother said to me, giving me a kiss, "Are you tired? You haven't had your tea, have you? Sit down. Have this chair, dear. It's more comfortable."

"Well, my boy," my father said.

"Want a wash?" my father said. "We've got a wash basin downstairs," he said. "I used not to mind about washing upstairs before. Now I couldn't do without it. Funny how your ideas change as you get older."

"How's business?" he said.

"Mustn't grumble," I said. "How's yours?"

"You knew," he said, "we took off the horses: except for one or two of the older families we have got motors now."

But he'd told me that the last time I was there. I'd been at him for years about motor hearses.

"You've forgotten I used to drive them," I said.

"Bless me, so you did," he said.

He took me up to my room. He showed me everything he had done to the house. "Your mother likes it," he said. "The traffic's company for her. You know what your mother is for company."

Then he gives me a funny look.

"Who's the girl?" he says.

My mother came in then and said:

"She's pretty, Arthur."

"Of course she's pretty," I said. "She's Irish."

"Oh," said the old man. "Irish! Got a sense of humour, eh?"

"She wouldn't be marrying me if she hadn't," I said. And then I gave *them* a look.

"Marrying her, did you say?" exclaimed my father.

"Any objection?" I said.

"Now Ernest dear," said my mother. "Leave the boy alone. Come down while I pop the kettle on."

She was terribly excited.

"Miss MacFarlane," the old man said.

"No sugar, thank you, Mrs. Humphrey. I beg your pardon, Mr. Humphrey?"

"The Glen Hotel at Swansea, I don't suppose you know that?" my father said.

"I wondered if you did being in the catering line," he said.

"It doesn't follow she knows every hotel," my mother said.

"Forty years ago," the old man said. "I was staying at the Glen in Swansea and the head waiter . . ."

"Oh no, not that one. I'm sure Miss MacFarlane doesn't want to hear that one," my mother said.

"How's business with you, Mr. Humphrey?" said Muriel. "We passed a large cemetery near the station."

"Dad's Ledger," I said.

"The whole business has changed so that you wouldn't know it, in my lifetime," said my father. "Silver fittings have gone clean out. Everyone wants simplicity nowadays. Restraint. Dignity," my father said.

"Prices did it," my father said.

"The war," he said.

"You couldn't get the wood," he said.

"Take ordinary mahogany, just an ordinary piece of mahogany. Or teak," he said. "Take teak. Or walnut."

"You can certainly see the world go by in this room," I said to my mother.

"It never stops," she said.

Now it was all bicycles over the new concrete road from the gun factory. Then traction engines and cars. They came up over the hill where the AA man stands and choked up round the tram stop. It was mostly holiday traffic. Everything with a wheel on it was out.

"On this stretch," my father told me, "they get three accidents a week." There was an ambulance station at the crossroads.

We had hardly finished talking about this, in fact the old man was still saying that something ought to be done when the telephone rang.

"Name of MacFarlane?" the voice said on the wire.

"No. Humphrey," my father said. "There is a Miss MacFarlane here."

"There's a man named Colin Mitchell lying seriously injured in an accident at the Cottage Hospital, gave me the name of MacFarlane as his nearest relative."

That was the Police. On to it at once. That fellow Colin had followed us down by road.

Cry, I never heard a girl cry, as Muriel cried, when we came back from the hospital. He had died in the ambulance. Cutting in, the old game he used to play on me. Clean off the saddle and under the Birmingham bus. The blood was everywhere, they said. People were still looking at it when we went by. Head on. What a mess! Don't let's talk about it.

She wanted to see him but they said "No." There wasn't anything recognisable to see. She put her arms round my neck and cried, "Colin. Colin," as if I were Colin and clung to me. I was feeling sick myself. I held her tight and I kissed her and I thought "Holiday ruined."

"Damn fool man," I thought. "Poor devil," I thought.

"I knew he'd do something like this."

"There, there," I said to her. "Don't think about Colin."

Didn't she love me, I said, and not Colin. Hadn't she got me? She said, yes, she had. And she loved me. But, "Oh Colin! Oh Colin!" she cried. "And Colin's mother," she cried. "Oh it's terrible." She cried and cried.

We put her to bed and I sat with her and my mother kept coming in.

"Leave her to me," I said. "I understand her." Before they went to bed they both came in and looked at her. She lay sobbing with her head in the pillow.

I could quite understand her being upset. Colin was a decent fellow. He was always doing things for her. He mended her electric lamp and he riveted the stem of a wine glass so that you couldn't see the break. He used to make things for her. He was very good with his hands.

She lay on her side with her face burning and feverish with misery and crying, scalded by the salt, and her lips shrivelled up. I put my arm under her neck and I stroked her forehead. She groaned. Sometimes she shivered and sometimes she clung to me, crying, "Oh Colin! Colin!"

My arm ached with the cramp and I had a crick in my back, sitting in the awkward way I was on the bed. It was late. There was nothing to do but to ache and sit watching her and thinking. It is funny the way your mind drifts. When I was kissing her and watching her I was thinking out who I'd show our new Autumn range to first. Her hand held my wrist tight and when I kissed her I got her tears on my lips. They burned and stung. Her neck and shoulders were soft and I could feel her breath hot out of her nostrils on the back of my hand. Ever noticed how hot a woman's breath gets when she's crying? I drew out my hand and lay down beside her and "Oh, Colin, Colin," she sobbed, turning over and clinging to me. And so I lay there, listening to the traffic, staring at the ceiling and shivering whenever the picture of Colin shooting right off that damned red thing into the bus came into my mind—until I did not hear the traffic any more, or see the ceiling any more, or think any more, but a change happened—I don't know when.

This Colin thing seemed to have knocked the bottom out of everything and I had a funny feeling we were going down and down and down in a lift. And the further we went the hotter and softer she got. Perhaps it was when I found with my hands that she had very big breasts. But it was like being on the mail steamer and feeling engines start under your feet, thumping louder and louder. You can feel it in every vein of your body. Her mouth opened and her tears dried. Her breath came through her open mouth and her voice was blind and husky. Colin, Colin, Colin, she said, and her fingers were hooked into me. I got out and turned the key in the door.

In the morning I left her sleeping. It did not matter to me what my father might have heard in the night, but still I wondered. She would hardly let me touch her before that. I told her I was sorry but she shut me up. I was afraid of her. I was afraid of mentioning Colin. I wanted to go out of the house there and then and tell someone everything. Did she love Colin all the time? Did she think I was Colin? And every time I thought of that poor devil covered over with a white sheet in the hospital mortuary, a kind of picture of her and me under the sheets with love came into my mind. I couldn't separate the two things. Just as though it had all come from Colin.

I'd rather not talk any more about that. I never talked to Muriel about it. I waited for her to say something but she didn't. She didn't say a word.

The next day was a bad day. It was grey and hot and the air smelled of oil fumes from the road. There's always a mess to clear up when things like this happen. I had to see to it. I had the job of ringing up the boy's mother. But I got round that, thank God, by ringing up the garage and getting them to go round and see the old lady. My father is useless when things are like this. I was the whole morning on the phone: to the hospital, the police, the coroner—and he stood fussing beside me, jerking up and down like a fat india-rubber ball. I found my mother washing up at the sink and she said:

"That poor boy's mother! I can't stop thinking of her." Then my father comes in and says,—just as though I was a customer—

"Of course if Mrs. Mitchell desires it we can have the remains of the deceased conveyed to his house by one of our new specially sprung motor hearses and can, if necessary, make all the funeral arrangements."

I could have hit him because Muriel came into the room when he was saying this. But she stood there as if nothing had happened.

"It's the least we can do for poor Mrs. Mitchell," she said. There were small creases of shadow under her eyes which shone with a soft strong light I had never seen before. She walked as if she were really still in that room with me, asleep. God, I loved that girl! God, I wanted to get all this over, this damned Colin business that had come right into the middle of everything like this, and I wanted to get married right away. I wanted to be alone with her. That's what Colin did for me.

"Yes," I said. "We must do the right thing by Colin."

"We are sometimes asked for long-distance estimates," my father said.

"It will be a little something," my mother said.

"Dad and I will talk it over," I said.

"Come into the office," my father said. "It occurred to me that it would be nice to do the right thing by this friend of yours."

We talked it over. We went into the cost of it. There was the return journey to reckon. We worked it out that it would come no dearer to old Mrs. Mitchell than if she took the train and buried the boy here. That is to say, my father said, if I drove it.

"It would look nice," my father said.

"Saves money and it would look a bit friendly," my father said. "You've done it before."

"Well," I said. "I suppose I can get a refund on my return ticket from the railway."

But it was not as simple as it looked, because Muriel wanted to come. She wanted to drive back with me and the hearse. My mother was very worried about this. It might upset Muriel, she thought. Father thought it might not look nice to see a young girl sitting by the coffin of a grown man.

"It must be dignified," my father said. "You see if she was there it might look as though she were just doing it for the ride—like these young women on bakers' vans."

My father took me out into the hall to tell me this because he did not want her to hear. But she would not have it. She wanted to come back with Colin.

"Colin loved me. It is my duty to him," she said. "Besides," she said, suddenly, in her full open voice—it had seemed to be closed and carved and broken and small—"I've never been in a hearse before."

"And it will save her fare too," I said to my father.

That night I went again to her room. She was awake. I said I was sorry to disturb her but I would go at once only I wanted to see if she was all right. She said, in the closed voice again, that she was all right.

"Are you sure?" I said.

She did not answer. I was worried. I went over to the bed.

"What is the matter? Tell me what is the matter," I said.

For a long time she was silent. I held her hand, I stroked her head. She was lying stiff in the bed. She would not answer. I dropped my hand to her small white shoulder. She stirred and drew up her legs and half turned and said, "I was thinking of Colin."

"Where is he?" she asked.

"They've brought him round. He's lying downstairs."

"In the front room?"

"Yes, ready for the morning. Now be a sensible girl and go back by train."

"No, no," she said. "I want to go with Colin. Poor Colin. He loved me and I didn't love him." And she drew my hands down to her breasts. "Colin loved me," she whispered.

"Not like this," I whispered.

It was a warm grey morning like all the others when we took Colin back. They had fixed the coffin in before Muriel came out. She came down wearing the bright blue hat she had got off Dormer's millinery man and she kissed my mother and father good-bye. They were very sorry for her. "Look after her, Arthur," my mother said. Muriel got in beside me without a glance behind her at the coffin. I started the engine. They smiled at us. My father raised his hat, but whether it was to Muriel and me or to Colin, or to the three of us, I do not know. He was not, you see, wearing his top hat. I'll say this for the old boy, thirty years in the trade have taught him tact.

After leaving my father's house you have to go down to the tram terminus before you get on to the by-pass. There was always one or two drivers, conductors or inspectors there, doing up their tickets, or changing over the trolley arms. When we passed I saw two of them drop their jaws, stick their pencils in their ears and raise their hats. I was so surprised by this that I nearly raised mine in acknowledgment, forgetting that we had the coffin behind. I had not driven one of my father's hearses for years.

Hearses are funny things to drive. They are well-sprung, smooth-running cars, with quiet engines and, if you are used to driving a smaller car, before you know where you are, you are speeding. You know you ought to go slow, say 25 to 30 maximum and it's hard to keep it down. You can return empty at 70 if you like. It's like driving a fire engine. Go fast out and come back slow—only the other way round. Open out in the country but slow down past houses. That's what it means. My father was very particular about this.

Muriel and I didn't speak very much at first. We sat listening to the engine and the occasional jerk of the coffin behind when we went over a pot hole. We passed the place where poor Colin—but I didn't say anything to Muriel, and she, if she noticed—which I doubt—did not say anything to me. We went through Cox Hill, Wammering and Yodley Mount, flat country, don't care for it myself. "There's a wonderful lot of building going on," Muriel said at last.

"You won't know these places in five years," I said.

But my mind kept drifting away from the road and the green fields and the dullness, and back to Colin,—five days before he had come down this way. I expected to see that Indian coming flying straight out of every corner. But it was all bent and bust up properly now. I saw the damned thing.

He had been up to his old game, following us, and that had put the end to following. But not quite; he was following us now, behind us in the coffin. Then my mind drifted off that and I thought of those nights at my parents' house, and Muriel. You never know what a woman is going to be like. I thought, too, that it had put my calculations out. I mean, supposing she had a baby. You see I had reckoned on waiting eighteen months or so. I would have eight hundred then. But if we had to get married at once, we should have to cut right down. Then I kept thinking it was funny her saying "Colin!" like that in the night; it was funny it made her feel that way with me, and how it made me feel when she called me Colin. I'd never thought of her in that way, in what you might call the "Colin" way.

I looked at her and she looked at me and she smiled but still we did not say very much, but the smiles kept coming to both of us. The light-railway bridge at Dootheby took me by surprise and I thought the coffin gave a jump as we took it.

"Colin's still watching us," I nearly said.

There were tears in her eyes.

"What was the matter with Colin?" I said. "Nice chap, I thought. Why didn't you marry him?"

"Yes," she said. "He was a nice boy. But he'd no sense of humour."

"And I wanted to get out of that town," she said.

"I'm not going to stay there, at that hotel," she said.

"I want to get away," she said. "I've had enough."

She had a way of getting angry with the air, like that. "You've got to take me away," she said. We were passing slowly into Muster, there was a tram ahead and people thick on the narrow pavements, dodging out into the road. But when we got into the Market Square where they were standing around, they saw the coffin. They began to raise their hats. Suddenly she laughed. "It's like being the King and Queen," she said.

"They're raising their hats," she said.

"Not all of them," I said.

She squeezed my hand and I had to keep her from jumping about like a child on the seat as we went through.

"There they go."

"Boys always do," I said.

"And another."

"Let's see what the policeman does."

She started to laugh but I shut her up. "Keep your sense of humour to yourself," I said.

Through all those towns that run into one another as you might say, we caught it. We went through, as she said, like royalty. So many years since I drove a hearse, I'd forgotten what it was like.

I was proud of her, I was proud of Colin and I was proud of myself. And, after what had happened, I mean on the last two nights, it was like a wedding. And although we knew it was for Colin, it was for us too, because Colin was with both of us. It was like this all the way.

"Look at that man there. Why doesn't he raise his hat? People ought to show respect for the dead," she said.

THE EVILS OF SPAIN

We took our seats at the table. There were seven of us.

It was at one of those taverns in Madrid. The moment we sat down Juliano, the little, hen-headed, red-lipped consumptive who was paying for the dinner and who laughed not with his mouth but by crinkling the skin round his eyes into scores of scratchy lines and showing his bony teeth—Juliano got up and said, "We are all badly placed." Fernando and Felix said, "No, we are not badly placed." And this started another argument shouting between the lot of us. We had been arguing all the way to the restaurant. The proprietor then offered a new table in a different way. Unanimously we said, "No," to settle the row; and when he brought the table and put it into place and laid a red and white check tablecloth on it, we sat down, stretched our legs and said, "Yes. This table is much better."

Before this we had called for Angel at his hotel. We shook his hand or slapped him on the back or embraced him and two hung on his arm as we walked down the street. "Ah, Angel, the rogue!" we said, giving him a squeeze. Our smooth Mediterranean Angel! "The uncle!" we said. "The old scoundrel." Angel smiled, lowering his black lashes in appreciation. Juliano gave him a prod in the ribs and asked him if he remembered, after all these years, that summer at Biarritz? When we had all been together? The only time we had all been together before?

Juliano laughed by making his eyes wicked and expectant, like one Andalusian reminding another of the great joke they had had the day poor So-and-So fell down the stairs and broke his neck.

"The day you were nearly drowned," Juliano said.

Angel's complexion was the colour of white coffee; his hair, crinkled like a black fern, was parted in the middle, he was rich, soft-palmed and patient. He was the only well-dressed man among us, the suavest shouter. Now he sat next door but one to Juliano. Fernando was between them, Juan next to me and, at the end, Felix. They had put Caesar at the head of the table, because he was the oldest and the largest. Indeed at his age he found his weight tiring to the feet.

Caesar did not speak much. He gave his silent weight to the dinner, letting his head drop like someone falling asleep, and listening. To the noise we made his silence was a balance and he nodded all the time slowly, making everything true. Sometimes someone told some story about him and he listened to that, nodding and not disputing it.

But we were talking chiefly of that summer, the one when Angel (the old uncle!) had nearly been drowned. Then Juan, the stout, swarthy one, banged the table with his hairy hands and put on his horn-rimmed glasses. He was the smallest and most vehement of us, the one with the thickest neck and the deepest voice, his words like barrels rumbling in a cellar.

"Come on! Come on! Let's make up our minds! What are we going to eat? Eat! Eat!" he roared.

"Yes," we cried. "Drink! What are we going to drink?"

The proprietor, who was in his shirt sleeves and braces, said it was for us to decide. We could have anything we wanted. This started another argument. He stepped back a pace and put himself in an attitude of self-defence.

"Soup! Soup? Make up your minds about soup! Who wants soup?" bawled Juan.

"Red wine," some of us answered. And others, "Not red, white."

"Soup I said," shouted Juan. "Yes," we all shouted. "Soup."

"Ah," said Juan, shaking his head, in his slow miserable disappointed voice. "Nobody have any soup. I want some soup. Nobody soup," he said sadly to the proprietor.

Juliano was bouncing in his chair and saying, God he would never forget that summer when Angel was nearly drowned! When we had all been together. But Juan said Felix had not been there and we had to straighten that matter out. Juliano said:

"They carried him on to the beach, our little Angel on to the beach. And the beach superintendent came through the crowd and said, 'What's happening?' 'Nothing,' we said. 'A man knocked out.' 'Knocked out?' said the beach superintendent. 'Nothing,' we said. 'Drowned!' A lot of people left the crowd and ran about over the beach saying, 'A man has been drowned.' 'Drowned,' said the beach superintendent. Angel was lying in the middle of them all, unconscious, with water pouring out of his mouth."

"No! No!" shouted Fernando. "No. It wasn't like that."

"How do you mean, it wasn't like that?" cried Juliano. "I was there." He appealed to us, "I was there."

"Yes, you were there," we said.

"I *was* there. I was there bringing him in. You say it wasn't like that, but it was like that. We were all there." Juliano jumped protesting to his feet, flung back his coat from his defying chest. His waistcoat was very loose over his stomach, draughty.

"What happened was better than that," Fernando said.

"Ah," said Juliano, suddenly sitting down and grinning with his eyes at everyone, very pleased at his show.

"It was better," he said. "How better?"

Fernando was a man who waited for silence and his hour. Once getting possession of the conversation he never let it go, but held it in the long, soothing ecstasy of a pliable embrace. All day long he lay in bed in his room in Fuencarral with the shutters closed, recovering from the bout of the day before. He was preparing himself to appear in the evening, spruce, grey-haired and meaty under the deep black crescents of his eyebrows, his cheeks ripening like plums as the evening advanced, his blue eyes, which got bloodshot early, becoming mistier. He was a man who ripened and moistened. He talked his way through dinner into the night, his voice loosening, his eyes misting, his walk becoming slower and stealthier, acting every sentence, as if he were swaying through the exalted phase of inebriation. But it was an inebriation purely verbal; an exaltation of dramatic moments, refinements upon situations; and hour after hour passed until the dawn found him sodden in his own anecdotes, like a fruit in rum.

"What happened was," Fernando said, "that I was in the sea. And after a while I discovered Angel was in the sea. As you know there is nothing more perilous than the sea, but with Angel in it the peril is tripled; and when I saw him I was preparing to get as far away as possible. But he was making faces in the water and soon he made such a face, so inhuman, so unnatural, I saw he was drowning. This did not surprise me for Angel is one of those men who, when he is in the sea, he drowns. There is some psychological antipathy. Now when I see a man drowning my instinct is to get away quickly. A man drowning is not a man. He is a lunatic. But a lunatic like Angel! But unfortunately he got me before I could get away. There he was," Fernando stood up and raised his arm, confronting the proprietor of the restaurant, but staring right through that defensive man, "beating the water, diving, spluttering, choking, spitting, and, seeing he was drowning, for the man *was* drowning, caught hold of me, and we both went under. Angel was like a beast. He clung to me like seaweed. I, seeing this, awarded him a knock-out—zum—but as the tenacity of man increases with unconsciousness, Angel stuck to me like a limpet, and in saving myself there was no escape from saving him."

"That's true," said Angel, admiring his finger nails. And Caesar nodded his head up and down twice, which made it true.

Juan then swung round and called out, "Eat! Food! Let us order. Let us eat. We haven't ordered. We do nothing but talk, not eat. I want to eat."

"Yes, come on," said Felix. "Eat. What's the fish?"

"The fish," said the proprietor, "is bacalao."

"Yes," everyone cried. "Bacalao, a good bacalao, a very good one. No, it must be good. No. I can't eat it unless it's good, very good *and* very good."

"No," we said. "Not fish. We don't want it."

"Seven bacalaos then?" said the proprietor.

But Fernando was still on his feet.

"And the beach inspector said, 'What's his name and address and has he any identity papers?' 'Man,' I said, 'he's in his bathing dress. Where could he keep his papers?' And Juan said, 'Get a doctor. Don't stand there asking questions. Get a doctor.'"

"That's true," said Juan gloomily. "He wasn't dead."

"Get a doctor, that was it," Angel said.

"And they got a doctor and brought him round and got half the Bay of Biscay out of him, gallons of it. It astonished me that so much water could come out of a man."

"And then in the evening," Juliano leaped up and clipped the story out of Fernando's mouth, "Angel says to the proprietor of the hotel . . ."

Juan's head had sunk to his chest. His hands were over his ears.

"Eat," he bawled in a voice of despair so final that we all stopped talking and gazed at him with astonishment for a few moments. Then in sadness he turned to me appealing. "Can't we eat? I am empty."

". . . said to the proprietor of the hotel," Fernando grabbed the tale back from Juliano, "who was rushing down the corridor with a face like a fish, 'I am the man who was drowned this morning.' And the proprietor who looked at Angel like a prawn, the proprietor said, 'M'sieu, whether you were drowned or not drowned this morning you are about to be roast. The hotel is on fire.'"

"That's right," we said. "The hotel was on fire."

"I remember," said Felix. "It began in the kitchen."

"How in the kitchen?"

This then became the argument.

"The first time ever I heard it was in the kitchen."

"But no," said Angel, softly rising to claim his life story for himself. Juliano clapped his hands and bounced with joy. "It was not like that."

"But we were all there, Angel," Fernando said, but Angel who spoke very rapidly said:

"No and no! And the proof of it is. What was I wearing?" He challenged all of us. We paused.

"Tripe," said Juan to me hopelessly wagging his head. "You like tripe? They do it well. Here! Phist!" he called the proprietor through the din. "Have you tripe, a good Basque tripe? No? What a pity! Can you get me some? Here! Listen," he shouted to the rest of the table. "Tripe," he shouted, but they were engrossed in Angel.

"Pyjamas," Fernando said. "When you are in bed you wear your pyjamas."

"Exactly, and they were not my pyjamas."

"You say the fire was not in the kitchen," shouted Fernando, "because the pyjamas you were wearing were not yours!" And we shouted back at Angel.

"They belonged to the Italian ambassador," said Angel, "the one who was with that beautiful Mexican girl."

Then Caesar, who, as I have said, was the oldest of us and sat at the head of the table, Caesar leaned his old big pale face forward and said in a hushed voice, putting out his hands like a blind man remembering:

"My God—but what a very beautiful woman she was," he said. "I remember her. I have never in my life," he said speaking all his words slowly and with grave concern, "seen such a beautiful woman."

Fernando and Angel, who had been standing, sat down. We all looked in awe at the huge, old-shouldered Caesar with his big pale face and the pockets under his little grey eyes, who was speaking of the most beautiful woman he had ever seen.

"She was there all that summer," Caesar said. "She was no longer young." He leaned forward with his hands on the table. "What must she have been when she was young?"

A beach, the green sea dancing down white upon it, that Mexican woman walking over the floor of a restaurant, the warm white houses, the night glossy black like the toe of a patent shoe, her hair black. We tried to think how many years ago this was. Brought by his voice to silence us, she was already fading.

The proprietor took his opportunity in our silence. "The bacalao is done in the Basque fashion with peppers and potatoes. Bring a bacalao," he snapped to a youth in the kitchen.

Suddenly Juan brought his fists on the table, pushed back his chair and beat his chest with one fist and then the other. He swore in his enormous voice by his private parts.

"It's eleven o'clock. Eat! For God's sake. Fernando stands there talking and talking and no one listens to anybody. It is one of the evils of Spain. Someone stop him. Eat."

We all woke up and glared with the defiance of the bewildered, rejecting everything he said. Then what he said to us penetrated. A wave roared over us and we were with him. We agreed with what he said. We all stood up and, by our private parts, swore that he was right. It was one of the evils of Spain.

The soup arrived. White wine arrived.

"I didn't order soup," some shouted.

"I said 'Red wine,'" others said.

"It is a mistake," the proprietor said. "I'll take it away." An argument started about this.

"No," we said. "Leave it. We want it." And then we said the soup was bad, and the wine was bad and everything he brought was bad, but the proprietor said the soup was good and the wine was good and we said in the end it was good. We told the proprietor the restaurant was good, but he said not very good, indeed bad. And then we asked Angel to explain about the pyjamas.

THE TWO BROTHERS

The two brothers went to Ballady to look at the house. It was ruinous but cheap, there were miles of bog and mountain alive with birds, there was the sea and not a soul living within two miles of it. As had always happened in their childhood and as had repeatedly happened since the war when "the Yank" had returned to the Old Country to look after his sick brother, "the Yank," with his voracious health, had his way.

"Sure it's ideal," yelled the Yank.

The time was the Spring.

"We'll take it for six months," he exclaimed.

"And after that?" asked Charlie, watching him like a woman for plans and motives he had not got.

"Och, we'll see. We'll see. Sure what's the use of worrying about the future?" said the Yank.

He knew and Charlie knew the question hung over them; the future watching them like an eagle on a rock, waiting to shadow them with its wing. In six months he would be left alone. He knew how the Yank, his brother, dealt with time. Out came his gun and he took a pot shot at it, went after it, destroyed it and then laughed at his own skill and forgot.

In the sky and land at Ballady there was the rugged wildness of farewell. This was the end of the land, prostrating itself in rags before the Atlantic. The wind stripped the soil so that there was no full-grown tree upon it, and rocks stood out like gravestones in the bigoted little fields. A few black cattle grazed, a few fields of oats were grown, the rest was mountain and the wide empty pans of bog broken into eyes of water. The house lay in a hollow out of sight of the sea, which was only half a mile away. It was a grey, rambling place of two storeys with outhouses and stables all going to pieces. It was damp, leaky and neglected and barely furnished. There were fuchsia bushes growing right up to the windows, beating against them and blinding them in the gales, pressed close as people in the night. The garden was feet deep in grasses, the gravel drive had become two grass ruts, and for a gate there was an iron hurdle propped against a gap in the stone wall. From the hill above Ballady Charlie and Micky had made out its slate roof silvery in the light, the ribs of the roofless stable, like a shining skeleton.

"The way it is," the Yank explained when he went in to Ballady alone for a drink now and then. "The poor bloody brother he's after having a breakdown." The Yank was a wild, tall, lean, muscular fellow, straight and springy as a whip, with eyes like dark pools, with bald brows, lips loose and thin, and large ears protruding from his bony skull. His black hair stood up straight and was cropped close like a convict's, so that the skin could be seen through it; his nose was straight and his face was reddened by the wind. He went about with a cigarette in the corner of lips askew in a conquering grin, and carried a gun all day. A breezy, sporting chap. He wandered up and down the bog and the fields or lay in the dunes waiting; then, bang went his gun, the seabirds screamed over the sand and up he got from his knees to pick up a rabbit or a bird. The sun burned him, the wind cut him, the squalls pitted him like shot. He had no secrets from anyone. Fifteen years of Canada, he told them, four years of war and now for a good time while his money lasted. Then, he said publicly to all, he would go back. All he wanted now was a bit of rough country, a couple of drinks, and a gun; and he had got them. It was what he had always wanted. He was out for the time of his life.

How different Charlie was, slight and wiry, nervous and private as a silvery fish. His hair was fair, almost white, and his eyes were a keen dark blue in the pupils and a fairer blue was ringed round them. His features were sharp and he kept his lips together and his head down as he walked, glancing nervously about him. He looked like a man walking in his thoughts. If, when he returned from the sea, he saw someone in his path, he dodged away and made a long detour back to the house. If taken by surprise and obliged to talk to a stranger, he edged away murmuring something. His voice was quiet, his look shrill, pleading and shy. He was absorbed in the most private of all pieties, the piety of fear to which his imagination devoted a rich and vivid ritual.

He did not badger his brother with speech. He followed him about the house, standing near him, asking with his eyes for the virtue of his brother's strength, courage, company and protection. He asked no more than his physical presence and to watch. In the mornings at first, after they had established themselves in the house, there was always this situation: Micky restless, burning to be out with his gun and Charlie's eyes silently asking him not to go. Micky bursting to be free, Charlie worrying to hold him. Sometimes Micky would be melted by an unguarded glance at his brother. For a moment he would forget his own strength and find himself moved by an awed tenderness for this clever man who had passed examinations, stayed in the Old Country, worked his way up in a bank and then, when the guns had started to popple, and "the troubles" began, had collapsed.

Micky was kind and humoured him. They would sit for hours together in the house, with the Spring growing in the world outside, while Charlie cajoled him with memories of their boyhood together, or listened to Micky's naive and boasting tales of travel. In those hours Charlie forgot the awful years, or he would have the illusion of forgetting. For the two surrounded themselves with walls of talk, and Charlie, crouching round the little camp fire of his heart, used every means to keep the talk going, to preserve this picture of life standing as still as a dreamy ship in haven and himself again a child.

But soon the sun would strike through the window and the fairness of the sky would make Micky restless. He would lead his brother, by a pretext, into the garden and slyly get him to work there, planting lettuces or digging, and when he had got him to work he would slip away, pick up his gun and be off to the dunes.

Shortly after moving into the house Micky went into Dill, got drunk as was his habit, and returned with a dog, a young black retriever very strong, affectionate and lively. He did not know why he had bought it and could hardly remember what he had paid for it. But when he got home he said on the impulse to Charlie:

"Here, Charlie boy. I've bought you a dog. One of the priest's pups."

Charlie smiled slightly and looked in wonder.

"There y'are, man," Micky cried. "Your dog."

"Hup! Go to your master," said Micky, giving the dog a push and sent it over to Charlie, who still incredulously gazed.

"Now that's kind of you," he murmured, flushing slightly. He was speechless with pleasure. Micky, who had given the animal to his brother on the spur of the moment, was now delighted with himself, sunned in his generosity.

"Sure now ye've got yer dog," Micky kept saying, "ye'll be all right. Ye'll be all right now ye've got the dog."

Charlie gazed at Micky and the animal, and slyly he smiled to himself; Micky had done this because he had a bad conscience. But Charlie put these thoughts aside.

Both brothers devoted themselves to the retriever, Micky going out and shooting rabbits for it, and Charlie cooking them and taking out the bones. But when Micky got up and took his gun and the retriever jumped up to go out with him, Charlie would whistle the dog back and say:

"Here! Stay here. Lie down. Ye're going out with me in a minute."

It was his dog.

At last Charlie went out and the watchful creature leaped out with him. Charlie drew courage from it as it loped along before him, sniffing at walls and standing stiff with ears cocked to see the sudden rise of a bird. Charlie talked to it in a low running murmur hardly made of words but easing to the mind. When it stopped he would pass his clever hands over its velvety nose and glossy head, feeling the strange life ripple under the hair and obtaining a curious strength from the tumult. Then he would press on and whistle the creature after him and make across the fields to the long finger bone of rock that ran down to the sea; but as the retriever ran it paused often, as Charlie began to note with bewilderment and then with dread, to listen for Micky's voice or the sound of his gun.

When he saw this Charlie redoubled his efforts to win the whole allegiance of the dog. Power was renewing itself in him. And so he taught the dog a trick. He called it over the rocks, slipping and yelping to the sea's edge. Here the sand was white, and as the worlds of clouds bowled over the sky to the mountains where the light brimmed like golden bees, the sea would change into deep jade halls, purple where the weeds lay and royal blue under the sparkling sun, and the air was sinewy and strong. Charlie took off his clothes and, shivering at the sight of his own thin pale body, his loose queasy stomach and the fair sickly hairs now picking up gold from the light, and with a desire to cleanse himself of sickness and fear, lowered himself cautiously into the green water, and wading out with beating heart called to the dog. It stood up whining and barking for a while, running up and down the rock, and at last plunged in pursuit. Then the man caught hold of its tail and let himself be towed out to sea, and for minutes they would travel out and out until, at a word, the dog returned, snorting, heart pumping, shoulders working and eyes gazing upwards and the green water swilling off its back until it had pulled Charlie back into his depth.

Then Charlie would sit drying himself and listening to the scream of the birds while the black retriever yelped and shivered at his side. And if Micky were late for his meal when he returned, through drinking with the schoolmaster or going away for a day to the races, Charlie would say nothing. He would build up a big turf fire in the empty room and wait with the dog at his side, murmuring to it.

But it took Charlie hours to make up his mind to these expeditions, and as time went on they became irregular. There were days when the absences of his brother left him alone with his fears, and on these days he would helplessly see the dog run after Micky and go off with him. Soon it would hardly obey Charlie's call.

"You're taking the dog from me," Charlie complained.

"Sure if ye'd go out the dog'd follow you," said Micky. "Dammit, what's the use of staying inside? I don't want the dog, but the poor bloody creature needs a run an't follows me. It's only natural."

"Natural. That's it," Charlie reflected. From him that hath not shall be taken even that which he hath. But he cried out sharply:

"Sure you have it trained away from me."

Then they quarrelled, and Micky, thinking his head was getting too hot for his tongue, went out to the dunes and stood in the wind staring at the sea. Why was he tied to this weak and fretful man? For three years since the end of the war he had looked after Charlie, getting him out of hospital and into a nursing home, then to houses in the country, sacrificing a lot of his own desire to have a good time before he returned to Canada, in order to get his brother back to health. Micky's money would not last for ever; soon he would have to go, and then what would happen?

But when he returned with cooler head, the problem carelessly thrown off, he was kind to his brother. They sat in eased silence before the fire, the dog dreaming at their feet, and to Charlie there returned the calm of the world. His jealousies, his suspicions, his reproaches, all the spies sent out by his reconnoitring fears, were called in and with Micky he was at peace and no shadow of the future was on him.

Yet as the months climbed higher out of July into August and swung there awhile, enchanted by their own halcyon weather, before declining into the cooler days, the question had to be faced. Micky knew and Charlie knew, but each wished the other to speak.

It was Micky who, without warning, became impatient and spoke out.

"Lookut here, Charlie," he said one evening as he washed blood off his hands in the kitchen—he had been skinning and cleaning a couple of rabbits—"are you coming back to Canada with me in September?"

"To Canada is it?" said the brother putting his thin fingers on the table and speaking in a gasping whisper. He stood incredulous. Yet he had expected this.

"And leave me here alone!"

"Not at all," said Micky. "I said 'You're coming with me.' You heard me. Will ye come with me to Canada?"

Charlie drew in his lips and his eyes were restless with agony.

"Sure, Micky, ye know I can't do that," he said.

"But what's to stop ye? Ye're all right. Ye're well. Ye've got your bit of pension and ye'll be as comfortable as in your own home. Get out of this damn country, that's what ye want. Sure 'tis no good at all except for old people and children," cried Micky.

But Charlie was looking out of the window towards the mountains. To go out into the world, to sit in trains with men, to sleep in houses with them, to stand bewildered, elbowed and shouldered by men in a new country! Or, as the alternative, to stay alone without Micky, left to his memories.

"You'll not leave me, Micky boy?" he stammered in panic.

Micky was bewildered by the high febrile voice, the thin body shivering like a featherless bird. Then Charlie changed. He hunched his shoulders, narrowing himself and cowering round his heart, hardening himself against the world, and his eyes shot out suspicions, jealousies, reproaches, the weapons of a sharp mind.

" 'Tis the schoolmaster has been putting you against me," he said.

Micky ridiculed the idea.

"Ye knew as well as I did, dammit, when we took the place, that I'd be going now," he said. Yes, this was true, Charlie had known it.

Micky took the matter to his friend the schoolmaster. He was a stout, hard-drinking old man with a shock of curly grey hair. His manner was theatrical and abrupt.

" 'Tis the poor bloody brother," Micky said. "What am I to do with him at all?"

"Ye've no more money," said the schoolmaster.

"Ye've been with him for years," he went on. He paused again.

"Ye can't live on him."

"And he must live with you."

He glowered at Micky and then his fierce look died away.

"Sure there's nothing you can do. Nothing at all," said the schoolmaster.

Micky filled their glasses again.

He continued his life. The Summer glided down like a beautiful bird scooping the light. The peasants stood in their long shadows in the fields and fishermen left their boats for the harvest. Micky was sad to be leaving this beautiful isolation.

But he had to return to the question. He and Charlie began to argue it continually day and night. Sometimes Charlie was almost acquiescent, but at last always retired within himself. Since he could not sit in the safety of the old talk, his cleverness found what comfort it could for him in the new. Soon it was clear to Micky that Charlie encouraged the discussion, cunningly played with it, tortured him with vacillations, cunningly played on his conscience. But to Charlie it seemed that he was struggling to make his brother aware of him fully; deep in the piety of his fear he saw in Micky a man who had never worshipped at its icy altars. He must be made to know. So the struggle wavered until one night it came out loudly into the open.

"God Almighty," cried out Micky as they sat in the lamplight. "If you'd been in France you'd have had something to cry about. That's what's wrong with this bloody country. All a pack of damn cowards, and ye can see it in their faces when they stare at you like a lot of bleating sheep."

"Oh, is that it?" said Charlie gripping the arms of his chair. "Is that what you're thinking all these years? Ye're saying I'm afraid, is it? You're saying I'm a coward. Is that what you were thinking when you came home like a red lord out of hell in your uniform, pretending to be glad to see me and the home? But thinking in your own heart I'm a coward not to be in the British army. Oh, is that it?"

His voice was quiet, high and monotonous in calculated contrast to Micky's shouting anger. But his body shook. A wound had been opened. He *was* a coward. He *was* afraid. He was terrified. But his clever mind quickly closed the wound. He was a man of peace. He desired to kill no one. He worshipped the great peace of God. This was why he had avoided factions, agreed with all sides, kept out of politics and withdrawn closer and closer into himself. At times it had seemed to him that the only place left in the world for the peace of God was in his own small heart.

And what had Micky done? In the middle of the war he had come home, the Destroyer. In five minutes by a few reckless words in the drink shop and streets of the town he had ruined the equilibrium Charlie had tended for years and had at last attained. In five minutes Charlie had become committed. He was no longer "Mr. Lough the manager," a man of peace. No, he was the brother of "that bloody pro-British Yank." Men were boycotted for having brothers in the British army, they were threatened, they were even shot. In an hour a village as innocent-looking as a green and white place in a postcard had become a place of windows hollow-eyed with evil vigils. Within a month he had received the first note threatening his life.

" 'Twas yourself," said Charlie—discovering at last his enemy. " 'Twas yourself, Micky, that brought all this upon me. Would I be sick and destroyed if you hadn't come back?"

"Cripes," said Micky, hearing the argument for the first time and pained by this madness in his brother. "Cripes, man, an' what was the rest of ye up to? Serving God Almighty like a lot of choir boys, shooting up some poor lonely policeman from a hedge and driving old women out of their homes."

"Stop it," shouted Charlie, as the memories broke upon him and he put his fingers to his ears.

Micky threw his cigarette into the fire and took his brother by the shoulder in compassion. He was sorry for having spoken so; but Charlie ignored him. He spoke, armouring himself.

"So it's a coward I am, is it!" he said. "Well, I stayed when they threatened me and I'll stay again. You're thinking I'm a coward." He was resolute. But behind the shrubs brushing against the window, in the spaces between the cool September stars, were the fears.

There was nothing else for it. Charlie watched Micky preparing to go, indifferent and resigned, feeding his courage on this new picture of his brother. He turned to it as to a secret revelation. Micky was no longer his brother. He was the Destroyer, the Prince of this World, the man of darkness. Micky, surprised that his good intentions were foiled, gave notice to the landlord, to force Charlie. Charlie renewed the agreement. He spoke little; he took no notice of the dog, which had now completely deserted him. When Micky had gone it would be his. Charlie kicked it once or twice as if to remind it. He gave up swimming in the sea. He was staying here. He had all the years of his life to swim in the sea.

Micky countered this by open neglect of his brother. He entered upon a life of wilder enjoyment. He gave every act the quality of a reckless farewell. He was out all day and half the night. In Ballady he drank the schoolmaster weeping under the table and came staggering home, roaring like an opera, and was up at dawn, no worse for it, after the duck.

"This is a rotten old wall," Micky said in the garden one day, and started pushing the stones off the top of it. A sign it was his wall no longer. He chopped a chair up for firewood. He ceased to make his bed. He took a dozen empty whisky bottles and, standing them at the end of the kitchen garden, used them as shooting targets. He shot three rabbits and threw two of them into the sea. He burned some old clothes, tore up his letters and gave away a haversack to the fisherman and a second gun to the schoolmaster. A careless enjoyment of destruction seized him. Charlie watched it, saying nothing. The Destroyer.

One evening as the yellow sun flared in the pools left by the tide on the sand, Micky came upon Charlie.

"Not a damn thing," Micky said, tapping his gun.

But as they stood there, some gulls which had been flying over the rocks came inland and one fine fellow flew out and circled over their heads, its taut wings deep blue in the shadow as it swung round. Micky suddenly raised his gun and fired and, before the echoes had broken in the rocks, the wings collapsed and the bird dropped warm and dead.

"God Almighty, man," cried Charlie, turning away with nausea, "is nothing sacred to ye?"

"It's no damned good," grinned Micky, picking up the bird by the wing, which squeaked open like a fan. "Let the fish have it." And he flung it into the sea. This was what he thought of wings.

Then with a week to go, without thinking he struck a bad blow. He went off to Dill to say good-bye to the boys, and the retriever followed him although Charlie called it back. The races were on at Dill, but Micky spent most of the time in the pubs telling everyone he was going back to Canada. A man hearing this said he'd change dogs with him. His dog, he said, was a spaniel. He hadn't it with him but he'd bring it down next fair. Micky was enthusiastic.

"I know ye will," said Micky. "Sure ye'll bring it."

"Ah, well now," said the man. "I will bring it."

"'Tis a great country the west," said Micky. "Will ye have another?"

"I will," said the man, and as he drank: "In the three countries there is not a place like this."

Micky returned the next day without the dog.

"Where's the dog?" said Charlie suspiciously.

"Och sure," began Micky evasively, realising for the first time what he had done. "D'you see the way it is, there is a man in Dill—"

"Ye've sold it. Ye've sold my dog," Charlie shouted out, rushing at his brother. His shout was the more unnerving because he had spoken so little for days. Micky drew back.

"Ah now, Charlie, be reasonable now. Sure you never did anything for the dog. You never took it out. You didn't care for it . . ."

Charlie gripped a chair and painfully sat down, laying his head in his hands on the table.

"You brought the war on me, you smash me up, you take the only things I have and leave me stripped and alone," he moaned. "Oh, God in heaven," he half sobbed in pleading voice, "will ye give me gentleness and peace!"

Now the dog was gone Charlie sat still. He would not move from the house, nor even from the sitting-room except to go to bed. He would scarcely speak. Sulking, Micky repeated to his uneasy conscience, sulking, sulking. He's either mad or he's sulking. What could he do? They sat estranged, already far apart, impatient for the act of departure.

When the eve of his departure came Micky was relieved to see that Charlie accepted it, and was even making it easy: and so touched was Micky by this that he found no difficulty in promising to spend that last night with Charlie alone. He remained in the house all day, and when the night came a misted moonlight gleamed on the cold roof and the sea was as quiet as the licking of a cat's tongue. Charlie drew the curtains, made up the fire and there they sat silently listening to the clock. They were almost happy: Charlie pleased to have this final brief authority over Micky; Micky relieved by the calm, both disinterested. Charlie spoke of his plans, the work he would do in the garden, the furniture he would buy, the girl he would get in to cook and clean.

" 'Twould be a fine place to bring a bride to," said Micky, giving Charlie a wink, and Charlie smiled.

But presently they heard footsteps on the drive.

"What's that?" exclaimed Charlie sharply, sitting up. The mild mask of peace left his face like a light, and his face set hard.

Without knocking at the door, in walked the schoolmaster. He was in the room before Charlie could get out. He stood up and retreated to the corner.

"Good evening to ye," said the schoolmaster, pulling a bottle out of his pocket, and spreading himself on to a seat. "I came to see your brother on his last night."

Charlie drew in his lips and gazed at the schoolmaster.

"Will ye have a drink?" said Micky nervously.

That began it. Gradually Micky forgot his promise. He paid no attention to Charlie's signs. They sat drinking and telling stories. The world span round. The alarm clock on the little bamboo table, the only table in the bare room, ticked on. Charlie waited in misery, his eyes craving his brother's, whose bloodshot eyes were merry with drinking and laughter at the schoolmaster's tales. The man's vehement voice shook the house. He told of the priest at Dill who squared the jockeys and long thick stories about some Archbishop and his so-called niece. The air to Charlie became profane.

"Isn't your wife afraid to be up and alone this time of night?" Charlie ventured once.

"Och, man, she's in bed long ago," shouted the schoolmaster. "She is that."

And Micky roared with laughter.

At two o'clock Charlie went to bed and left him to it. But he was awake at five when Micky stumbled into his room.

"Before God, man," Micky said. "I'm bloody sorry, Charlie man. Couldn't turn out a friend."

"It's too late now," said Charlie.

Micky left at seven to catch a man who would give him a lift to the eight-o'clock train.

———

The Autumn gales broke loose upon the land a month after Micky's departure and the nights streamed black and loud. The days were cold and fog came over the sea. The fuchsias were blown back and the under leaves blew up like silver hands. The rain lashed on the windows like gravel. There were days of calm and then the low week-long mist covered the earth, obliterating the mountains, melting all shapes. All day long the moisture dripped from the sheds and windows and glistened on the stone walls.

At first Charlie did not change. Forced to go to the village for groceries he would appear there two or three times a week, saying little and walking away quickly. A fisherman would call and the post-boy lingered. Letters came from Micky. Charlie took little heed of all this. But as the weather became wilder he hung curtains over the windows day and night and brought his bed down to the sitting-room. He locked the doors upstairs, those that had still keys to them. He cooked on the sitting-room fire. He was narrowing his world, making a smaller and closer circle to live in. And as it grew smaller, the stranger the places beyond its boundaries seemed. He was startled to go into the empty kitchen, and looked with apprehension up the carpetless stairs to the empty landing where water dripped through the fanlight and was already staining the ceiling below. He lay awake in the night as the fire glowed in the room.

One morning when he found the noises of his isolation supportable no more, he put on his hat and coat and packed his things and walked out of the house. He would stay no longer. But with his fear his brain had, as always, developed a covering cunning. He went up the lane to see if anyone was coming first. He wanted to be away from people, yet among them; with them, yet alone. And on this morning the Ballady sailor was reloading a load of turf that had fallen off his cart. Charlie returned into the house. He took off his hat and coat. He had not been out for a week because of this dread.

There was still food in tins for a few days. It was the thought that he could last if he liked, that he could keep the world off, that made him satisfied. No letters came now. Micky no longer wrote; effusive in the first weeks, his letters had become rare. Now there had been no news for a month. Charlie scarcely thought of him.

But when late in December the mists held the country finally, the twigs creaked on the drive like footsteps and the dark bushes divided in the wind as if they had been parted by hidden hands, he cowered into his beating heart, eating little, and the memories began to move and creep in his head. A letter threatened him with death. He drove alone with the bank's money. At Carragh-cross road the signpost stood emptily gesticulating like some frightened speaker with the wind driving back the words into his mouth, and the two roads dangling from its foot. He knew what had happened at Carragh-cross road. He knew what had been found there lying with one leg out of the ditch. He saw it. And Micky, the Destroyer, with his convict's head and his big red ears, shooting down the Holy Ghost like a beautiful bird, grinned there blowing smoke down his nose.

These memories came and went. When they came they beat into his head like wings, and though he fought them off with prayers, they beat down and down on him and he cried out fast to the unanswering house:

"God give me peace," he prayed. "Holy Mother of God, give me peace for the sake of thy sweet Son . . ."

When the beating wings went his cleverness took possession of him again. He prepared a little food, and once or twice walked around the garden within the shelter of the walls. The ground was frozen, the air still and a lace of snow was on the paths. But if the days passed in peace, his heart quickened at the early darkness, and when the turf smoke blew back down the chimney it was as if someone had blown down a signal. One night he had a terrible dream. He was dead, he had been caught at last on the road at Carragh-cross. "Here's the man with the pro-British brother," they cried and threw him into a bog pool, sinking deeper and deeper into soft and sucking fires that drew him down and down. He was in hell. And there in the flames calling to him was a woman with dark hair and with pale insects walking over her skin. It was the schoolmaster's wife. "And he thinking you were in bed," said Charlie, amazed by the justice of revenge. He woke up gasping in the glow of the sitting-room fire, and feeling that a load was still pressing down on his chest.

In the morning the dream was still in his mind; mingling with some obscure sense of triumph it ceased to be a dream and became reality. It became like a new landscape imposed upon the world. The voice of the woman was more real to his ear than his own breathing.

He felt free, was protected and cleansed, and his dream seemed to him like an impervious world within a world, a mirage in which he musically walked. In the afternoon he was exalted. He walked out of the house and taking the long way round by the lanes went to the schoolmaster's. The frost still held and the air was windless, the land fixed and without colour. As it happened the schoolmaster had taken it into his head to go as far as his gate.

"Man, I'm glad to see ye about," cried the schoolmaster at the sight of Charlie. "I meant to see ye. Come in now. Come in. 'Tis terrible lonely for you in that place."

Charlie stood still and looked icily through him.

"Ye thought she was in bed," he said. "But I'm after seeing her in the flames of hell fire."

Without another word he walked away. The schoolmaster made a rush for him. But Charlie had climbed the stone wall and had dropped into the field opposite.

"Come here. Come back. What's that you say?" called the schoolmaster. But Charlie walked on, gathering speed as he dropped behind the hill out of sight going to his house. Then he ran for his life.

The schoolmaster did not wait. He went in for his coat, bicycled into Ballady Post Office and rang up the Guards at Dill.

"There's a poor feller here might do harm to himself," he said. "Will you send someone down?"

But on the way back to the house Charlie's accompanying dream and its dazed exaltation left him. Speaking had dissolved it. It lifted like a haze and suddenly he was left alone, exposed, vulnerable in the middle of the fields. He began to run, shying at every corner, and when he got to the house he clawed at the door and ran in gasping to throw himself on the bed. He lay there on his face, his eyes closed. There had been brief excitement in the run, but as he recovered his breath the place resumed its normal aspect and its horror became real as slowly he turned over and opened his eyes to it. And now they were open he could not close them again. They stared and stared. Slowly it came to him there was nothing in life left for him but emptiness. Career gone, peace gone, God gone, Micky gone, dog—all he had ever had trooped with bleak salute of valediction through his mind. He was left standing in the emptiness of himself. And then a shadow was cast upon the emptiness; looking up he saw the cold wing of a great and hovering bird. So well he knew it that in this last moment his mind cleared and he had no fear. " 'Tis yourself, Micky, has me destroyed," he said. He took out a razor and became absorbed in the difficulty of cutting his throat. He was not quite dead when the Guards broke in and found him.

The Upright Man

Calvert was an upright man, tall, shy, short-stepping. His eyes were lowered and his narrow shoulders square. Proud in his poverty he kept to himself, he feared to know himself to be known. He came to the office punctually, he hung up his raincoat and hat in the cloakroom reserved for the male staff, he changed into a grey jacket in order to save his better one, he used his own towel when he washed his thin hands. He did not stand as the other clerks did, with dejected buttocks to the cashier's fire, defying him in his absence and scattering to their stools when the blowing of a nose announced that he had arrived. Calvert did not spend himself in gestures or extravagances. He kept himself apart. He went straight to his desk, took out his blotting paper, cleaned his pens, took down his books and, before all others, bent his body and bowed his head. The clerks smiled at him. He was fair.

The carpenter bends over his bench, the cobbler over his shoe, the mechanic over his machine, the priest over his altar, the clerk over his desk. By day, the heads of all men are bowed and their bodies bent. Not one of them is upright. Yet Calvert, the first to bow, was an upright man. Soldierly in duty, remembering his mother, scrupulous in poverty, when others laughed only smiling, saying two words while others spoke ten, eating sparingly alone, secret in life and parsimonious of himself. He trod the path of a single preoccupation, an instinctive loneliness. He conserved himself, every sinew was restraining. There were iron bars to the windows of his office. Through them if a bowed man looked up, he saw not the sky but across the street the flat walls of windows where other bowed men worked.

At first he had been restless, his mouth had the desire to speak, his legs fidgeted on the stool—the chains unfamiliar—his hands reckoning his money, his grey eyes looking at the window-bars for a space to squeeze through and escape. "Calvert," the cashier warned him. And the chant of the office went on. He bowed his head and ducked with the rest repentant. Then cautiously at twenty-two he let a little of himself go. He lit his eyes, guiltily conscient of his mother and their poverty, permitted himself a little of the great secrecy of love. He cautiously looked up at the bars expecting to see a miracle, a vision, the appearance of an angel. For months he continued this deep espionage. No vision came. He bowed his head at last. He was an upright man.

Now there were two women, his mother and this other. It was his duty not to look up. She and he must save themselves. They must not speak too much, nor smile too much, nor touch too much each other's skin, in case they should love too much and exclaim out of their hearts. How long the old live! They sat in the evenings with his mother and with hers, looking through the fine lace curtains to the sky, waiting for the miracle. But there was no sky. There were the walls of lace curtains in the houses opposite and behind them invisible presences looking up. For ten years looking through lace curtains for a miracle they brought laughter to others.

Clerks flung their lives about and committed follies. One married to a voracious wife drank on Thursdays a glass of stout. One who copied weighing slips gave imitations of the voice of the cashier. One who was bald put his hand down the blouse of his secretary and was slapped in the face. One would absent himself for twenty minutes in the morning to read the newspaper in the lavatory. One going deaf turned to an Oriental religion. One made use of the office telephone to communicate with a bookmaker. One told the Port of London Authority of an error in demurrage; it was his own. One staying after six lit his pipe. The oldest, in charge of stamps, went up in an aeroplane for a few minutes at a resort; he had married a widow. But Calvert did not so defy the gods, his gaolers.

So the gods, his gaolers, got drunk and went mad. They opened the doors of the cell, they flung in the keys. "You are not a slave. You are not a tame man," they whispered in his ears. "You are a beast and brute fighting for survival. You have saved yourself too long. Go outside," they said to him, patting him on the back. "Stand out in the air, draw yourself up to your full height, take a deep breath. Do you see? You are a man already. Your pale face is tanned by the sun, your neck is golden. Your hair which had gone dead and greasy is alive again like corn. Your shoulders are like walls, your muscles are hard. Do not lower your eyes! Do not bow your head any more! That day has passed and gone. My dear fellow, those red spots in front of your eyes have nothing to do with your liver, they are made of blood."

"Blood?" murmured Calvert incredulously.

"Yes, yes," they said. "Blood. Life. You're a hero. Go and kill."

Women, above all, they said, expected this of him. Now was the time to save nothing but to spend all.

He mistrusted them until they said, remembering his tradition, that it was his duty. He had bowed but now at last had come the time of freedom and uprightness.

And indeed the whole world of men was changed. The carpenter no longer bent over his bench, nor the mechanic over his screw, nor the cobbler at his last, nor the clerk at his desk. They were not many bowed men. They were all upright, bolt upright, chins up, shoulders back, forefinger on the seam of trousers, and they marched on grass under the sky. Like upright gods they marched, strong, healthy and beautiful. Women watched them. They would never go back they said. Many indeed did not.

For it appeared that this was a trick. They were made to stand in rows in trenches as they had sat in rows at desks, but the pens they now used required two arms to lift. The cashiers had three stripes on their arms, the partners red bands to their hats. The bars of the office windows had become bars of wire. Accounts were opened and kept, but not of bales. It soon became the habit not to be an upright man, but to duck the head once more. Looking at the sky, they saw miracles but they were sulphurous, and there was a tone of hoarse, consumptive wailing in the voices of the angels as they passed over to be entertained unawares.

But Calvert was an upright man. He had waited long with great passion. He had waited to make a life for himself. He had come to the end of his loneliness. Recklessly he talked, loudly he laughed. He entered into fellowship. He had to spend himself and all his life, to laugh with his whole body, to love and die and live again with his whole nature. This was a supreme duty. All his life he had waited, to stand in all his stature and fullness, attending the Passion. And after sundown between the lights of day and night when the bowed men stand up, he looked up through the wire bars at the sky, and the miracle occurred. He was shot by a sniper in the head.

First of all it was as if, angered with his standing, the earth had swung up with all its metals like a pick and hit with full might upon the head, that his life leapt from his feet and all parts of his body to that place. He fell. It seemed he was whipped off his feet while his head pealed like a helpless belfry. Now there was nothing left of him, he was scattered into fragments and flung together in an iron ball of pain, to be struck and struck until he broke into nothing but clangorous and bloody echoes; and then great toothed pliers picked him up by the skull and flung him away down into a black pit that had no end to it and measured only by the wail of his pain as he dropped down. He had not imagined a death so extravagant.

They carried Calvert away on a stretcher. He was written off the books. His name appeared in many entries. By goods, cash. His account closed, he entered into heaven where all men were lying down full length and only the angels bowed their heads over them. For a long time the hammer-on-anvil clangour of the earth was there, but slowly as he sank into heaven there was the tolerable melody of bells and endurable singing. God came in white coat and held his head together by the pressure of his hands so that these sounds died and after God had held his head it was rigid. Calvert slept, and in his sleep lived many lives and enacted dreams. After many months his eyes, which had long been open, saw a white ceiling and a human face looking down at him. He closed his eyes, unwilling to return from the fevers of heaven from which he was drifting on the sweet stream of sleep. He could have wept that he was not dead. When again he opened his eyes two women were looking at him. One of them was old and one desired. "Save yourself," their eyes pleaded. He had nothing now to save. He had spent. "Do not let him bend his head," they said in one voice. "HE CANNOT MOVE HIS HEAD," said the doctor. "The bullet is still in it."

At this the gods sobered and grabbed back the keys. "All men to the cells," they said. "All men back to the bars. No more holidays—work!"

The clerks in this new freedom were gay. One who had come to suspect Divine Justice took to games of chance. One who was bald consummated love with a telephone operator and was presented with a clock on his marriage; one saddened by an adding machine took drugs which gave him visions; one moved into a town whose train service had been electrified; one who could imitate the voice of the cashier played in an orchestra; one sold his house at a profit; a typist given to the circulation of religious pamphlets had a week's leave to serve on a jury; many grew flowers and had newborn children.

But what can a man do in the world who cannot bend his head? Even the inspired blind are led erect, tapping, can bend their heads and work. They can lean down to kiss, they can grope into the convulsions of love. But a man screwed upright by a bullet in his neck, a bullet like the clot of a spirit level to be steadily carried, cannot bend over tools or ledger, nor grovel with fingers.

In this new world returning to life Calvert walked now rigid as the memory of the fear of death. Eyes now wide open, face narrow, shoulders fixed, body bleak, he was fixed in uprightness for ever. Many pitied him. But life requires pliable men. Regimentation of the pliable, they said; it was the lesson of the war. All must bend to the wheel together. No head out of alignment.

What could he do, fixed now in the discipline of uprightness for ever, not of men, lately of heaven, but not of the angels, needing to eat? He sank from plane to plane. There were two women. He had been, he said, staring, a clerk. He went from place to place asking. "There," they said, "that is what you can do." He could go from place to place, he could be a pair of hands, impersonal. Take this. Bring that. Fetch me . . . Give him . . . A messenger, walking from room to room, standing in lifts, waiting at desks, an intermediary, lifeless. Not a live man, not a dead man, a man now without all means of desiring anything, a man indelibly alone not looking up nor down. An upright man.

You Make Your Own Life

Upstairs from the street a sign in electric light said "Gent's Saloon." I went up. There was a small hot back room full of sunlight, with hair clippings on the floor, towels hanging from a peg and newspapers on the chairs. "Take a seat. Just finishing," said the barber. It was a lie. He wasn't anywhere near finishing. He had in fact just begun a shave. The customer was having everything.

In a dead place like this town you always had to wait. I was waiting for a train, now I had to wait for a haircut. It was a small town in a valley with one long street, and a slow mud-coloured river moving between willows and the backs of houses.

I picked up a newspaper. A man had murdered an old woman, a clergyman's sister was caught stealing gloves in a shop, a man who had identified the body of his wife at an inquest on a drowning fatality met her three days later on a pier. Ten miles from this town the skeletons of men killed in a battle eight centuries ago had been dug up on the Downs. That was nearer. Still, I put the paper down. I looked at the two men in the room.

The shave had finished now, the barber was cutting the man's hair. It was glossy black hair and small curls of it fell on the floor. I could see the man in the mirror. He was in his thirties. He had a swarthy skin and brilliant long black eyes. The lashes were long too and the lids when he blinked were pale. There was just that suggestion of weakness. Now he was shaved there was a sallow glister to his skin like a Hindu's and as the barber clipped away and grunted his breaths, the dark man sat engrossed in his reflection, half smiling at himself and very deeply pleased.

The barber was careful and responsible in his movements but nonchalant and detached. He was in his thirties too, a young man with fair receding hair, brushed back from his forehead. He did not speak to his customer. His customer did not speak to him. He went on from one job to the next silently. Now he was rattling his brush in the jar, wiping the razor, pushing the chair forward to the basin. Now he gently pushed the man's head down, now he ran the taps and was soaping the head and rubbing it. A peculiar look of amused affection was on his face as he looked down at the soaped head.

"How long are you going to be?" I said. "I've got a train."

He looked at the clock. He knew the trains.

"Couple of minutes," he said.

He wheeled a machine on a tripod to the back of the man. A curved black thing like a helmet enclosed the head. The machine was plugged to the wall. There were phials with coloured liquids in them and soon steam was rushing out under the helmet. It looked like a machine you see in a Fun Fair. I don't know what happened to the man or what the barber did. Shave, hot towels, haircut, shampoo, this machine and then yellow liquid like treacle out of a bottle—that customer had everything.

I wondered how much he would have to pay.

Then the job was over. The dark man got up. The clippers had been over the back of his neck and he looked like a guardsman. He was dressed in a square-shouldered grey suit, very dandyish for this town, and he had a silk handkerchief sticking out of his breast pocket. He wore a violet and silver tie. He patted it as the barber brushed his coat. He was delighted with himself.

"So long, Fred," he smiled faintly.

"Cheero, Albert," said the upright barber and his lips closed to a small, hardly perceptible smile too. Thoughtfully, ironically, the barber watched his handiwork go. The man hadn't paid.

I sat in the chair. It was warm, too warm, where the man had sat. The barber put the sheet round me. The barber was smiling to himself like a man remembering a tune. He was not thinking about me.

The barber said that machine made steam open the pores. He glanced at the door where the man had gone. "Some people want everything," he said, "some want nothing." You had to have a machine like that.

He tucked in the cotton wool. He got out the comb and scissors. His fingers gently depressed my head. I could see him in the mirror bending to the back of my head. He was clipping away. He was a dull young man with pale blue eyes and a look of ironical stubbornness in him. The small dry smile was still like claw marks at the corners of his lips.

"Three bob a time," he said. He spoke into the back of my neck, and nodded to the door. "He has it every week."

He clipped away.

"His hair's coming out. That's why he has it. Going bald. You can't stop that. You can delay it but you can't stop it. Can't always be young. He thinks you can." He smiled drily but with affection.

"But he wasn't so old."

The barber stood up.

"That man!" he said. He mused to himself with growing satisfaction. He worked away in long silence as if to savour every possible flavour of my remark. The result of his meditation was to make him change his scissors for a finer pair.

"He ought to be dead," he said.

"TB," he said with quiet scorn.

He looked at me in the mirror.

"It's wonderful," he said, as if to say it was nothing of the sort.

"It's wonderful what the doctors can do," I said.

"I don't mean doctors," he said. "Consumptives! Tuh! They're wonderful." As much as to say a sick man can get away with anything—but you try if you're healthy and see what happens!

He went on cutting. There was a glint in his pale-blue eyes. He snipped away amusedly as if he were attending to every individual hair at the back of my head.

"You see his throat?" he said suddenly.

"What about his throat?" I asked.

"Didn't you notice anything? Didn't you see a mark a bit at the side?" He stood up and looked at me in the mirror.

"No," I said.

He bent down to the back of my neck again. "He cut his throat once," he said quietly. "Not satisfied with TB," he said with a grin. It was a small firm, friendly grin. So long, Fred. Cheero, Albert. "Tried to commit suicide."

"Wanted everything," I said.

"That's it," he said.

"A girl," the barber said. "He fell in love with a girl."

He clipped away.

"That's an item," said the barber absently.

He fell in love with a local girl who took pity on him when he was in bed, ill. Nursed him. Usual story. Took pity on him but wasn't interested in him in that way.

"A very attractive girl," said the barber.

"And he got it badly?"

"They get it badly, consumptives."

"Matter of fact," said the barber, stepping over for the clippers and shooting a hard sideways stare at me. "It was my wife."

"Before she was my wife," he said. There was a touch of quiet, amused resolution in him.

He'd known that chap since he was a kid. Went to school with him. Used to be his best friend. Still was. Always a lad. Regular nut. Had a milk business, was his own guv'nor till he got ill. Doing well.

"He knew I was courting her," he smiled. "That didn't stop him." There was a glint in his eye.

"What did you do?" I asked.

"I lay low," he said.

She had a job in the shop opposite. If you passed that shop you couldn't help noticing her in the cash desk near the door. "It's not for me to say—but she was the prettiest girl in this town," he said. "Still is," he mused.

"You've seen the river? You came over it by the station," he said. "Well he used to take her on the river when I was busy. I didn't mind. I knew my mind. She knew hers. I knew it was all right."

"I knew him," he grinned. "But I knew her. 'Let him take you on the river,' I said."

I saw the barber's forehead and his dull blue eyes looking up for a moment over my head in the mirror.

"Damp river," he said reflectively. "Damp mists, I mean, on the river.

Very flat, low lying, unhealthy," he said. "That's where he made his mistake. It started with him taking her on the river."

"Double pneumonia once," he said. "Sixty cigarettes a day, burning the candle at both ends."

He grunted.

"He couldn't get away with it," he said.

When he got ill, the girl used to go and look after him. She used to go and read to him in the afternoons. "I used to turn up in the evenings too when we'd closed."

The barber came round to the front and took the brushes lazily. He glanced sardonically at the door as if expecting to see the man standing there. That cocksure irony in the barber seemed to warm up.

"Know what he used to say to her?" he said sharply and smiled when I was startled. " 'Here, Jenny,' he used to say. 'Tell Fred to go home and you pop into bed with me. I'm lonely.' " The young barber gave a short laugh.

"In front of me," he said.

"What did you say?"

"I told him to keep quiet or there'd be a funeral. Consumptives want it, they want it worse than others, but it kills them," he said.

"I thought you meant *you'd* kill him," I said.

"Kill him?" he said. "Me kill him?" He smiled scornfully at me: I was an outsider in this. "He tried to kill *me*," he said.

"Yeah," he said, wiping his hands on a towel. "Tried to poison me. Whisky. It didn't work. Back OK?" he said, holding up a mirror. "I don't drink."

"I went to his room," he said. "I was his best friend. He was lying on the bed. Thin! All bones and blue veins and red patches as if he'd been scalded and eyes as bright as that bottle of bath salts. Not like he is now. There was a bottle of whisky and a glass by the side of the bed. He wanted me to have a drop. He knew I didn't drink.

" 'I don't want one,' I said. 'Yes, you do,' he said. 'You know I never touch it,' I said. 'Well, touch it now,' he said. 'I tell you what,' he said; 'you're afraid.' 'Afraid of what?' I said. 'Afraid of catching what I've got.' 'Touch your lips to it if you're not afraid. Just have a sip to show.'

"I told him not to be a fool. I took the bottle from him. He had no right to have whisky in his state. He was wild when I took it. 'It'll do some people a bit of good,' I said, 'but it's poison to you.'

" 'It *is* poison,' he said.

"I took the bottle away. I gave it to a chap in the town. It nearly finished him. We found out it *was* poison. He'd put something in it."

I said I'd have a singe. The barber lit the taper. I felt the flame warm against my head. "Seals up the ends," the barber said. He lifted up the hair with the comb and ran the flame along. "See the idea?" he said.

"What did you do?"

"Nothing," he said. "Just married my girl that week," the barber said. "When she told him we were going to get married he said, 'I'll give you something Fred won't give you.' We wondered what it would be. 'Something big,' he said. 'Best man's present,' he said. He winked at her. 'All I've got. I'm the best man.' That night he cut his throat." The barber made a grimace in the mirror, passed the scissors over his throat and gave a grin.

"Then he opened the window and called out to a kid in the street to fetch *her*. The kid came to me instead. Funny present," he said. He combed, he patted, he brushed. He pulled the wool out of the back of my neck. He went round it with the soft brush. Coming round to the front he adroitly drew off the sheet. I stood up.

"He got over it," he said. "Comes round and plays with my kids on Sundays. Comes in every Friday, gets himself up. See him with a different one every week at the Pictures. It's a dead place this, all right in the summer on the river. You make your own life. The only thing is he don't like shaving himself now, I have to go over every morning and do it for him."

He stood with his small grin, his steady eyes amused and resolute. "I never charge him," he said. He brushed my coat, he brought my hat.

THE SAILOR

He was lifting his knees high and putting his hand up, when I first saw him, as if, crossing the road through that stinging rain, he were breaking through the bead curtain of a Pernambuco bar. I knew he was going to stop me. This part of the Euston Road is a beat of the men who want a cup of tea or their fare to a job in Luton or some outlying town.

"Beg pardon, chum," he said in an anxious hot-potato voice. "Is that Whitechapel?"

He pointed to the traffic clogged in the rain farther down where the electric signs were printing off the advertisements and daubing them on the wet road. Coatless, with a smudged trilby hat on the back of his head so that a curl of boot polish black hair glistered with raindrops over his forehead, he stood there squeezing the water in his boots and looking at me, from his bilious eyes, like a man drowning and screaming for help in two feet of water and wondering why the crowd is laughing.

"That's St. Pancras," I said.

"Oh, Gawd," he said, putting his hand to his jaw like a man with toothache. "I'm all messed up." And he moved on at once, gaping at the lights ahead.

"Here, wait," I said. "Which part of Whitechapel do you want? Where have you come from?"

"Surrey Docks," he said. "They said it was near Surrey Docks, see, but they put me wrong. I bin on the road since ten this morning."

"Acton," he read a bus sign aloud, recalling the bottom of the day's misery. "I bin there," and fascinated, watched the bus out of sight.

The man's worried mouth dropped open. He was sodden. His clothes were black with damp. The smell of it came off him. The rain stained from the shoulders of his suit past the armpits over the ribs to the waist. It spread from dark blobs over his knees to his thighs. He was a greasy-looking man, once fat and the fat had gone down unevenly like a deflating bladder. He was calming as I spoke to him.

A sailor, of course, and lost. Hopelessly, blindly lost. I calculated that he must have wandered twenty miles that day exhausting a genius for misdirection.

"Here," I said. "You're soaked. Come and have a drink."

There was a public-house nearby. He looked away at once.

"I never touch it," he said. "It's temptation."

I think it was that word which convinced me the sailor was my kind of man. I am, on the whole, glad to say that I am a puritan and the word temptation went home, painfully, pleasurably, excitingly and intimately familiar. A most stimulating and austerely gregarious word, it indicates either the irresistible hypocrite or the fellow-struggler with sin. I couldn't let him go after that.

Presently we were in a café drinking acrid Indian tea.

"Off a ship?" I said.

He looked at me as if I were a magician who could read his soul.

"Thank Gawd I stopped you," he said. "I kep' stopping people all day and they messed me up, but you been straight."

He gave me his papers, his discharge paper, his pension form, official letters, as he said this, like a child handing himself over. Albert Edward Thompson, they said, cook, born '96, invalided out of the service two years before. So he was not just off a ship.

"They're clean," he said suspiciously when I asked him about this. "I got ulcers, riddled with ulcers for fourteen years."

He had no job and that worried him, because it was the winter. He had ganged on the road, worked in a circus, had been a waiter in an Italian restaurant. But what worried him much more was getting to Whitechapel. He made it sound to me as though for two years he had been threshing about the country, dished by one job and another, in a less and less successful attempt to get there.

"What job are you going to do?" I said.

"I don't know," he said.

"It's a bad time," I said.

"I fall on my feet," he said, "like I done with you."

We sat opposite to each other at the table. He stared at the people in the café with his appalled eyeballs. He was scared of them and they looked scared too. He looked as though he was going to give a yell and spring at them; in fact, he was likelier to have gone down on his knees to them and to have started sobbing. They couldn't know this. And then he and I looked at each other and the look discovered that we were the only two decent, trustworthy men in a seedy and grabbing world. Within the next two hours I had given him a job. I was chum no longer, but "Sir." "Chum" was anarchy and the name of any twisty bleeder you knocked up against, but "sir" (for Thompson, out of the naval nursery) was hierarchy, order, pay-day and peace.

I was living alone in the country in those days. I had no one to look after me. I gave Albert Thompson some money, I took him to Whitechapel and wrote down the directions for his journey to my house.

The bungalow where I lived was small and stood just under the brow of a hill. The country was high and stony there. The roads broke up into lanes, the lanes sank into woods and cottages were few. The oak woods were naked and as green as canker. They stood like old men, and below them were sweet plantations of larch where the clockwork pheasants went off like toys in the rainy afternoons. At night you heard a farm dog bark like a pistol and the oceanic sound of the trees and sometimes, over an hour and half's walk away, the whistle of a train. But that was all. The few people looked as though they had grown out of the land, sticks and stones in cloth; they were old people chiefly. In the one or two bigger houses they were childless. It was derelict country; frost with its teeth fast in the ground, the wind running finer than sand through a changeless sky or the solitary dribble of water in the butts and the rain legging it over the grass—that was all one heard or saw there.

"Gawd!" said Thompson when he got there. "I thought I'd never strike the place." Pale, coatless again in the wet, his hat tipped back from a face puddingy and martyred, he came up the hill with the dancing step of a man treading on nails. He had been lost again. He had travelled by the wrong train, even by the wrong line, he had assumed that, as in towns, it was safest to follow the crowd. But country crowds soon scatter. He had been following people—it sounded to me—to half the cottages for miles around.

"Then I come to the common," he said. "I didn't like the look of that. I kept round it."

At last some girl had shown him the way.

I calmed him down. We got to my house and I took him to his room. He sat down on the bed and told me the story again. He took off his boots and socks and looked at his blistered feet, murmuring to them as if they were a pair of orphans. There was a woman in the train with a kid, he said, and to amuse the kid he had taken out his jack-knife. The woman called the Guard.

After we had eaten and I had settled in, I went for a walk that afternoon. The pleasure of life in the country for me is in its monotony. One understands how much of living is habit, a long war to which people, plants and animals have settled down. In the country one expects nothing of people; they are themselves, not bringers of gifts. In towns one asks too little or too much of them.

The drizzle had stopped when I went out, the afternoon was warmer and inert and the dull stench of cattle hung over the grass. On my way down the hill I passed the bungalow which was my nearest neighbour. I could see the roof as pink as a slice of salt ham, from the top of my garden. The bungalow was ten years old. A chicken man had built it. Now the woodwork was splitting and shrinking, the garden was rank, two or three larches, which the rabbits had been at, showed above the dead grass and there was a rose-bush. The bush had one frozen and worm-eaten flower which would stick there half the winter. The history of the bungalow was written in the tin bath by the side door. The bath was full of gin, beer and whisky bottles, discarded after the weekend parties of many tenants. People took the place for ever and then, after a month or two, it changed hands. A business man, sentimental about the country, an invalid social worker, a couple with a motor bicycle, an inseparable pair of school-teachers with big legs and jumping jumpers; and now there was a woman I hardly saw, a Colonel's daughter, but the place was said to belong to a man in the Northampton boot trade.

A gramophone was playing when I walked by. Whenever I passed, the Colonel's daughter was either playing the gramophone or digging in the garden. She was a small girl in her late twenties, with a big knowledgeable-looking head under tobacco-brown curls, and the garden fork was nearly as big as herself. Her gardening never lasted long. It consisted usually of digging up a piece of the matted lawn in order to bury tins; but she went at it intensely, drawing back the fork until her hair fell over her face and the sweat stood on her brow. She always had a cigarette in her mouth, and every now and then the carnation skin of her face, with its warm, dark blue eyes, would be distorted and turned crimson by violent bronchial coughing. When this stopped she would straighten up, the delicacy came back to her skin and she would say, "Oh, Christ. Oh, bloody hell" and you noticed at the end of every speech the fine right eyebrow would rise a little and the lid of the eye below it would quiver. This wink, the limpid wink of the Colonel's daughter, you noticed at once. You wondered what it meant and planned to find out. It was as startling and enticing as a fish rising, and you discovered when you went after it that the Colonel's daughter was the hardest drinking and most blasphemous piece of apparent childish innocence you had ever seen. Old men in pubs gripped their sticks, went scarlet and said someone ought to take her drawers down and give her a tanning. I got a sort of fame from being a neighbour of the Colonel's daughter. "Who's that piece we saw down the road?" people asked.

"Her father's in the Army."

"Not," two or three of them said, for this kind of wit spreads like measles, "the Salvation Army." They said I was a dirty dog. But I hardly knew the Colonel's daughter. Across a field she would wave, utter her obscenity, perform her wink and edge off on her slight legs. Her legs were not very good. But if we met face to face on the road she became embarrassed and nervous; this was one of her dodges. "Still alone?" she said.

"Yes. And you?"

"Yes. What do you do about sex?"

"I haven't got any."

"Oh, God, I wish I'd met you before."

When I had friends she would come to the house. She daren't come there when I was alone, she said. Every night, she said, she locked and bolted up at six. Then the wink—if it was a wink. The men laughed. She did not want to be raped, she said. Their wives froze and some curled up as if they had got the blight and put their hands hard on their husbands' arms. But the few times she came to the house when I was alone, the Colonel's daughter stood by the door, the full length of the room away, with a guilty look on her face.

When I came back from my walk the gramophone had stopped. The Colonel's daughter was standing at the door of her bungalow with her sleeves rolled up, a pail of water beside her and a scrubbing brush in her hand.

"Hullo," she said awkwardly.

"Hullo," I said.

"I see you've got the Navy down here. I didn't know you were that way."

"I thought you would have guessed that straight away," I said.

"I found him on the common crying this morning. You've broken his heart." Suddenly she was taken by a fit of coughing.

"Well," she said. "Every day brings forth something."

When I got to the gate of my bungalow I saw that at any rate if Thompson could do nothing else he could bring forth smoke. It was travelling in thick brown funnel puffs from the short chimney of the kitchen. The smoke came out with such dense streaming energy that the house looked like a destroyer racing full steam ahead into the wave of hills. I went down the path to the kitchen and looked inside. There was Thompson, not only with his sleeves rolled up but his trousers also, and he was shovelling coal into the kitchener with the garden spade, the face of the fire was roaring yellow, the water was throbbing and sighing in the boiler, the pipes were singing through the house.

"Bunkering," Thompson said.

I went into the sitting-room. I thought I had come into the wrong house. The paint had been scrubbed, the floors polished like decks, the reflections of the firelight danced in them, the windows gleamed and the room was glittering with polished metal. Door-knobs, keyholes, fire-irons, window-catches, were polished; metal which I had no idea existed flashed with life.

"What time is supper piped—er ordered," said Thompson, appearing in his stockinged feet. His big round eyes started out of their dyspeptic shadows and became enthusiastic when I told him the hour.

A change came over my life after this. Before Thompson everything had been disorganised and wearying. He drove my papers and clothes back to their proper places. He brought the zest and routine of the Royal Navy into my life. He kept to his stockinged feet out of tenderness for those orphans, a kind of repentance for what he had done to them; he was collarless and he served food with a splash as if he allowed for the house to give a pitch or a roll which didn't come off. His thumbs left their marks on the plates. But he was punctual. He lived for "Orders." "All ready, sir," he said, planking down the dish and looking up at the clock at the same moment. Burned, perhaps, spilling over the side, invisible beneath Bisto—but on time!

The secret of happiness is to find a congenial monotony. My own housekeeping had suffered from the imagination. Thompson put an end to this tiring chase of the ideal. "What's orders for lunch, sir?

"Do you a nice fried chop and chips?" he said. That was settled. He went away but soon he came back.

"What pudding's ordered, sir?" That stumped both of us, or it stumped me. Thompson watched me to time his own suggestion.

"Do you a nice spotted dick?" So it was. We had this on the second day and the third, we changed on the fourth, but on the fifth we came back to it. Then Thompson's mind gave a leap.

"Do you grilled chop, chips, spotted dick *and custard*?" he said. That became almost our fixed menu. There were bouts of blancmange, but spotted dick came back.

Thompson had been sinking towards semi-starvation, I to the insidious Oblomovism of the country. Now we were reformed and happy.

"I always fall on my feet," he said, "like I done with you." It was his refrain.

The winter dripped like a tap, the fog hardly left our hill. Winter in England has the colourless, steaming look of a fried-fish shop-window. But we were stoking huge fires, we bunkered, the garden spade went through coal by the hundredweight. We began to talk a more tangy dialect. Things were not put away; they were "stowed." String appeared in strange knots to make things "fast," plants were "lashed" in the dying garden, washing was "hoist" on the lines, floors were "swabbed." The kitchen became the "galley." The postman came "alongside," all meals were "piped" and at bedtime we "piped down." At night, hearing the wind bump in the chimneys and slop like ocean surf in the woods, looking out at the leather darkness, I had the sensation that we were creeping down the Mersey in a fog or lumping about in the Atlantic swell off Ushant.

I was happy. But was Thompson happy? He seemed to be. In the mornings we were both working, but in the afternoons there was little more to do. He sat on a low chair with his knees close to the bars of the range or on the edge of his bed, darning his clothes. (He lived in a peculiar muddle of his own and he was dirty in his own quarters.) In the evenings he did the same and sometimes we talked. He told me about his life. There was nothing in it at all. It was buried under a mumble of obscurity. His memories were mainly of people who hadn't "behaved right," a dejecting moral wilderness with Thompson mooching about in it, disappointed with human nature. He didn't stay to talk with me much. He preferred the kitchen where, the oil-lamp smoking, the range smoking and himself smoking, he sat chewing it all over, gazing into the fire.

"You can go out, you know," I said, "whenever you want. Do what you like."

"I'm OK," he said.

"See some of the people," I said. Thompson said he'd just as lief stand by.

Everyone knows his own business best. But I was interested one night when I heard the sound of voices in the kitchen. Someone had come in. The voices went on on other nights. Who was it? The milker from the farm probably or the cowman who cleaned out cess pits by lantern light at night and talked with nostalgia about burying bodies during the war. "If there hadn't been a war," this man used to say, "I wouldn't have seen nothing. It was an education."

I listened. Slow in question, slow in answer, the monotonous voices came. The woodcutter, the postman? I went into the kitchen to see who the profound and interminable crony was.

There was no one. There was only Thompson in the kitchen. Sitting close to the fire with all windows closed, a sallow, stupefied, oil-haired head in his own fug, Thompson was spelling out a story from a

Wild West Magazine. It was old and dirty and his coal-blackened finger was moving from word to word.

So far Thompson had refused to go out of the house except as far as the coal-shed, but I was determined after this discovery that he should go out. I waited until pay-day.

"Here's your money," I said. "Take the afternoon off."

Thompson stepped back from the money.

"You keep it," he said, in a panic. "You keep it for me."

"You may need it," I said. "For a glass of beer or cigarettes or something."

"If I have it I'll lose it," he said. "They'll pinch it."

"Who?" I said.

"People," Thompson said. I could not persuade him.

"All right, I'll keep it for you," I said.

"Yes," he said eagerly. "If I want a bob I'll ask you. Money's temptation," he said.

"Well, anyway," I said, "take the afternoon off. It's the first sunny afternoon we've had. I'll tell you where to go. Turn to the right in the lane . . ."

"I don't like them lanes," said Thompson, looking suspiciously out of the window. "I'll stay by you."

"Well, take a couple of hours," I said. "We all need fresh air."

He looked at me as if I had suggested he should poison himself; indeed as if I were going to do the poisoning.

"What if I do an hour?" he began to bargain.

"No, the afternoon," I said.

"Do you half an hour?" he pleaded.

"All right, I don't want to force you," I said. "This is a free country. Go for an hour."

It was like an auction.

"Tell you what," he said, looking shifty. "I'll do you twenty minutes." He thought he had tricked me, but I went back into the kitchen and drove him to it. I had given him an overcoat and shoes, and it was this appeal to his vanity which got him. Out he went for his twenty minutes. He was going straight down the lane to where it met the main road and then straight back; it would take a smart walker about twelve minutes on a winter's day.

When an hour passed I was pleased with myself. But when four hours had gone by and darkness came I began to wonder. I went out to the gate. The land and the night had become one thing. I had just gone in again when I heard loud voices and saw the swing of a lamp. There came Thompson with a labourer. The labourer, a little bandy man known as Fleas, stood like a bent bush with a sodden sack on his shoulders, snuffling in the darkness, and he grinned at me with the malevolence of the land.

"He got astray," he said, handing Thompson over.

"Gawd," exclaimed Thompson, exhausted. His face was the familiar pale suety agony. He was full of explanations. He was sweating like a scared horse and nearly hysterical. He'd been on the wrong course. He didn't know where to steer. One thing looked like another. Roads and lanes, woods and fields, mixed themselves together.

"Woods I seen," he said in horror. "And that common! It played me up proper."

"But you weren't anywhere near the common," I said.

"Then what was it?" he said.

That night he sat by the fire with his head in his hands.

"I got a mood," he said.

The next morning cigarette smoke blew past my window and I heard coughing. The Colonel's daughter was at the kitchen door talking to Thompson. "Cheero," I heard her say and then she came to my door and pushed it open. She stood there gravely and her eye winked. She was wearing a yellow jersey and looked as neat as a bird.

"You're a swine," she said.

"What have I done?"

"Raping women on the commons," she said. "Deserting your old friends, aren't you?"

"It's been too wet on the common," I said.

"Not for me," she said. "I'm always hopeful. I came across last night. There was the Minister's wife screaming in the middle of it. I sat on her head and calmed her down and she said a man had been chasing her. 'Stop screaming,' I said. 'You flatter yourself, dear.' It was getting dark and I carried her shopping-bag and umbrella for her and took her to her house. I often go and see her in the evenings. I've got to do something, haven't I? I can't stick alone in that bungalow all day and all night. We sit and talk about her son in China. When you're old you'll be lonely too."

"What happened on the common?"

"I think I'm drunk," said the Colonel's daughter, "but I believe I've been drunk since breakfast. Well, where was I? I'm losing my memory too. Well, we hadn't gone five minutes before I heard someone panting like a dog behind us and jumping over bushes. Old Mrs. Stour started screaming again. 'Stand still,' I said, and I looked and then a man came out of a tree about ten yards away. 'What the hell do you want?' I said. A noise came back like a sheep. 'Ma'am, ma'am, ma'am, ma'am,' it said."

"So that's where Thompson was," I said.

"I thought it was you," the Colonel's daughter said. " 'There's a woman set about me with a stick on the common,' he said. 'I didn't touch her, I was only following her,' he said. 'I reckoned if I followed her I'd get home.' "

When they got to the wood Thompson wouldn't go into it and she had to take his hand; that was a mistake. He took his hand away and moved off. So she grabbed his coat. He struggled after this, she chased him into the thicket and told him not to be a fool, but he got away and disappeared, running on to the common.

"You're a damn swine," the Colonel's daughter said to me. "How would you like to be put down in the middle of the sea?"

She walked away. I watched her go up the path and lean on the gate opposite to stroke the nose of a horse. She climbed into the field and the horses, like hairy yokels, went off. I heard her calling them but they did not come.

When she was out of sight, the door opened behind me and Thompson came in.

"Beg pardon, sir," he said. "That young lady, sir. She's been round my kitchen door."

"Yes," I said.

He gaped at me and then burst out:

"I didn't touch her, straight I didn't. I didn't lay a finger on her."

"She didn't say you did. She was trying to help you."

He calmed down. "Yes, sir," he said.

When he came back into the room to lay the table I could see he was trying to catch my eye.

"Sir," he said at last, standing at attention. "Beg pardon, sir, the young lady . . ."

His mouth was opening and shutting, trying to shape a sentence.

"The young lady—she'd had a couple, sir," he said in a rush.

"Oh," I said, "don't worry about that. She often has."

"It's ruination, sir," said Thompson evangelically.

She did not come to the house again for many days, but when she came I heard him lock both kitchen doors.

Orders at the one extreme, temptation at the other, were the good and evil of Thompson's life. I no longer suggested that he went out. I invented errands and ordered him to go. I wanted, in that unfortunate way one has, to do good to Thompson. I wanted him to be free and happy. At first he saw that I was not used to giving orders and he tried to dodge. His ulcers were bad, he said. Once or twice he went about barefoot, saying the sole was off one of his boots. But when he saw I meant what I said, he went. I used to watch him go, tilted forward on his toes in his half-running walk, like someone throwing himself blindly upon the mercy of the world. When he came back he was excited. He had the look of someone stupefied by incomprehensible success. It is the feeling a landsman has when he steps off a boat after a voyage. You feel giddy, canny, surprised at your survival after crossing that bridge of deep, loose water. You boast. So did Thompson—morally.

"There was a couple of tramps on the road," Thompson said. "I steered clear. I never talked to them," he said.

"Someone asked me who I was working for." He described the man. "I never told him," he said shrewdly. "I just said 'A gentleman.' Meaning you," he said.

There was a man in an allotment who had asked him for a light and wanted to know his business.

"I told him I didn't smoke," said Thompson. "You see my meaning—you don't know what it's leading up to. There warn't no harm, but that's how temptation starts."

What was temptation? Almost everything was temptation to Thompson. Pubs, cinemas, allotments, chicken-runs, tobacconists—in these, everywhere, the tempter might be. Temptation, like Othello's jealousy, was the air itself.

"I expect you'd like to go to church," I said. He seemed that kind.

"I got nothing *against* religion," Thompson said. "But best keep clear. They see you in church and the next thing they're after you."

"Who?" I asked.

"People," he said. "It's not like a ship."

I was like him, he said, I kept myself to myself. I kept out of temptation's way. He was glad I was like that, he said.

It was a shock to me that while I observed Thompson, Thompson observed me. At the same time one prides oneself, the moment one's character is defined by someone else, on defeating the definition. I kept myself to myself? I avoided temptation? That was all Thompson knew! There was the Colonel's daughter. I might not see her very often; she might be loud, likeable, dreary or alarming by turns, but she was Temptation itself. How did he know I wasn't tempted? Thompson's remark made me thrill. I began to see rather more of the Colonel's daughter.

And so I discovered how misleading he had been about his habits and how, where temptation was concerned, he made a difference between profession and practice. So strong was Thompson's feeling about temptation that he was drawn at once to every tempter he saw. He stopped them on the road and was soon talking about it. The postman was told. The shopkeepers heard all his business and mine. He hurried after tramps, he detained cyclists, he sat down on the banks with roadmakers and ditchers, telling them the dangers of drink, the caution to be kept before strangers. And after he had done this he always ended by telling them he kept himself to himself, avoided drink, ignored women and, patting his breast pocket, said that was where he kept his money and his papers. He behaved to them exactly as he had behaved with me two months before in the Euston Road. The Colonel's daughter told me. She picked up all the news in that district.

"He's a decent, friendly soul," muttered the Colonel's daughter thickly. "You're a prig. Keep your hair on. You can't help it. I expect you're decent, too, but you're like all my bloody so-called friends."

"Oh," I said hopefully, "are prigs your special line?"

I found out, too, why Thompson was always late when he came home from his errands. I had always accepted that he was lost. And so he was in a way, but he was lost through wandering about with people, following them to their doorsteps, drifting to their allotments, backyards and, all the time, telling them, as he clung to their company,

about the dangers of human intercourse. "I never speak to nobody"—
it was untrue, but it was not a lie. It was simply a delusion.

"He lives in two worlds at once," I said to the Colonel's daughter
one morning. I had sent Thompson to the town to buy the usual chops,
and I was sitting in her bungalow. This was the first time I had ever
been in it. The walls were of varnished match-boarding like the inside
of a gospel hall and the room was heated by a paraffin stove which
smelled like armpits. There were two rexine covered chairs, a rug and
a table in the room. She was sorting out gramophone records as I
talked and the records she did not like she dropped to the floor and
broke. She was listening very little to what I said but walked to the
gramophone, put on a record, stopped it after a few turns and then,
switching it off, threw the record away.

"Oh, you know a hell of a lot, don't you?" she said. "I don't say
you're not an interesting man, but you don't get on with it, do you?"

"How old are you? Twenty-five?" I said.

Her sulking, ironical expression went. She was astonished.

"Good God!" she exclaimed with a smile of sincerity. "Don't be a
damn fool." Then she frowned. "Or are you being professionally
clever?"

"Here," she said. "I was damn pretty when I was twenty-five. I'm
thirty-nine. I've still got a good figure."

"I would have put you at twenty-seven at the most," I said truth-
fully.

She walked towards me. I was sitting on the arm-chair and she stood
very close. She had never been as close to me before. I had thought her
eyes were dark blue but now I saw they were green and grey, with a
moist lascivious haze in them and yet dead and clock-like, like a cat's
on a sunless day. And the skin, which had seemed fresh to me, I saw in
its truth for the first time. It was clouded and flushed, clouded with
that thickened pimpled ruddiness which the skin of heavy drinkers has
and which in middle-age becomes bloated and mottled. I felt: this is
why she has always stood the length of the room away before.

She saw what was in my mind and she sat down on the chair opposite to me. The eye winked.

"Keep control of yourself," she said. "I came down here for a rest
and now you've started coming round."

"Only in the mornings," I said.

She laughed. She went to a bookshelf and took down a bottle of whisky and poured out half a tumblerful.

"This is what you've done coming in here, early bird," she said. "Exciting me on an empty stomach. I haven't touched it for ten days. I had a letter this morning. From my old man."

"Your father?"

I had always tried to imagine the Colonel. She gave a shout of cheerful laughter and it ended in coughing till tears came to her eyes.

"That's rich. God, that's rich. Keen observer of women! No, from my husband, darling. He's not my husband, damn him, of course, but when you've lived with someone for ten years and he pays the rent and keeps you, he is your husband, isn't he? Or ought to be. Ten years is a long time and his family thought he ought to be married. He thought so too. So he picked up a rich American girl and pushed me down here to take it easy in the country. I'm on the dole like your sailor boy. Well, I said, if he felt that way, he'd better have his head. In six months he'll tire of the new bitch. So I left him alone. I didn't want to spoil his fun. Well, now, he writes me, he wants to bring his *fiancée* down because she's heard so much about me and adores the country . . ."

I was going to say something indignant.

"He's nice too," she said casually. "He sells gas-heaters. You'd like him all the same. But blast that bloody woman," she said raising her cool voice. "She's turned him into a snob. I'm just his whore now."

"Don't look so embarrassed," she said. "I'm not going to cry."

"For ten years," she said, "I read books, I learned French, educated myself, learned to say 'How d'you do,' instead of 'Pleased to meet you,' and look down my nose at everything in his sort of way. And I let him go about saying my father was in the Army too, but they were such bloody fools they thought he must be a Colonel. They'd never heard of sergeant-majors having children. Even my old man, bless his heart," she smiled affectionately, "thought or let himself think they did. I was a damn silly little snob."

"I don't know him," I said. "But he doesn't sound much good to me."

"That's where you're wrong," she said sharply. "Just weak, poor kid, that's all. You don't know what it is to be ashamed your mother's a housemaid. I got over it—but he didn't, that's all."

She paused and the wink gave its signal.

"This is more embarrassing than I thought," she said.

"I am very sorry," I said. "Actually I am in favour of snobbery, it is a sign of character. It's a bad thing to have, but it's a bad thing not to have had. You can't help having the diseases of your time."

"There you go," she said.

The suffering of others is incredible. When it is obscure it seems like a lie; when it is garish and raw, it is like boasting. It is a challenge to oneself. I got up from my chair and went towards her. I was going to kiss her.

"You are the sentimental type," she said.

So I didn't kiss her.

Then we heard someone passing the bungalow and she went to the window. Thompson was going by. The lock of black hair was curling over his sweating forehead and he gave a hesitant staggering look at the bungalow. There was a lump of fear on his face.

"He'd better not know where you've been," she said. She moved her lips to be kissed, but I walked out.

I was glad of the steady sense of the fresh grey air when I got outside. I was angry and depressed. I stood at the window of my house. Thompson came in and was very talkative. He'd been lost, of course. He'd seen people. He'd seen fields. He'd heard trees. He'd seen roads. I hardly listened. I was used to the jerky wobbling voice. I caught the words "legion" and "temptation," and thought he was quoting from the Bible. Presently I realised he was talking about the British Legion. The postman had asked him to go to a meeting of the British Legion that night. How simple other people's problems are! Yet "No" Thompson was saying. He was not going to the British Legion. It was temptation.

I ought to have made love to her and kissed her, I was thinking. She was right, I was a prig.

"You go," I said to Thompson, "if you want to. You'd enjoy it."

But how disgusting, obvious, stupid, to have made love to her then, I thought.

"Do as you like," I said.

"I'm best alongside you," said Thompson.

"You can't always be by me," I said. "In a month, perhaps less, as you know, I'll be leaving here and you'll have to go."

"Yes," he said. "You tol' me. You been straight. I'll be straight with you. I won't go to the Legion."

We ate our meal and I read.

"In every branch of our spiritual and material civilisation we seem to have reached a turning point," I read. "This spirit shows itself not only in the actual state of public affairs . . ."

Well, I thought, I can ask her over tonight. I needn't be a fool twice. I went out for an hour. When I returned Thompson was fighting Temptation hard. If he went to the Legion how would he get back? No, best not. He took the Legion on in its strength. (She is a type, I thought.) At four he was still at it. At five he asked me for his money. (Well, we are all types, I was thinking.) Very shortly he brought the money back and asked me to keep his pension papers. At half-past six I realised this meant that Thompson was losing and the Legion and all its devils winning. (What is a prig, anyway?) He was looking out at the night. Yet, just when I thought he had lost, he had won. There was the familiar sound of the Wild West monologue in the kitchen. It was half-past eight. The Legion was defeated.

I was disappointed in Thompson. Really, not to have had more guts than that! Restlessly I looked out of the window. There was a full moon spinning on the tail of a dying wind. Under the moonlight the fields were like wide-awake faces, the woods like womanish heads of hair upon them. I put on my hat and coat and went out. I was astonished by the circle of stars. They were as distinct as figures on a clock. I took out my watch and compared the small time in my hand with the wide time above. Then I walked on. There was a sour smell at the end of the wood, where, no doubt, a dead rabbit or pigeon was rotting.

I came out of the wood on to the metalled road. Suddenly my heart began to beat quickly as I hurried down the road, but it was a long way round now. I cut across fields. There was a cottage and a family were listening to a dance-band on the wireless. A man was going the rounds of his chickens. There was a wheelbarrow and there were spades and steel bars where a water mill was being built.

Then I crossed the last fields and saw the bungalow. My heart throbbed heavily and I felt all my blood slow down and my limbs grow heavy. It was only when I got to the road that I saw there were no lights in the bungalow. The Colonel's daughter, the Sergeant's daughter, had gone to bed early like a child. While I stood I heard men's voices singing across the fields. It must have gone ten o'clock and people were coming out of the public-house. In all the villages of England, at this hour, loud-voiced groups were breaking up and dispersing into the lanes.

I got to my house and lit a candle. The fire was low. I was exhausted and happy to be in my house among my own things, as if I had got into my own skin again. There was no light in the kitchen. Thompson had gone to bed. I grinned at the thought of the struggles of poor Thompson. I picked up a book and read. I could hear still the sound of that shouting and singing. The beer was sour and flat in this part of the country but it made people sing.

The singing voices came nearer. I put down the book. An argument was going on in the lane. I listened. The argument was nearing the cottage. The words got louder. They were going on at my gate. I heard the gate go and the argument was on my path. Suddenly—there could be no doubt—people were coming to the door. I stood up, I could recognise no voice. Loud singing, stumbling feet, then bang! The door broke open and crashed against the wall. Tottering, drunk, with their arms round each other, Thompson and the Colonel's daughter nearly fell into the room.

Thompson stared at me with terror.

"Stand up, sailor," said the Colonel's daughter, clinging to him.

"He was lonely," she said unsteadily to me. "We've been playing gramophone records. Sing," she said.

Thompson was still staring.

"Don't look at him. Sing," she said. Then she gave a low laugh and they fell, bolt upright on the sofa like prim, dishevelled dolls.

A look of wild love of all the world came into Thompson's eyes and he smiled as I had never seen him smile before. He suddenly opened his twitching mouth and bawled:

"You've robbed every tailor,
And you've skinned every sailor,
But you won't go walking Paradise Street no more."

"Go on. That's not all," the Colonel's daughter cried and sang, "Go on—something—something, deep and rugged shore."

She put her arms round his neck and kissed him. He gaped at her with panic and looked at her skirt. It was undone.

He pointed at her leg in consternation. The sight sobered him. He pulled away his arms and rushed out of the room. He did not come back. She looked at me and giggled. Her eyes were warm and shining. She picked leaves off her skirt.

"Where's he gone? Where's he gone?" she kept asking.

"He's gone to bed," I said.

She started a fit of coughing. It strained her throat. Her eyes were dilated like an animal's caught in a trap, and she held her hand to her chest.

"I wish," she cried hysterically, pointing at me in the middle of her coughing, "I wish you could see your bloody face."

She got up and called out.

"Thompson! Thompson!" And when he did not answer she sang out, "Down by the deep and rugged shore—ore-ore-ore."

"What's the idea?" I said.

"I want Thompson," she said. "He's the only man up here."

Then she began to cry. She marched out to his room, but it was locked. She was wandering through the other rooms calling him and then she went out, away up the path. She went calling him all the way down to her bungalow.

In the morning Thompson appeared as usual. He brought the breakfast. He came in for "orders." Grilled chop, did I think? And what about spotted dick? He seemed no worse. He behaved as though nothing had happened. There was no guilty look in his eyes and no apprehension. He made no apology. Lunch passed, tea-time and the day. I finished my work and went into the kitchen.

"Tell me," I said, "about last night."

Thompson was peeling potatoes. He used to do this into a bucket on the floor, as if he were peeling for a whole crew. He put down the clasp-knife and stood up. He looked worried.

"That was a terrible thing," Thompson said, as if it was something he had read about in the papers.

"Terrible, sir. A young lady like that, sir. To come over here for me, an educated lady like that. Someone oughter teach her a lesson. Coming over and saying she wanted to play some music. I was took clean off my guard.

"It wasn't right," said Thompson. "Whichever way you look at it, it wasn't right. I told her she'd messed me up."

"I'm not blaming you. I want to know."

"And she waited till you was out," Thompson said. "That's not straight. She may class herself as an educated young lady, but do you know what I reckon she is? I reckon she's a jane."

I went down to the bungalow. I was beginning to laugh now. She was in the garden digging. Her sleeves were rolled up and she was sweating over the fork. The beds were thick with leaves and dead plants. I stood there watching her. She looked at me nervously for a moment. "I'm making the garden tidy," she said. "For Monday. When the bitch comes down."

She was shy and awkward. I walked on and, looking back, saw her go into the house. It was the last I ever saw of her. When I came back the fork she had been using was stuck in the flower bed where she had left it. She went to London that night and did not return.

"Thank Gawd," Thompson said.

There was a change in Thompson after this and there was a change in me. Perhaps the change came because the dirty February days were going, the air softer and the year moving. I was leaving soon. Thompson mentioned temptation no more. Now he went out every day. The postman was his friend. They used to go to the pub. He asked for his money. In the public-house the labourers sat around muttering in a language Thompson didn't understand. He stood them drinks. At his first pint he would start singing. They encouraged him. He stood them more drinks. The postman ordered them for him and then tapped him on the pocket book. They emptied his pockets every night. They despised him and even brought complaints to me about him after they had emptied his pockets.

Thompson came back across the common alone, wild, enthusiastic and moaning with suspicion by turns. The next day he would have a mood. All the countryside for ten miles around knew the sailor. He became famous.

Our last week came. He quietened down.

"What are you going to do?" I asked.

"I'll stay by you."

"You can't," I said. "I'll be going abroad."

"You needn't pay me," he said. "I'll stay by you." It was hard to make him understand he could not stay with me. He was depressed.

"Get me out of here safe," he pleaded at last. "Come with me to the station." He could not go on his own because all the people he knew would be after him. He had told them he was going. He had told them I was saving his pension and his last fortnight's pay. They would come creeping out of cottage doors and ditches for him. So I packed his things and got a taxi to call for us. How slowly we had lived and moved in these fields and lanes. Now we broke through it all with a rush as the car dropped down the hill and the air blew in at the window. As we passed the bungalow with the sun on its empty windows I saw the fork standing in the neglected bed. Then we swept on. Thompson sat back in the car so that no one should see him, but I leaned forward to see everything for the last time and forget it.

We got to the town. As the taxi slowed down in the streets people looked out of shops, doors, a potman nodded from the pub.

"Whatcha, Jack," the voices called.

The police, the fishmonger, boys going to school, dozens of people waved to him. I might have been riding with royalty. At the station a large woman sweeping down the steps of the bank straightened up and gave a shout.

"Hi, Jacko!" she called, bending double, went into shrieks of laughter and called across to a friend at a first-floor window. It was a triumph. But Thompson ignored them all. He sat back out of sight.

"Thank Gawd I've got you," he said. "They skin you of everything."

We sat in the train. It was a two-hour journey.

"Once I strike Whitechapel," he said in the voice of one naming Singapore, "I'll be OK." He said this several times, averting his face from the passing horror of the green fields.

"Don't you worry," he said. "Don't fret yourself for me. Don't you worry." His optimism increased as mine dwindled as we got nearer London. By the time we reached London he was almost shouting. "I'll fall on my feet, don't you worry. I'll send you my address."

We stood on the kerb and I watched him walk off into the yellow rain and the clogged, grunting and mewing traffic. He stepped right into it without looking. Taxis braked to avoid him. He was going to walk to Whitechapel. He reckoned it was safer.

THE LION'S DEN

"Oh, there you are, that's it, dear," said the mother, timidly clawing her son out of the darkness of the doorway and kissing him. "You got here all right. I couldn't look out for you; they've boarded up the window. We've had a land-mine. All the glass went last week. Have you had your tea? Have a cup of tea?"

"Well, let's see the boy," said the father. "Come in here to the light."

"I've had tea, thanks," Teddy said.

"Have another cup. It won't take a tick. I'll pop the kettle on . . ."

"Leave the boy alone, old dear," the father said. "He's had his tea. Your mother's just the same, Teddy."

"I only thought he'd like a cup of tea. He must be tired," said the mother.

"Sit down, do, there's a good girl," said the father.

"Now—can Father speak? Thank you. Would you like to wash your hands, old chap?" the father said. "We've got the hot water back, you know."

"Yes, go on," said the mother, "wash your hands. They did the water yesterday."

"There she goes again," the father said. "Wonderful, isn't it?"

"No, I don't want to wash," said Teddy.

"He doesn't want to wash his hands," said the father, "so leave him alone."

"It's hot if he wants to."

"We know it's hot," said the father. "Well, my boy, sit down and make yourself comfortable."

"Take this chair. Don't have that one. It's a horrible old thing. Here, take this one," the mother said.

"He's all right. He's got a chair," the father said.

"Let him sit where he likes," the mother said. "You do like that chair, Teddy, don't you?"

"Well," said Teddy, "you're looking well, Mother." This was not true; the mother looked ill. Her shoulders were hunched, her knees were bent and her legs bowed stiffly as she walked. When she smiled, tears ran to the corners of her eyes as if age were splitting them; and dirty shadows like fingermarks gave them the misplaced stare of anxiety. Her fingers, too, were twisting and untwisting the corners of her cardigan.

"Of course she's looking well. Nothing wrong with her, is there? What I keep saying," the father said.

He was a bit of a joker. He resembled a doll-like colonel from a magazine cover, but too easy in manner for that.

"I'm well now," said the mother. "It's just these old raids. They upset me, but I get over it."

"We worry about you," Teddy said.

"You shouldn't worry," said the father. "There's nothing to worry about, really. We're here, that's the chief point. We just don't worry at all."

"It doesn't do any good, Teddy dear," said the mother. She was sitting by the fire and she leaned over to him and gripped his knee hard. "We've had our life. I'm seventy, don't forget."

"Seventy," laughed his father. "She can't forget she's seventy. She doesn't look it."

"But I am," said his mother fiercely.

"Age is what you make it," the father said. "That's how I feel."

"There's a lot in that," said the son.

"I go to bed ... and I lie there listening," the mother said. "I just wait for it to go. Your father, of course, he goes to sleep at once. He's tired. He has a heavy day. But I listen and listen," the mother said, "and when it goes I give him a shake and say 'It's gone.'"

"I don't want to sound immodest," the father laughed, "but she nearly has my—my confounded pyjamas off me sometimes."

"He just lies there. He'd sleep through it, guns and all," the mother went on. "But I couldn't do that. I sit on the edge of the bed. If it's bad I sit on the top of the stairs."

"We both do if it's bad," the father said. "I get up if it's bad."

"You ought to sit under the staircase, not on top," said Teddy.

"Just in case," said the mother. "I like to feel I can get out."

"You see, you want to get out," the father said. "It isn't that one's afraid, but—well—you feel more comfortable."

"I sit there and I know it's wrong of me, I think of you all, if I'll ever see any of you again. I wish you were with me. I never see you all, not together like we used to be . . ."

"It is natural for a mother to feel like that," said the father.

"I mean if we could be not so far apart."

"We wish you'd come down to us," Teddy said.

"I wish I could, dear," said the mother.

"Why don't you? You could, easily."

"I'd like to, but I can't."

"I don't see why not. Why don't you send her, Dad? Just for the rest."

"I've got to stay with Dad," she said.

"Your mother feels she's got to stay with me."

"But," Teddy said, "you could look after yourself for a while."

"I could look after myself all right," said the father. "Don't you worry about that."

"Well," said Teddy, "what's against it?"

"Nothing's against it," said his father. "Just herself. She feels her place is here. She just feels this is her place."

His father raised his chin and lowered his eyes bashfully. He had a small white moustache as slight as a monkey's, and it seemed to give a twist to the meaning of his words, putting them between sets of inverted commas.

The mother read his eyes slowly and fidgeted on her stool by the fire. She nodded from habit when she had got through her husband's words, but she glanced furtively at her son. She put on an air of light-heartedness, to close the subject.

"Some day I'll come," she said. "The Miss Andersons are very kind. They had us down last Sunday when the windows went . . . It's safer downstairs."

"You know what I feel?" said his father, in a sprightly way. "I feel it's safe everywhere."

The son and the mother both looked at the father with very startled concern and sympathy, recognising that in danger everyone lives by his own foible. Then guiltily they glanced at each other.

"I feel it," said the father apologetically, when he saw their expression.

"I know it," he asserted, feebly scowling. Seeing he had embarrassed them, he escaped into a business-like mood. "Now I'm going down to see about the coal for the morning. I always do it at this time."

"He's wonderful," said the mother. "He always does the coal."

When the father left the room a great change came over the mother and son.

"Come nearer the fire, dear," said the mother. They were together. They came closer together like lovers.

"Just a minute, dear," she said. And she went to the curtains and peeped into the night. Then she came back to the stool.

"You see how it is, dear," she said. "He has faith." The son scowled.

"It's wonderful, his faith," she said. "He trusts in God."

A look of anger set on the son's jaw for a moment, then he wagged his head resignedly.

"He always did. You remember, when you were a boy?" said the mother, humouring her son. "I never could. He did from the beginning when I met him. Mind you, Teddy, I don't say it's a bad thing. It's got him on. When one of those old things starts he goes to his room and he prays. I know he's praying. Really he's praying all the time, for me, for you children . . ."

"For us!" exclaimed the son.

"Yes, for everyone," said the mother. "The world—oh, I don't understand. If there's a God why did He let it happen in the first place?—but your father, he always did do things on a big scale."

She was speaking in a whisper and glancing now and then at the door.

"Too big," she murmured.

"If there is a God," said the son. "He is pitiable, weak, small. Hardly born . . ."

He checked himself when he saw that his mother looked at him without comprehension. "I am old," she shivered and he saw the tears cracking in her eyes. "I used to live in hope—you know for the future. You know, hope things would go right, hoping things for you children, but now I haven't even got hope." She looked wildly. "It's gone."

She stared over his shoulder to the walls of the room and the heavy curtains.

"It isn't this old war and these old raids," she said. "Life's gone, it's gone too quickly. There's nothing, Ted, that's how it seems to me, except if we could just be together as we were."

"Don't cry, Mother."

"No, mustn't cry, mustn't let him see I cried. Women do cry. It's silly. What shall we talk about? Let's think of something else."

She became sly and detached like a young girl running away, daring him to catch her. He knew these changes of mood in his mother very well. She began to talk in a bold taunting way.

"It's the house," she said scornfully. "He doesn't like the house to be left. Someone must be in the house. It won't run away I tell him. Good thing if it was bombed. But his mother was just the same, cling on, cling on, scrubbing, polishing. 'You can't take it with you,' I used to say to her. She used to give me a look. 'Eh,' she said, 'you want me to die.' I can see her now. 'You wicked woman,' I said. And when they carried her out, the men bumped the coffin, dear, on the chest of drawers and I thought: 'If you could see that scratch!' Some call it faith. I call it property. Property."

His mother's eyes became sly and malicious. She laughed.

"Oh, there are things I could tell you," she cried recklessly, looking at the door. "When it starts and I hear the guns, I think of you. Things you don't know about, you were just a baby at the time. No one knows them. It's my life. All those years. Can you hear him? Is he coming upstairs?"

"No, I don't hear him."

"No, he'll be another minute or two. Quick, I'll show you something. Come along."

She got up and seizing her son's sleeve she nearly ran with him from the room.

"You're not to say anything," she said.

"His bedroom," she said. "Look at it."

It was simply a bedroom with too much furniture in it.

"Three chests of drawers," the son said. "What does he want with three?" A look of wicked delight came into his mother's face, a look so merry that he knew he was saying what she wanted him to say.

"Two wardrobes," he exclaimed.

"Three with this!" exclaimed his mother, touching a cupboard in the corner, as if she were selling it.

"And then—just in case you want to read," his mother said satirically. She pointed one by one to several reading lamps by the bed, on the chests, on the dressing-table.

"What's he want five for?" said the son.

"Shave?" said his mother excitedly, opening a heavy drawer. Inside was a number of razors and shaving things of all kinds. She bent to the drawer below.

"Locked," she said. Undismayed, she led him to the far wall. "Count," she said. The son began to count. At seventeen he stopped. There were many more than seventeen pairs of boots lined up, and at the end the son stopped with astonishment.

"Riding-boots. When does he ride?"

"He's never ridden in his life, my dear."

"Waders, climbing boots . . ." the son began to laugh. "He never fished, did he?—"

"When did he buy all this gear?"

"Oh, we haven't begun, dear. Look at this."

One by one she opened the wardrobes swiftly, allowed her son to glance, even to touch for a moment, and then swiftly closed the door. She showed him some thirty suits of clothes and more hats than he could count.

"I'll try one on," said the son laughing.

"No," said the mother, "he'd know you'd touched them."

"What's the idea of this hoard? It's madness," he said.

The word madness came to his head because, at this triumph of her secret-telling, she looked mad herself. Her eyes stared with all the malice of the mad, intent on their message. Then quickly as a mouse she scurried to the door and listened.

The son stood by the fireplace when she went to the door and looked at a picture over the mantelpiece. It was the only picture in the room. It was a picture of a tall, bareheaded, austere man in ancient robes, standing in the shadows of a crowded place, alone. And in those shadows crouched a prowling group of lions, their surly faces barred with scowls of anger and fear.

"Daniel in the Lion's Den. He loves old Daniel," said his mother, coming up behind him. "He's always talking of Daniel."

The son gaped at the picture. The room was filled with his father's life, but this picture seemed to be more profoundly his father's life than anything in the room. He suddenly felt ashamed of being in his father's room.

"Let's go back to the fire," the son said.

"Look, dear," the mother was pulling at his sleeve. "Something else, quick."

She took him to a chest of drawers and opened the drawers one by one.

"Pants," she said in her deceptive voice, and as she spoke she carefully lifted one or two of the garments. Underneath them was a silver cruet.

"Solid silver," she said. "Wait. Two dozen teaspoons. A set of fish-knives. All silver."

"Come along, Mother. I know, I know."

"Silver tea-tray. Kettle," she was at another drawer, ignoring him.

"Fish-knives, spoons, ink-stands . . ."

"Mother, stop . . ."

"You move this. It's heavy. Look at this one. Shirts." She was lifting the shirts and revealing under them a cache of silver cream-jugs, hot-water jugs . . .

"Oh dear," said his mother. "We never use them. We never see them. He thinks I don't know. He just comes home and goes straight to his bedroom and slips them in."

"Where does he pick up all this?" said the son.

"Ask no questions, hear no lies," said his mother.

"No, seriously, what's the idea?"

The old lady's face was marked suddenly by all the bewilderment of a lifetime. She was helpless.

"Don't ask me, dear," she said. "It's him. It's how he's always been."

She looked at her son, exhausted and enquiring. She had suddenly lost interest. She was also frightened.

"Come out, in case he comes. You see, dear, how it is. We couldn't leave all that."

She turned out the lights and they walked back into the sitting-room. "You're looking tired, dear," she said, in an unnatural voice, making conversation. "Do you sleep well?"

She went over to the curtain again and peeped out as she said this.

"Pretty well."

She came back to the fire.

"I know. You dream. Do you dream? I dream something chronic. Every night. Your father doesn't dream, of course. He just sleeps. He's always been like that. Sometimes I have a terrible dream. I dream, dear, that I'm in a palace, a king's palace, something like Windsor Castle, and I go into a great hall and it's filled with—treasure: well, things, beautiful—you know, armour, pictures, china, and I stand there and I can't get my breath and I say 'Oh. I must get out.' And I go out of a door just to get air to breathe . . ."

"Indigestion," said her son.

"Is it? Well, through this door there's another room, just the same, but it's filled with commoner things—crockery, ironmongery, furniture—just like a second-hand shop, but thousands, dear, and I think, 'Oh, let me breathe,' and I hurry out of it by the door, and beyond that door," said the mother, holding his hand, "is another room. Ted, it's full of everything decaying, filthy. Oh, it's horrible, dear. I wake up feeling sick."

"What is that?" asked the son, nodding to the ceiling. "Up there."

"On the ceiling?" she said. "Oh, that's our crack. It's getting bigger," she said. "It's a bad one."

"That was the land-mine, dear, the one that broke the windows. The one that killed old Mrs. Croft . . ."

"I know, Mother, don't . . ."

"I thought we had gone and I said, 'Oh Dad. We've gone.' Ted, dear, the dust!"

They looked at the ceiling. Beginning at the wall by the window, the crack was like a cut that has not closed.

"And perhaps it would have been a good thing if we had gone," she said, narrowing her eyes and searching her son's face with a look that terrified him. "We've had our life. What is your life? I watch that old crack and I say, 'Let's see. Are you getting larger?' But he sits there, quiet at his table, and says 'Remember Daniel. There's nothing to be afraid of.' It's wonderful, really. He believes it. It does him good.

There's just ourselves, dear, you see. You've all grown up, you've gone your own ways, you can't be here with me and it wouldn't be right if you could be. I always feel I've got you. I think to myself, I've got something, I've got you children. But he's got nothing. You mustn't take any notice of the things I say. I expect you know women just say things and don't know why they say them ... When I see him sitting there under the lamp, praying for me and you and all of us, I think, 'Poor old Daddy, that's all he's got—his faith. But I've got him.'"

"Ssh, Mother, don't cry. He's coming now," the son said. Quickly she sat on the stool by the fire and put her head forward so that the disorder of her face should be hidden in the glow of the flame.

The father tapped his fingers comically on the panel of the door.

"May I come in? Sure I'm not interrupting? Thank you. Mother and son," he smiled, nodding his head. "The old, old story, mother and son."

A flush of annoyance and guilt passed over the son's body and came to his lips in a jaunty, uneasy laugh.

The father frowned.

"I say, old girl," he said. "I've just been outside. There was a chink of light showing in my room. We must be careful ..."

"I was just showing Ted round," said the mother.

"Showing me round the estate," Ted said.

"I've switched it off," the mother said.

"Switch it on, old girl. Let's have that tea." He settled himself innocently on the edge of his chair with his legs tucked under it, and his pleased fingers joined over his waistcoat.

"It's a good thing I know your mother. How old are you, my boy—forty? In forty-five years I've got to know her," the father smiled.

The old lady nodded her head as she went over his words, and then she got up from her stool to make the tea.

"I don't think they'll come tonight, dear," she said with spirit.

"I'm here," the son laughed.

"Run along, old girl. Of course they won't," the father said, ordering and defending his own. "I just *know* they won't."

The Saint

When I was seventeen years old I lost my religious faith. It had been unsteady for some time and then, very suddenly, it went as the result of an incident in a punt on the river outside the town where we lived. My uncle, with whom I was obliged to stay for long periods of my life, had started a small furniture-making business in the town. He was always in difficulties about money, but he was convinced that in some way God would help him. And this happened. An investor arrived who belonged to a sect called the Church of the Last Purification, of Toronto, Canada. Could we imagine, this man asked, a good and omnipotent God allowing his children to be short of money? We had to admit we could not imagine this. The man paid some capital into my uncle's business and we were converted. Our family were the first Purifiers—as they were called—in the town. Soon a congregation of fifty or more were meeting every Sunday in a room at the Corn Exchange.

At once we found ourselves isolated and hated people. Everyone made jokes about us. We had to stand together because we were sometimes dragged into the courts. What the unconverted could not forgive in us was first that we believed in successful prayer and, secondly, that our revelation came from Toronto. The success of our prayers had a simple foundation. We regarded it as "Error"—our name for Evil—to believe the evidence of our senses and if we had influenza or consumption, or had lost our money or were unemployed, we denied the reality of these things, saying that since God could not have made them they therefore did not exist. It was exhilarating to look at our congregation and to know that what the vulgar would call miracles were performed among us, almost as a matter of routine, every day. Not very big miracles, perhaps; but up in London and out in Toronto, we knew that deafness and blindness, cancer and insanity, the great scourges, were constantly vanishing before the prayers of the more advanced Purifiers.

"What!" said my schoolmaster, an Irishman with eyes like broken glass and a sniff of irritability in the bristles of his nose. "What! Do you have the impudence to tell me that if you fell off the top floor of this building and smashed your head in, you would say you hadn't fallen and were not injured?"

I was a small boy and very afraid of everybody, but not when it was a question of my religion. I was used to the kind of conundrum the Irishman had set. It was useless to argue, though our religion had already developed an interesting casuistry.

"I *would* say so," I replied with coldness and some vanity. "And my head would not be smashed."

"You would not say so," answered the Irishman. "You would not say so." His eyes sparkled with pure pleasure. "You'd be dead."

The boys laughed, but they looked at me with admiration.

Then, I do not know how or why, I began to see a difficulty. Without warning and as if I had gone into my bedroom at night and had found a gross ape seated in my bed and thereafter following me about with his grunts and his fleas and a look, relentless and ancient, scored on his brown face, I was faced with the problem which prowls at the centre of all religious faith. I was faced by the difficulty of the origin of evil. Evil was an illusion, we were taught. But even illusions have an origin. The Purifiers denied this.

I consulted my uncle. Trade was bad at the time and this made his faith abrupt. He frowned as I spoke.

"When did you brush your coat last?" he said. "You're getting slovenly about your appearance. If you spent more time studying books"—that is to say, the Purification literature—"and less with your hands in your pockets and playing about with boats on the river, you wouldn't be letting Error in."

All dogmas have their jargon; my uncle as a business man loved the trade terms of the Purification. "Don't let Error in," was a favourite one. The whole point about the Purification, he said, was that it was scientific and therefore exact; in consequence it was sheer weakness to admit discussion. Indeed, betrayal. He unpinched his pince-nez, stirred his tea and indicated I must submit or change the subject. Preferably the latter. I saw, to my alarm, that my arguments had defeated my uncle. Faith and doubt pulled like strings round my throat.

"You don't mean to say you don't believe that what our Lord said was true?" my aunt asked nervously, following me out of the room. "Your uncle does, dear."

I could not answer. I went out of the house and down the main street to the river where the punts were stuck like insects in the summery flash of the reach. Life was a dream, I thought; no, a nightmare, for the ape was beside me.

I was still in this state, half sulking and half exalted, when Mr. Hubert Timberlake came to the town. He was one of the important people from the headquarters of our Church and he had come to give an address on the Purification at the Corn Exchange. Posters announcing this were everywhere. Mr. Timberlake was to spend Sunday afternoon with us. It was unbelievable that a man so eminent would actually sit in our dining-room, use our knives and forks, and eat our food. Every imperfection in our home and our characters would jump out at him. The Truth had been revealed to man with scientific accuracy—an accuracy we could all test by experiment—and the future course of human development on earth was laid down, finally. And here in Mr. Timberlake was a man who had not merely performed many miracles—even, it was said with proper reserve, having twice raised the dead—but who had actually been to Toronto, our headquarters, where this great and revolutionary revelation had first been given.

"This is my nephew," my uncle said, introducing me. "He lives with us. He thinks he thinks, Mr. Timberlake, but I tell him he only thinks he does. Ha, ha." My uncle was a humorous man when he was with the great. "He's always on the river," my uncle continued. "I tell him he's got water on the brain. I've been telling Mr. Timberlake about you, my boy."

A hand as soft as the best quality chamois leather took mine. I saw a wide upright man in a double-breasted navy blue suit. He had a pink square head with very small ears and one of those torpid, enamelled smiles which were said by our enemies to be too common in our sect.

"Why, isn't that just fine?" said Mr. Timberlake who, owing to his contacts with Toronto, spoke with an American accent. "What say we tell your uncle it's funny he thinks he's funny."

The eyes of Mr. Timberlake were direct and colourless. He had the look of a retired merchant captain who had become decontaminated from the sea and had reformed and made money. His defence of me had made me his at once. My doubts vanished. Whatever Mr. Timberlake believed must be true and as I listened to him at lunch, I thought there could be no finer life than his.

"I expect Mr. Timberlake's tired after his address," said my aunt.

"Tired?" exclaimed my uncle, brilliant with indignation. "How can Mr. Timberlake be tired? Don't let Error in!"

For in our faith the merely inconvenient was just as illusory as a great catastrophe would have been, if you wished to be strict, and Mr. Timberlake's presence made us very strict.

I noticed then that, after their broad smiles, Mr. Timberlake's lips had the habit of setting into a long depressed sarcastic curve.

"I guess," he drawled, "I guess the Al-mighty must have been tired sometimes, for it says He re-laxed on the seventh day. Say, do you know what I'd like to do this afternoon," he said turning to me. "While your uncle and aunt are sleeping off this meal let's you and me go on the river and get water on the brain. I'll show you how to punt."

Mr. Timberlake, I saw to my disappointment, was out to show he understood the young. I saw he was planning a "quiet talk" with me about my problems.

"There are too many people on the river on Sundays," said my uncle uneasily.

"Oh, I like a crowd," said Mr. Timberlake, giving my uncle a tough look. "This is the day of rest, you know." He had had my uncle gobbling up every bit of gossip from the sacred city of Toronto all the morning.

My uncle and aunt were incredulous that a man like Mr. Timberlake should go out among the blazers and gramophones of the river on a Sunday afternoon. In any other member of our Church they would have thought this sinful.

"Waal, what say?" said Mr. Timberlake. I could only murmur.

"That's fixed," said Mr. Timberlake. And on came the smile as simple, vivid and unanswerable as the smile on an advertisement. "Isn't that just fine!"

Mr. Timberlake went upstairs to wash his hands. My uncle was deeply offended and shocked, but he could say nothing. He unpinched his glasses.

"A very wonderful man," he said. "So human," he apologised.

"My boy," my uncle said. "This is going to be an experience for you. Hubert Timberlake was making a thousand a year in the insurance business ten years ago. Then he heard of the Purification. He threw everything up, just like that. He gave up his job and took up the work. It was a struggle, he told me so himself this morning. 'Many's the time,' he said to me this morning, 'when I wondered where my next meal was coming from.' But the way was shown. He came down from Worcester to London and in two years he was making fifteen hundred a year out of his practice."

To heal the sick by prayer according to the tenets of the Church of the Last Purification was Mr. Timberlake's profession.

My uncle lowered his eyes. With his glasses off the lids were small and uneasy. He lowered his voice too.

"I have told him about your little trouble," my uncle said quietly with emotion. I was burned with shame. My uncle looked up and stuck out his chin confidently.

"He just smiled," my uncle said. "That's all."

Then we waited for Mr. Timberlake to come down.

I put on white flannels and soon I was walking down to the river with Mr. Timberlake. I felt that I was going with him under false pretences; for he would begin explaining to me the origin of evil and I would have to pretend politely that he was converting me when, already, at the first sight of him, I had believed. A stone bridge, whose two arches were like an owlish pair of eyes gazing up the reach, was close to the landing-stage. I thought what a pity it was the flannelled men and the sunburned girls there did not know I was getting a ticket for *the* Mr. Timberlake who had been speaking in the town that very morning. I looked round for him and when I saw him I was a little startled. He was standing at the edge of the water looking at it with an expression of empty incomprehension. Among the white crowds his air of brisk efficiency had dulled. He looked middle-aged, out of place and insignificant. But the smile switched on when he saw me.

"Ready?" he called. "Fine!"

I had the feeling that inside him there must be a gramophone record going round and round, stopping at that word.

He stepped into the punt and took charge.

"Now I just want you to paddle us over to the far bank," he said, "and then I'll show you how to punt."

Everything Mr. Timberlake said still seemed unreal to me. The fact that he was sitting in a punt, of all commonplace material things, was incredible. That he should propose to pole us up the river was terrifying. Suppose he fell into the river? At once I checked the thought. A leader of our Church under the direct guidance of God could not possibly fall into a river.

The stream is wide and deep in this reach, but on the southern bank there is a manageable depth and a hard bottom. Over the clay banks the willows hang, making their basket-work print of sun and shadow on the water, while under the gliding boats lie cloudy, chloride caverns. The hoop-like branches of the trees bend down until their tips touch the water like fingers making musical sounds. Ahead in midstream, on a day sunny as this one was, there is a path of strong light which is hard to look at unless you half close your eyes and down this path on the crowded Sundays, go the launches with their parasols and their pennants; and also the rowing boats with their beetle-leg oars, which seem to dig the sunlight out of the water as they rise. Upstream one goes, on and on between the gardens and then between fields kept for grazing. On the afternoon when Mr. Timberlake and I went out to settle the question of the origin of evil, the meadows were packed densely with buttercups.

"Now," said Mr. Timberlake decisively when I had paddled to the other side. "Now I'll take her."

He got over the seat into the well at the stern.

"I'll just get you clear of the trees," I said.

"Give me the pole," said Mr. Timberlake standing up on the little platform and making a squeak with his boots as he did so. "Thank you, sir. I haven't done this for eighteen years but I can tell you, brother, in those days I was considered some poler."

He looked around and let the pole slide down through his hands. Then he gave the first difficult push. The punt rocked pleasantly and we moved forward. I sat facing him, paddle in hand, to check any inward drift of the punt.

"How's that, you guys?" said Mr. Timberlake looking round at our eddies and drawing in the pole. The delightful water sished down it.

"Fine," I said. Deferentially I had caught the word.

He went on to his second and his third strokes, taking too much water on his sleeve, perhaps, and uncertain in his steering, which I corrected, but he was doing well.

"It comes back to me," he said. "How am I doing?"

"Just keep her out from the trees," I said.

"The trees?" he said.

"The willows," I said.

"I'll do it now," he said. "How's that? Not quite enough? Well, how's this?"

"Another one," I said. "The current runs strong this side."

"What? More trees?" he said. He was getting hot.

"We can shoot out past them," I said. "I'll ease us over with the paddle."

Mr. Timberlake did not like this suggestion.

"No, don't do that. I can manage it," he said. I did not want to offend one of the leaders of our Church, so I put the paddle down; but I felt I ought to have taken him farther along away from the irritation of the trees.

"Of course," I said. "We could go under them. It might be nice."

"I think," said Mr. Timberlake, "that would be a very good idea."

He lunged hard on the pole and took us towards the next archway of willow branches.

"We may have to duck a bit, that's all," I said.

"Oh, I can push the branches up," said Mr. Timberlake.

"It is better to duck," I said.

We were gliding now quickly towards the arch, in fact I was already under it.

"I think I should duck," I said. "Just bend down for this one."

"What makes the trees lean over the water like this?" asked Mr. Timberlake. "Weeping willows—I'll give you a thought there. How

Error likes to make us dwell on sorrow. Why not call them *laughing* willows?" discoursed Mr. Timberlake as the branch passed over my head.

"Duck," I said.

"Where? I don't see them," said Mr. Timberlake turning round.

"No, your head," I said. "The branch," I called.

"Oh, the branch. This one?" said Mr. Timberlake finding a branch just against his chest and he put out a hand to lift it. It is not easy to lift a willow branch and Mr. Timberlake was surprised. He stepped back as it gently and firmly leaned against him. He leaned back and pushed from his feet. And he pushed too far. The boat went on, I saw Mr. Timberlake's boots leave the stern as he took an unthoughtful step backwards. He made a last minute grasp at a stronger and higher branch, and then, there he hung a yard above the water, round as a blue damson that is ripe and ready, waiting only for a touch to make it fall. Too late with the paddle and shot ahead by the force of his thrust, I could not save him.

For a full minute I did not believe what I saw; indeed our religion taught us never to believe what we saw. Unbelieving I could not move. I gaped. The impossible had happened. Only a miracle, I found myself saying, could save him.

What was most striking was the silence of Mr. Timberlake as he hung from the tree. I was lost between gazing at him and trying to get the punt out of the small branches of the tree. By the time I had got the punt out there were several yards of water between us and the soles of his boots were very near the water as the branch bent under his weight. Boats were passing at the time but no one seemed to notice us. I was glad about this. This was a private agony. A double chin had appeared on the face of Mr. Timberlake and his head was squeezed between his shoulders and his hanging arms. I saw him blink and look up at the sky. His eyelids were pale like a chicken's. He was tidy and dignified as he hung there, the hat was not displaced and the top button of his coat was done up. He had a blue silk handkerchief in his breast pocket. So unperturbed and genteel he seemed that as the tips of his shoes came nearer and nearer to the water, I became alarmed. He could perform what are called miracles. He would be thinking at this moment that only in an erroneous and illusory sense was he hanging from the branch of the tree over six feet of water. He was probably praying one of the closely reasoned prayers of our faith which were more like conversations with Euclid than appeals to God. The calm of his face suggested this. Was he, I asked myself, within sight of the main road, the town Recreation Ground and the landing-stage crowded with people, was he about to re-enact a well-known miracle? I hoped that he was not. I prayed that he was not. I prayed with all my will that Mr. Timberlake would not walk upon the water. It was my prayer and not his that was answered.

I saw the shoes dip, the water rise above his ankles and up his socks. He tried to move his grip now to a yet higher branch—he did not succeed—and in making this effort his coat and waistcoat rose and parted from his trousers. One seam of shirt with its pant-loops and brace-tabs broke like a crack across the middle of Mr. Timberlake. It was like a fatal flaw in a statue, an earthquake crack which made the monumental mortal. The last Greeks must have felt as I felt then, when they saw a crack across the middle of some statue of Apollo. It was at this moment I realised that the final revelation about man and society on earth had come to nobody and that Mr. Timberlake knew nothing at all about the origin of evil.

All this takes long to describe, but it happened in a few seconds as I paddled towards him. I was too late to get his feet on the boat and the only thing to do was to let him sink until his hands were nearer the level of the punt and then to get him to change hand-holds. Then I would paddle him ashore. I did this. Amputated by the water, first a torso, then a bust, then a mere head and shoulders, Mr. Timberlake, I noticed, looked sad and lonely as he sank. He was a declining dogma. As the water lapped his collar—for he hesitated to let go of the branch to hold the punt—I saw a small triangle of deprecation and pathos between his nose and the corners of his mouth. The head resting on the platter of water had the sneer of calamity on it, such as one sees in the pictures of a beheaded saint.

"Hold on to the punt, Mr. Timberlake," I said urgently. "Hold on to the punt."

He did so.

"Push from behind," he directed in a dry businesslike voice. They were his first words. I obeyed him. Carefully I paddled him towards the bank. He turned and, with a splash, climbed ashore. There he stood, raising his arms and looking at the water running down his swollen suit and making a puddle at his feet.

"Say," said Mr. Timberlake coldly, "we let some Error in that time."
How much he must have hated our family.

"I am sorry, Mr. Timberlake," I said. "I am most awfully sorry. I should have paddled. It was my fault. I'll get you home at once. Let me wring out your coat and waistcoat. You'll catch your death . . ."

I stopped. I had nearly blasphemed. I had nearly suggested that Mr. Timberlake had fallen into the water and that to a man of his age this might be dangerous.

Mr. Timberlake corrected me. His voice was impersonal, addressing the laws of human existence, rather than myself.

"If God made water it would be ridiculous to suggest He made it capable of harming his creatures. Wouldn't it?"

"Yes," I murmured hypocritically.

"OK," said Mr. Timberlake. "Let's go."

"I'll soon get you across," I said.

"No," he said. "I mean let's go on. We're not going to let a little thing like this spoil a beautiful afternoon. Where were we going? You spoke of a pretty landing-place farther on. Let's go there."

"But I must take you home. You can't sit there soaked to the skin. It will spoil your clothes."

"Now, now," said Mr. Timberlake. "Do as I say. Go on."

There was nothing to be done with him. I held the punt into the bank and he stepped in. He sat like a bursting and sodden bolster in front of me while I paddled. We had lost the pole of course.

For a long time I could hardly look at Mr. Timberlake. He was taking the line that nothing had happened and this put me at a disadvantage. I knew something considerable had happened. That glaze, which so many of the members of our sect had on their faces and persons, their minds and manners, had been washed off. There was no gleam for me from Mr. Timberlake.

"What's the house over there?" he asked. He was making conversation. I had steered into the middle of the river to get him into the strong sun. I saw steam rise from him.

I took courage and studied him. He was a man, I realised, in poor physical condition, unexercised and sedentary. Now the gleam had left him one saw the veined empurpled skin of the stoutish man with a poor heart. I remembered he had said at lunch:

"A young woman I know said, 'Isn't it wonderful. I can walk thirty miles in a day without being in the least tired.' I said, 'I don't see that bodily indulgence is anything a member of the Church of the Last Purification should boast about.'"

Yes, there was something flaccid, passive and slack about Mr. Timberlake. Bunched in swollen clothes, he refused to take them off. It occurred to me, as he looked with boredom at the water, the passing boats and the country, that he had not been in the country before. That it was something he had agreed to do but wanted to get over quickly. He was totally uninterested. By his questions—what is that church? Are there any fish in this river? Is that a wireless or a gramophone?—I understood that Mr. Timberlake was formally acknowledging a world he did not live in. It was too interesting, too eventful a world. His spirit, inert and preoccupied, was elsewhere in an eventless and immaterial habitation. He was a dull man, duller than any man I have ever known; but his dullness was a sort of earthly deposit left by a being whose diluted mind was far away in the effervescence of metaphysical matters. There was a slightly pettish look on his face as (to himself, of course) he declared he was not wet and that he would not have a heart attack or catch pneumonia.

Mr. Timberlake spoke little. Sometimes he squeezed water out of his sleeve. He shivered a little. He watched his steam. I had planned when we set out to go up as far as the lock but now the thought of another two miles of this responsibility was too much. I pretended I wanted to go only as far as the bend which we were approaching, where one of the richest buttercup meadows was. I mentioned this to him. He turned and looked with boredom at the field. Slowly we came to the bank.

We tied up the punt and we landed.

"Fine," said Mr. Timberlake. He stood at the edge of the meadow just as he had stood at the landing-stage—lost, stupefied, uncomprehending.

"Nice to stretch our legs," I said. I led the way into the deep flowers. So dense were the buttercups there was hardly any green. Presently I sat down. Mr. Timberlake looked at me and sat down also. Then I turned to him with a last try at persuasion. Respectability, I was sure, was his trouble.

"No one will see us," I said. "This is out of sight of the river. Take off your coat and trousers and wring them out."

Mr. Timberlake replied firmly:

"I am satisfied to remain as I am."

"What is this flower?" he asked to change the subject.

"Buttercup," I said.

"Of course," he replied.

I could do nothing with him. I lay down full length in the sun; and, observing this and thinking to please me, Mr. Timberlake did the same. He must have supposed that this was what I had come out in the boat to do. It was only human. He had come out with me, I saw, to show me that he was only human.

But as we lay there I saw the steam still rising. I had had enough.

"A bit hot," I said getting up.

He got up at once.

"Do you want to sit in the shade," he asked politely.

"No," I said. "Would you like to?"

"No," he said. "I was thinking of you."

"Let's go back," I said. We both stood up and I let him pass in front of me. When I looked at him again I stopped dead. Mr. Timberlake was no longer a man in a navy blue suit. He was blue no longer. He was transfigured. He was yellow. He was covered with buttercup pollen, a fine yellow paste of it made by the damp, from head to foot.

"Your suit," I said.

He looked at it. He raised his thin eyebrows a little, but he did not smile or make any comment.

The man is a saint, I thought. As saintly as any of those gold-leaf figures in the churches of Sicily. Golden he sat in the punt; golden he sat for the next hour as I paddled him down the river. Golden and bored. Golden as we landed at the town and as we walked up the street back to my uncle's house. There he refused to change his clothes or to sit by a fire. He kept an eye on the time for his train back to London. By no word did he acknowledge the disasters or the beauties of the world. If they were printed upon him, they were printed upon a husk.

———

Sixteen years have passed since I dropped Mr. Timberlake in the river and since the sight of his pant-loops destroyed my faith. I have not seen him since, and today I heard that he was dead. He was fifty-seven. His mother, a very old lady with whom he had lived all his life, went into his bedroom when he was getting ready for church and found him lying on the floor in his shirt-sleeves. A stiff collar with the tie half in-serted was in one hand. Five minutes before, she told the doctor, she had been speaking to him.

The doctor who looked at the heavy body lying on the single bed saw a middle-aged man, wide rather than stout and with an extraordinarily box-like thick-jawed face. He had got fat, my uncle told me, in later years. The heavy liver-coloured cheeks were like the chaps of a hound. Heart disease, it was plain, was the cause of the death of Mr. Timberlake. In death the face was lax, even coarse and degenerate. It was a miracle, the doctor said, that he had lived as long. Any time during the last twenty years the smallest shock might have killed him.

I thought of our afternoon on the river. I thought of him hanging from the tree. I thought of him, indifferent and golden in the meadow. I understood why he had made for himself a protective, sedentary blandness, an automatic smile, a collection of phrases. He kept them on like the coat after his ducking. And I understood why—though I had feared it all the time we were on the river—I understood why he did not talk to me about the origin of evil. He was honest. The ape was with us. The ape that merely followed me was already inside Mr. Timberlake eating out his heart.

The Wheelbarrow

"Robert," Miss Freshwater's niece called down from the window of the dismantled bedroom, "when you have finished that, would you mind coming upstairs a minute? I want you to move a trunk."

And when Evans waved back from the far side of the rumpled lawn where he was standing by the bonfire, she closed the window to keep out the smoke of slow-burning rubbish—old carpeting, clothes, magazines, papers, boxes—which hung about the waists of the fir trees and blew towards the house. For three days the fire had been burning and Evans, red-armed in his shirt sleeves and sweating along the seams of his brow, was prodding it with a garden fork. A sudden silly tongue of yellow flame wagged out: some inflammable piece of family history— who knew what?—perhaps one of her aunt's absurd summer hats or a shocking year of her father's day-dream accountancy was having its last fling. She saw Evans pick up a bit of paper from the outskirts of the fire and read it. What was it? Miss Freshwater's niece drew back her lips and opened her mouth expectantly. At this stage all family privacy had gone. Thirty, forty, fifty years of life were going up in smoke.

Evans took up the wheelbarrow and swaggered back with it across the lawn towards the house, sometimes tipping it a little to one side to see how the rubber-tyred wheel was running and to admire it. Miss Freshwater's niece smiled. With his curly black hair, his sun-reddened face and his vacant blue eyes, and the faint white scar or chip on the side of his nose, he looked like some hard-living, hard-bitten doll. "Burn this? This lot to go?" was his cry. He was an impassioned and natural destroyer. She could not have found a better man. "Without you, Robert," she said on the first day and with real feeling, "I could never have faced it."

It was pure luck getting him but, lazy, smiling and drifting, she always fell on her feet. She had stepped off the morning train from London at the beginning of the week and had stood on the kerb in the station yard, waiting for one of the two or three taxi drivers who were talking there to take notice of her. Suddenly, Evans drove in fast from the street outside, pulled up beside her, pushed her in and drove off. It was like an abduction. The other taxi drivers shouted at him in the bad language of law-abiding men, but Evans slowly moved his hand up and down, palm downwards, silently and insultingly telling them to shut up and keep their hair on. He looked very pious as he did this. It made her laugh out loud.

"They are manner-less," he said in a slow, rebuking voice, giving each syllable its clear value as if he were speaking the phrase of a poem. "I am sorry I did not ask you where you want me to take you."

They were going in the wrong direction and he had to swing round the street. She now saw him glance at her in the mirror and his doll's eyes quickly changed from shrewd pleasure to vacancy: she was a capture.

"This is not the first time you are here, I suppose?" he said.

"I was born here," she said. "I haven't been here for twenty-five years, well perhaps just for a day a few years ago. It has changed. All this building!"

She liked friendly conversations.

They were driving up the long hill out of the town towards her aunt's house. Once there had been woodland here but now, like a red hard sea flowing in to obliterate her memory, thousands of sharp villas replaced the trees in angular waves.

"Yes," he said simply. "There is money everywhere."

The car hummed up the long, concrete hill. The villas gave way to ribbons of shacks and bungalows. The gardens were buzzing with June flowers. He pointed out a bungalow which had a small grocery shop in the lean-to at the side, a yard where a couple of old cars stood, and a petrol pump. That was his place, he said. And then, beyond that, were the latest municipal housing estates built close to the Green which was only half a mile from her aunt's house. As they passed, she saw a white marquee on the Green and a big, sagging white banner with the words Gospel Mission daubed on it.

"I see the Gospellers still keep it up," she said. For it was all bad land outside the town, a place for squatters, poor craftsmen, smallholders, little men with little sheds, who in their flinty way had had for generations the habit of breaking out into little religious sects.

"Oh, yes," said Evans in a soft voice, shocked that she could doubt it. "There are great openings. There is a mighty coming to the Lord. I toil in the vineyard myself. You are Miss Freshwater's niece?" he said. "She was a toiler too. She was a giantess for the Lord."

She saw she had been reckless in laughing. She saw she was known. It was as if he had knowingly captured her.

"You don't come from these parts, do you?" she said.

"I am from Wales," he said. "I came here from the mines. I ob-ject-ed to the starvation."

They arrived at the ugly yellow house. It could hardly be seen through the overgrown laurels and fir trees which in some places fingered the dirty windows. He steadied her as she got out for she had put on weight in the last year or so and while she opened her bag to find some money, he walked to the gate and looked in.

"It was left to you in the will, I suppose?" he said.

"Yes," she said. She was a woman always glad to confide. "I've come down to clear up the rubbish before the sale. Do you know anyone here who would give me a hand?"

"There are many," he pronounced. "They are too handy." It was like a line from an anthem. He went ahead, opened the gate and led the way in and when she opened the front door, splitting it away from the cobwebs, he went in with her, walking into the stale, sun-yellowed rooms. He looked up the worn carpet of the stairs. He looked at the ceilings, measuring the size of everything.

"It will fetch a high price," he said in a sorrowful voice and then, looking over her figure like a farmer at the market, in case she might go with the property, he added enthusiasm to his sorrow.

"The highest!" he said. "Does this door go to the back?" She lost him for a while. When she found him he was outside, at the back of the house, looking into sheds. He had opened the door of one that contained gardening tools and there he was, gazing. He was looking at a new green metal wheelbarrow with a red wheel and a rubber tyre and he had even pulled it out. He pushed it back, and when he saw her he said accusingly:

"This door has no lock. I do not like to see a door without a lock. I will bring one this afternoon."

It was how she knew he had appointed himself.

"But who will do your taxi work?"

"My son will do that," he said.

From that moment he owned her and the house.

"There will be a lot of toil in this vineyard," she said to him maliciously and wished she had not said it; but Evans's eyes lost their vacancy again and quickened and sparkled. He gave a shout of laughter.

"Oh boy, there will!" he said admiring her. And he went off. She walked from room to room, opening windows, and from an upper one she saw distantly the white sheet of the Gospel tent through the fir trees. She could settle to nothing.

It was an ugly house of large mean rooms, the landings dark, the stairs steep. The furniture might have come out of old-fashioned hotels and had the helpless look of objects too large, ill-met commercially and too gregarious. After her mother's death, her father had moved his things into his sister's house. Taste had not been a strong point in the family. The books, mainly sermons, were her grandfather's; his son had lived on a hoard of engineering textbooks and magazines. His sister read chiefly the Bible and the rest of her time changed her clothes, having the notion that she might be going out.

What paralysed Miss Freshwater's niece was the emptiness of the place. She had expected to disturb ghosts if she opened a drawer. She had expected to remember herself. Instead, as she waited for Evans to come on the first day she had the sensation of being ignored. Nothing watched in the shadows, nothing blinked in the beams of sunlight slanting across the room. The room she had slept in meant nothing. To fit memories into it was a task so awkward and artificial that she gave up trying. Several times she went to the window, waiting for Evans to walk in at the gate and for the destruction to begin.

When he did come he seized the idea at once. All files marked A.H.F.—that was her father—were "rubbish."

"Thorpe?" he said. "A.H.F. more A.H.F.! Burn it?" He was off with his first load to lay the foundation to the fire.

"And get this carpet up. We shall trip on it, it is torn," she said. He ripped the carpet off the stairs. He tossed the door mats, which were worn into holes, outside. By the barrow load out went the magazines. Every now and then some object took his eye—a leather strap, a bowl, a pipe rack, which he put into a little heap of other perquisites at the back door.

But to burn was his passion, to push the wheelbarrow his joy. He swaggered with it. He unloaded it carefully at the fire, not putting it down too near or roughly tipping it. He often tried one or two different grips on the handles before he started off. Once, she saw him stop in the middle of the lawn and turn it upside down and look it over carefully and make the wheel spin. Something wrong? No, he lovingly wiped the wheel with a handful of grass, got an oilcan from his pocket, and gave the wheel a squirt. Then he righted the wheelbarrow and came on with it round the house, singing in a low and satisfied voice. A hymn, it sounded like. And at the end of the day, when she took him a cup of tea and they stood chatting, his passion satisfied for the time being, he had a good look at her. His eye was on the brooch she was carelessly wearing to fasten her green overall. He came closer and put his hand to the brooch and lifted it.

"Those are pearls, I shouldn't wonder?" he said.

"Yes," she said. He stepped nimbly away, for he was as quick as a flea.

"It is beautiful," he said, considering the brooch and herself together. "You would not buy it for fifty pounds, nor even a hundred, I suppose. A present, I expect?" And before she could answer, he said gravely: "Half past five! I will lock the sheds. Are you sleeping here? My wife would go off her head, alone in the house. When I'm at the Mission, she's insane!"

Evans stared at Miss Freshwater's niece, waiting for a response to his drama. She did not know what to do, so she laughed. Evans gave a shout of laughter too. It shook the close black curls of his hair and the scar on the side of his nose went white.

"I have the key," he said seriously and went off.

"Robert," Miss Freshwater's niece opened the window and called again. "Can you come now? I can't get on."

Evans was on his way back to the house. He stamped quickly up the bare stairs.

"I'm in here," she called. "If you can get in!"

There was a heap of old brown paper knee high at the door. Some of the drawers of a chest had been taken out, others were half open; a wardrobe's doors were open wide. There were shoes, boxes and clothes piled on the bed which was stripped. She had a green scarf in a turban round her head, and none of her fair hair could be seen. Her face, with its strong bones and pale skin marked by dirty fingers, looked hard, humorous and naked. Her strong lips were dry and pale with dust.

They understood each other. At first he had bossed her but she had fought back on the second day and they were equals now. She spoke to him as if they were in a conspiracy together, deciding what should be "saved" and what should be "cast into the flames." She used those words purposely, as a dig of malice at him. She was taller than he. She couldn't get over the fact that he preached every night at the Mission and she had fallen into the habit of tempting him by some movement of arm or body, when she caught him looking at her. Her aunt had used the word "inconvenient," when her niece was young, to describe the girl's weakness for dawdling about with gardeners, chauffeurs, errand boys. Miss Freshwater's niece had lost the sense of the "convenient" very early in life.

"I've started upstairs now," she said to Evans. "It's worse than downstairs. Look at it."

Evans came a step further into the room and slowly looked round, nodding his head.

She leaned a little forward, her hands together, eagerly awaiting for him to laugh so that they could laugh together.

"She never threw away a scrap of paper. Not even paper bags. Look at this," she said.

He waded into the heap and peeped into a brown paper bag. It contained a bun, as hard as stone.

"Biscuits too," she said. "Wrapped up! Like a larder. They must have been here for years. In the top drawer."

Evans did not laugh.

"She feared starvation," he said, "old people are hungry. They are greedy. My grandmother nibbled like a little rat, all day. And in the night too. They wake up in the night and they are afraid. They eat for comfort. The mice did not get in, I hope," he said, going to look in the drawer.

"She was eighty-four," she said.

"My grandmother was ninety," he said. "My father's mother. She liked to hear a mouse. It was company, she said."

"I think my aunt must have been fond of moths," she said. "They came out in clouds from that wardrobe. Look at all those dresses. I can hardly bear to touch them."

She shook a couple of dresses in the wardrobe and then took them out. "There you are, did you see it? There goes one."

She held up an old-fashioned silk dress.

"Not worn for twenty years, you can see by the fashion. There!" She gave the dress a pull. "Did you hear? Perished. Rotten. They are all like that. You can't give them away. They'd fall off you."

She threw the dresses on the floor and he picked up one and he saw where moths had eaten it.

"It is wicked," he said. "All that money has gone to waste."

"Where moth and dust doth corrupt," she mocked him, and took an armful of the clothes and threw them on the floor. "Why did she buy them if she did not want them? And all those hats we had to burn? You haven't seen anything yet. Look at this."

On the bed was lying a pile of enormous lace-up corsets. Evans considered them.

"The men had patience," he said.

"Oh, she was not married," she said.

He nodded.

"That is how all the property comes to you, I suppose," he said. There was a shrewd flash in his blue eyes and she knew he had been gazing at her all this time and not at the clothes; but even as she caught his look the dissembling, still, vacant light slid back into it.

"Shoes!" she said, with excitement. "Do you want any shoes?" A large number of shoes of all kinds, little worn or not worn at all, were rowed in pairs on the bed and some had been thrown into a box as well.

"Fifty-one pairs I counted," she said. "She never went out but she went on ordering them. There's a piece of paper in each pair. Have a look. Read it. What does it say?"

He took a piece of paper out of a shoe.

" 'Comfortable for the evening,' " he read out. He took another. " 'For wet weather.' Did it rain indoors?"

She took one and read out:

" 'With my blue dress!' Can you imagine? 'Sound walking pair,' " she laughed but he interrupted her.

"In Wales they lacked them," he said. "In the bad times they were going barefoot. My sisters shared a pair for dances."

"What shall I do with them?" she asked. "Someone could wear them."

"There are good times now. They have the money," he said, snubbing her. "They buy new."

"I mean—anyone," she said. "They are too big for me. I'll show you."

She sat down on a packing case and slipped her foot into a silver evening shoe.

"You can see, my feet are lost in them," she said.

"You have small feet," he said. "In Wales the men would be chasing you."

"After chapel, I've no doubt," she said. "Up the mountain—what was the name of it? You told me."

"It has the best view in Wales. But those who go up it never see it," he laughed. "Try this pair," he said, kneeling down and lifting her foot. "Ah no, I see. But look at those legs, boy!"

Miss Freshwater's niece got up.

"What size does your wife take?" she asked.

"I don't know," he said, very pleased with himself. "Where is this trunk you said we had to move?"

"Out in the landing cupboard. I'll show you. I can't move it."

She led the way to the landing and bent down to tug at it.

"You must not do that," he said, putting his hands on her waist and moving her out of the way. He heaved at the trunk and tipped it on end. She wanted it, she said, in the light, where she could see.

"Here on the chest," she said.

He lifted it up and planked it down on the chest.

"Phew!" he said. "You have a small waist for a married woman. Soft.

My wife is a giantess, she weighs thirteen stone. And yet, you're big, too, oh yes, you are. But you have light bones. With her, now, it is the bones that weigh. Shall we open it?"

She sat down on a chair and felt in her pocket for a mirror.

"Why didn't you tell me I looked such a sight?" she said, wiping her face. "Yes, open it."

The trunk was made of black leather: it was cracked, peeling, stained and squashed by use. Dimly printed on it was her father's fading name in white large letters. The trunk had been pitched and bumped and slithered out of ships' holds and trains, all over the world. Its lid, now out of the true, no longer met the lock and it was closed by a strap. It had lain ripening and decaying in attics and lofts for half a lifetime.

"What is in it?" she called, without looking from her mirror.

"Clothes," he said. "Books. A pair of skates. Did the old lady go skating?"

He pulled out a Chinese hat. There was a pigtail attached to it and he held it up.

"Ah," he called. "This is the job." He put the hat on his head and pulled out a mandarin coat.

Miss Freshwater's niece stared and then she flushed.

"Where did you get that?" she cried jumping up, taking the hat from his head and snatching the coat. "They're mine! Where were they?"

She pushed him aside and pulled one or two things from the trunk. "They're mine!" she accused him. "All mine."

She aged as she looked at him. A photograph fell to the floor as she lifted up a book. "To darling Laura," she read out. "Tennyson."

"Who is this?" he said, picking up the photograph.

She did not hear. She was pulling out a cold, sequined evening dress that shrank almost to nothing as she picked it up.

"Good God," she said and dropped it with horror. For under the dress was an album. "Where," she said, sharply possessive, "did you put the skates?" She opened the album. She looked at a road deep in snow leading to an hotel with eaves a yard wide. She had spent her honeymoon there.

"Kitzbühel," she said. "Oh, no!"

She looked fiercely at him to drive him away. The house, so anonymous, so absurd, so meaningless and ghostless, had suddenly got her. There was a choke of cold wonder in her throat.

She turned on him: "Can't you clear up all that paper in the room?" She did not want to be seen by him.

Evans went to the door of the bedroom and, after a glance inside, came back. He was not going to leave her. He picked up the book of poems, glanced at a page or two and then dropped it back in the trunk.

"Everyone knows," he said scornfully, "that the Welsh are the founders of all the poetry of Europe."

She did not hear him. Her face had drained of waking light. She had entered blindly into a dream in which she could hardly drag herself along. She was looking painfully through the album, rocking her head slowly from side to side, her mouth opening a little and closing on the point of speech, a shoulder rising as if she had been hurt, and her back moving and swaying as she felt the clasp of the past like hands on her. She was looking at ten forgotten years of her life, her own life, not her family's, and she did not laugh when she saw the skirts too long, the top-heavy hats hiding the eyes, her face too full and fat, her plainness so sullen, her prettiness too open-mouthed and loud, her look too grossly sly. In this one, sitting at the café table by the lake when she was nineteen, she looked masterful and at least forty. In this garden picture she was theatrically fancying herself as an ancient Greek in what looked like a nightgown! One of her big toes, she noticed, turned up comically in the sandal she was wearing. Here on a rock by the sea, in a bathing dress, she had got thin again—that was her marriage—and look at her hair! This picture of the girl on skis, sharp-faced, the eyes narrowed—who was that? Herself—yet how could she have looked like that! But she smiled a little at last at the people she had forgotten. This man with the crinkled fair hair, a German—how mad she had been about him. But what pierced her was that in each picture of herself she was just out of reach, flashing and yet dead; and that really it was the things that burned in the light of permanence—the chairs, the tables, the trees, the car outside the café, the motor launch on the lake. These blinked and glittered. They had lasted and were ageless, untouched by time, and she was not. She put the album back into the trunk and pulled out an old tweed coat and skirt. Under it was an exercise book with the word "Diary" written on it in a hand more weakly rounded than the hand she wrote today. Part of a letter fell out of the diary, the second page, it seemed, of a letter of her own. She read it.

". . . the job at any rate," she read. "For a whole week he's forgotten his chest, his foot, his stomach. He's not dying any more!!! He conde (crossed out) congratulates himself and says it just shows how doctors are all fools. Inner self-confidence is what I need, he tells me!! It means giving up the flat and that's what I keep thinking—Oxford will be much more difficult for you and me. Women, he says, aren't happy unless they're sacrificing themselves. Darling, he doesn't know; it's the thought of You that keeps . . ."

She turned over the page. Nothing. She looked through the diary. Nothing. She felt sick and then saw Evans had not gone and was watching her. She quickly put the letter back into the diary.

"Ah," she said nervously. "I didn't know you were here. I'll show you something." She laughed unnaturally and opened the album until she found the most ludicrous and abashing picture in the book, one that would humiliate her entirely. "Here, look at this."

There was a see-saw in the foreground surrounded by raucously laughing people wearing paper hats and looking as though they had been dipped in glycerine: she was astride at the higher end of the see-saw, kicking her legs, and on the lower end was a fat young man in a pierrot costume. On her short, fuzzy fair hair was a paper hat. She showed the picture to Evans and picked out the terrible sequin dress from the trunk.

"That's the dress!" she said, pointing to the picture. "I was engaged to him. Isn't it terrible?" And she dropped the dress back again. It felt cold and slippery, almost wet. "I didn't marry him."

Evans scowled.

"You were naked," he said with disgust.

"I remember now. I left it all here. I kept that dress for years. I'll have to go through it all." And she pulled down the lid.

"This photograph fell out," he said.

It was the picture of another young man.

"Is this your husband?" Evans asked, studying the man.

"My husband is dead," she said sharply. "That is a friend." And she threw the picture back into the trunk. She realised now that Evans had been holding her arm a long time. She stepped away from him abruptly.

The careless friendliness, the sense of conspiracy she had felt while they worked together, had all gone. She drew away and said, in the hostile voice of unnecessary explanation:

"I mean," she said, "my husband died a few years ago. We were divorced. I mustn't waste any more time."

"My wife would not condescend to that," he said.

"She has no reason, I am sure," said Miss Freshwater's niece, severely, and returned to the bedroom.

"Now! We can't waste time like this. You'd better begin with what is on the bed. And when you've cleared it you can put the kettle on."

When Evans had gone downstairs with his load, she went to the landing and glared at the trunk. Her fists were clenched; she wished it was alive and that she could hit it. Glancing over the banisters to be sure she was alone, she opened it again, took out the photograph and the letter from her diary and put them in her handbag. She thought she was going to be sick or faint for the past was drumming, like a train coming nearer and nearer, in her head.

"My God!" she said. And when she saw her head in its turban and her face hardened by shock and grief in her absurd aunt's dressing-table mirror, she exclaimed with real horror. She was crying. "What a mess," she said and pulled the scarf off her head. Her fair, thick hair hung round her face untidily. Not once, in all those photographs, had a face so wolfish with bitterness and without laughter looked back at her.

"I'm taking the tea out," Evans called from below.

"I'm just coming," she called back and hurriedly tried to arrange her hair and then, because she had cried a little, she put on her glasses. Evans gave a keen look at the change in her when she got downstairs and walked through the hall to the door.

He had put the tray on the grass near a yew hedge in the hot corner at the side of the house and was standing a few yards away drinking his tea. In the last two days he had never drunk his tea near her but had chatted from a distance.

In her glasses and with her hair girlishly brushed back, Miss Freshwater's niece looked cold, tall and grand, like a headmistress.

"I hope we shan't get any more smoke here," she said. "Sit down. You look too restless."

She was very firm, nodding to the exact place on the lawn on which she required him to sit. Taken aback, Evans sat precisely in that place. She sat on the grass and poured herself a cup of tea.

"How many souls came to Jesus last night?" she asked in her lady-like voice. Evans got up and squatted cheerfully, but watchfully, on his heels.

"Seventeen," he said.

"That's not very good," she said. "Do you think you could save mine?"

"Oh, yes," he said keenly.

"You look like a frog," she said mocking. He had told her miners always squat in this way after work. "It's too late," she went on. "Twenty years too late. Have you always been with the Mission?"

"No," he said.

"What was it? Were you converted, did you see the light?" she mocked, like a teacher.

"I had a vision," he said seriously.

"A vision!" she laughed. She waved her hand. "What do you mean—you mean, you—well, where? Up in the sky or something?"

"No," he said. "It was down the mine."

"What happened?"

He put down his cup and he moved it away to give himself more room. He squatted there, she thought, not like a frog at all, but like an imp or a devil, very grave and carven-faced. She noticed now how wide his mouth was and how widely it opened and how far the lips drew back when he spoke in his declamatory voice. He stared a long time waiting for her to stop fidgeting. Then he began:

"I was a drunkard," he declaimed, relishing each syllable separately. "I was a liar. I was a hypocrite. I went with women. And married women too!" His voice rose. "I was a fornicator. I was an adulterer. Always at the races, too, gambling, it was senseless. There was no sin the Devil did not lead me into, I was like a fool. I was the most noteworthy sinner in the valley, everyone spoke of it. But I did not know the Lord was lying in wait for me."

"Yes, but what happened?" she said.

He got to his feet and gazed down at her and she was compelled to look up at him.

"I will tell you," he said. "It was a miracle." He changed his manner and after looking round the garden, he said in a hushing and secretive voice:

"There was a disaster in the mine," he said. "It was in June. I was twenty-three and I was down working and I was thinking of the sunlight and the hills and the evening. There was a young girl called Alys Davies, you know, two or three had been after her and I was thinking I would take her up the rock, that is a quiet place, only an old mountain ram would see you . . ."

"You were in the mine," she said. "You are getting too excited about this Alys Jones . . ."

"Davies," he said with a quick grin. "Don't worry about her. She is married now." He went back to his solemn voice.

"And suddenly," he said, "there was a fall, a terrible fall of rock like thunder and all the men shouting. It was at eleven in the morning when we stopped work for our tea. There were three men in there working with me and they had just gone off. I was trapped alone."

"Were you hurt?" she said anxiously.

"It was a miracle, not a stone touched me. I was in a little black cave. It was like a tomb. I was in that place alone for twelve hours. I could hear them working to get at me but after the first fall there was a second and then I thought I was finished. I could hear nothing."

"What did you do? I would have gone out of my mind," she said. "Is that how you got the scar on your nose?"

"That was in a fight," he said, offhand. "Madness is a terrible thing. I stared into the blackness and I tried to think of one thing to stop my mind wandering but I could not at first for the fear, it was chasing and jumping like a mad dog in my head. I prayed and the more I prayed the more it chased and jumped. And then, suddenly, it stopped. I saw in my mind a picture. I saw the mantelpiece at home and on it a photograph of our family—my father and mother, my four sisters and my brother. And we had an aunt and uncle just married, it was a wedding photograph. I could see it clearly as if I had been in my home. They were standing there looking at me and I kept looking at them and thinking about them. I held on to them. I kept everything else out of my mind; wherever I looked that picture was before my eyes. It was like a vision. It saved me."

"I have heard people say they hear voices," said Miss Freshwater's niece, kindly now.

"Oh, no! They were speechless," said Evans. "Not a word! I spoke to them," he said. "Out loud. I promised God in front of all my family that I would cleanse my soul when I got out."

Evans stood blazing in his trance and then he picked up his cup from the grass and took it to her.

"May I please have some more tea?" he said.

"Of course," she said. "Sit down."

He considered where he should sit and then put himself beside her.

"When I saw you looking at your photographs," he said, "I thought, 'She is down the mine.'"

"I have never been down a mine in my life. I don't know why. We lived near one once when I was in the north," she evaded.

"The mine of the past," he said. "The dark mine of the past."

"I can see why you are a preacher, Robert," she smiled. "It's funny how one cannot get one's family out of one's head. I could feel mine inside me for years—but not now."

She had entirely stopped mocking him.

"I can't say they ever saved me," she said. "I think they nearly ruined me. Look at that ugly house and all that rubbish. Did you ever see anything like their furniture? When I was a girl I used to think, Suppose I got to look like that sideboard! And then money was all they ever talked about—and good and nice people, and nice people always had money. It was like that in those days, thank God that has gone. Perhaps it hasn't. I decided to get away from it and I got married. They ought to have stopped me—all I wanted was to get away—but they thought my husband had money, too. He just had debts and a bad stomach. When he had spent all my money, he just got ill to punish me . . . You don't know anything about life when you're young and when you are old it's too late . . ."

"That's a commonplace remark," she went on, putting her cup on the tray and reaching for his. "My mother used to make it." She picked up her scarf and began to tie it on her head, but as she was tying it Evans quickly reached for it and pulled it off. His hand held the nape of her neck gently.

"You are not old," he shouted, laughing and sparkling. "Your hair is golden, not a grey one in it, boy."

"Robert, give me that scarf. It is to keep out the dust," she said, blushing. She reached for the scarf and he caught her wrist.

"When I saw you standing at the station on Monday, I said, Now, there is a woman! Look at the way she stands, a golden woman, that is the first I have seen in this town, she must be a stranger," he said.

"You know all the others, I expect," she said with amusement.

"Oh, indeed, yes I do! All of them!" he said. "I would not look at them twice."

His other hand slipped from her neck to her waist.

"I can trust myself with them, but not with you," he said, lowering his voice and speaking down to her neck. "In an empty house," he whispered, nodding to the house, letting go of her hand and stroking her knee.

"I am far past that sort of thing," said Miss Freshwater's niece, choosing a lugubrious tone. She removed his arm from her waist. And she stood up, adroitly picking up the tray, and from behind that defence, looked round the garden. Evans sprang up but instead of coming near her, he jumped a few yards away and squatted on his heels, grinning at her confidently.

"You look like the devil," she said.

He had placed himself between her and the way to the house.

"It is quiet in the garden, too," he said with a wink. And then she saw the wheelbarrow which he had left near the fire.

"That barrow ought to go well in the sale," she said. "It is almost new. How much do you think it will fetch?"

Evans stood up at once and his grin went. An evasive light, almost the light of tears, came into his hot blue eyes and he stared at her with an alarm that drove everything else out of his head.

"They'll put it with the tools, you will not get much for it."

"I think every man in the town will be after it," she said, with malice.

"What price did you want for it?" he said, uncertain of her.

"I don't know what they cost," she said carelessly and walked past him very slowly back to the house, maddening him by her walk. He followed her quickly and when she turned, still carrying the tray, to face him in the doorway, she caught his agitation.

"I will take the tray to the kitchen," he said politely.

"No," she said, "I will do that. I want you to go upstairs and fetch down all those shoes. And the trunk. It can all go."

And she turned and walked through the house to the kitchen. He hesitated for a long time; at last she heard him go upstairs and she pottered in the kitchen where the china and pans were stacked on the table, waiting for him to come down. He was a very long time. He came down with the empty trunk.

"It can all go. Burn it all. It's no good to anyone, damp and rotten. I've put aside what I want," she said.

He looked at her sullenly. He was startled by her manner and by the vehemence of her face, for she had put on the scarf and her face looked strong-boned, naked and ruthless. She was startled herself.

His sullenness went; he returned to his old excitement and hurried the barrow to the fire and she stood at the door impatiently waiting for the blaze. When he saw her waiting he came back.

"There it goes," he said with admiration.

The reflection of the flame danced in points of light in her eyes, her mouth was set, hard and bitter. Presently the flame dropped and greenish smoke came out thickly.

"Ah!" she gasped. Her body relaxed and she smiled at Evans, tempting him again.

"I've been thinking about the barrow," she said. "When we've finished up here, I'll make you a present of it. I would like to give it to you, if you have a use for it?"

She could see the struggle going on inside him as he boldly looked at her; and she saw his boldness pass into a small shrug of independent pride and the pride into pretence and dissembling.

"I don't know," he said, "that I have a use—well, I'll take it off you. I'll put the shoes in it, it will save bringing the car." He could not repress his eagerness any longer. "I'll put the shoes into it this evening. Thank you." He paused. "Thank you, ma'am," he said.

It was the first time he had called her ma'am. The word was like a blow. The affair was over. It was, she realised, a dismissal.

An hour later she heard him rumbling the barrow down the path to the gate. The next day he did not come. He had finished with her. He sent his son up for his money.

It took Miss Freshwater's niece two more days to finish her work at the house. The heavy jobs had been done, except for putting the drawers back into the chests. She could have done with Evans's help there, and for the sweeping which made her hot but she was glad to be alone because she got on more quickly with the work. She hummed and even sang as she worked, feeling light and astonishingly happy. Once or twice, when she saw the white sheet of the Mission tent distantly through the trees, she laughed:

"He got what he wanted! And I'm evidently not as old as I look."

The last hours buzzed by and she spun out the time, reluctant to go. She dawdled, locking the sheds, the windows and doors, until there was nothing more to keep her. She brought down a light suitcase in which she had put the few things she wanted to take away and she sat in the dining-room, now as bare as an office, to go through her money. After the destruction she was having a fit of economy and it had occurred to her that instead of taking a taxi to the station, she could walk down to the bus stop on the Green. She knew that the happiness she felt was not ebbing, but had changed to a feeling she had not had for many years: the feeling of expectancy, and as this settled in her she put her money and papers back into her bag. There was a last grain of rubbish here: with scarcely a glance at them, she tore up the photograph and the unfinished letter she had found in the trunk.

"I owe Evans a lot," she thought.

Nothing retained her now.

She picked up her case. She left the house and walked down the road in the strong shade of the firs and the broad shade of the oak trees, whose leaves hardened with populous contentment in the long evening light. When she got to the open Green children were playing round the Gospel Tent and, in twos and threes, people were walking from the houses across the grass towards it. She had twenty minutes to wait until her bus arrived. She heard the sound of singing coming from the tent. She wondered if Evans would be there.

"I might give him the pleasure of seeing what he missed," she thought.

She strolled across to the tent.

A youth who had watered his hair and given it a twirl with a comb was standing in his best clothes at the entrance to the tent.

"Come to Jesu! Come to Jesu!" he said to her as she peeped inside.

"I'm just looking for someone," she said politely.

The singing had stopped when she looked in but the worshippers were still standing. They were packed in the white light of the tent and the hot smell of grass and somewhere at the far end, invisible, a man was shouting like a cheapjack selling something at an auction. He stopped suddenly and a high, powerful country voice whined out alone: "Ow in the vale . . ." and the congregation joined in for another long verse.

"Is Mr. Evans here tonight?" she asked the youth.

"Yes," he said. "He's witnessing every night."

"Where is he? I don't see him."

The verse came to an end and once more a voice began talking at the other end of the tent. It was a woman's voice, high and incomprehensible and sharp. The hymn began again and then spluttered into an explosive roar that swept across the Green.

"They've fixed it. The loudspeaker!" the youth exclaimed. Miss Freshwater's niece stepped back. The noises thumped. Sadly, she looked at her watch and began to walk back to the bus stop. When she was about ten yards from the tent, the loudspeaker gave a loud whistle and then, as if God had cleared his throat, spoke out with a gross and miraculous clearness.

"Friends," it said, sweeping right across the Green until it struck the furthest houses and the trees. "My friends . . ."

The word seemed to grind her and everyone else to nothing, to mill them all into the common dust.

"When I came to this place," it bellowed, "the serpent . . ." (An explosion of noise followed but the voice cleared again) ". . . heart. No bigger than a speck it was at first, as tiny as a speck of coal grit in your eye . . ."

Miss Freshwater's niece stopped. Was it Evans's voice? A motor coach went by on the road and drowned the next words, and then she heard, spreading into an absurd public roar:

"I was a liar. I was an adulterer. Oh my friends, I was a slave of the strange woman the Bible tells about, the whore of Babylon, in her palace where moth and dust . . ." Detonations again.

But it was Evans's voice. She waited and the enormously magnified voice burst through:

"And then by the great mercy of the Lord I heard a voice cry out, 'Robert Evans, what are you doing, boy? Come out of it' . . ." But the voice exploded into meaningless concussions, suddenly resuming:

". . . and burned the adulteress in the everlasting fire, my friends—and all her property."

The hymn started up again.

"Well, not quite all, Robert," said Miss Freshwater's niece pleasantly aloud, and a child eating an ice-cream near her watched her walk across the grass to the bus stop.

The Fall

It was the evening of the Annual Dinner. More than two hundred accountants were at that hour changing into evening clothes, in the flats, villas and hotel rooms of a large, wet, Midland city. At the Royal was Charles Peacock, slender in his shirt, balancing on one leg and gazing with frowns of affection in the wardrobe mirror at the other leg as he pulled his trousers on; and then with a smile of farewell as the second went in. Buttoned up, relieved of nakedness, he visited other mirrors—the one at the dressing table, the two in the bathroom, assembling the scattered aspects of the unsettled being called Peacock "doing"—as he was apt to say—"no so badly" in this city which smelled of coal and where thirty-eight years ago he had been born. When he left his room there were mirrors in the hotel lift and down below in the foyer and outside in the street. Certain shop windows were favourable and assuring. The love affair was taken up again at the Assembly Rooms by the mirrors in the tiled corridor leading towards the bullocky noise of two hundred-odd chartered accountants in black ties, taking their drinks under the chandeliers that seemed to weep above their heads.

Crowds or occasions frightened Peacock. They engaged him, at first sight, in the fundamental battle of his life: the struggle against nakedness, the panic of grabbing for clothes and becoming someone. An acquaintance in a Scottish firm was standing near the door of the packed room as Peacock went in.

"Hullo, laddie," Peacock said, fitting himself out with a Scottish accent, as he went into the crowded, chocolate-coloured buffet.

"What's to do?" he said, passing on to a Yorkshireman.

"Are you well now?" he said, in his Irish voice. And, gaining confidence, "Whatcha cock!" to a man up from London, until he was shaking hands in the crowd with the President himself, who was leaning on a stick and had his foot in plaster.

"I hope this is not serious, sir," said Peacock in his best southern English, nodding at the foot.

"Bloody serious," said the President sticking out his peppery beard. "I caught my foot in a grating. Some damn fools here think I've got gout."

No one who saw Peacock in his office, in Board Rooms, on committees, at meetings, knew the exhausting number of rough sketches that had to be made before the naked Peacock could become Peacock dressed for his part. Now, having spoken to several human beings, the fragments called Peacock closed up. And he had one more trick up his sleeve if he panicked again: he could drop into music hall Negro.

Peacock got a drink at the buffet table and pushed his way to a solitary island of carpet two feet square, in the guffawing corral. He was looking at the back of the President's neck. Almost at once the President, on the crest of a successful joke he had told, turned round with appetite.

"Hah!" he shouted. "Hah! Here's friend Peacock again."

Why "again"? thought Peacock.

The President looked Peacock over.

"I saw your brother this afternoon," shouted the President. The President's injured foot could be said to have made his voice sound like a hilarious smash. Peacock's drink jumped and splashed his hand. The President winked at his friends.

"Hah!" said the President. "That gave our friend Peacock a scare!"

"At the Odeon," explained a kinder man.

"Is Shelmerdine Peacock your brother? The actor?" another said, astonished, looking at Peacock from head to foot.

"Shelmerdine Peacock was born and bred in this city," said the President fervently.

"I saw him in *Waste*," someone said. And others recalled him in *The Gun Runner* and *Doctor Zut*.

Four or five men stood gazing at Peacock with admiration, waiting for him to speak.

"Where is he now?" said the President, stepping forward, beard first. "In Hollywood? Have you seen him lately?"

They all moved forward to hear about the famous man.

Peacock looked to the right—he wanted to do this properly—but there was no mirror in that direction; he looked to the left, but there was no mirror there. He lowered his head gravely and then looked up shaking his head sorrowfully. He brought out the old reliable Negro voice:

"The last time I saw l'il ole brudder Shel," he said, "he was being thrown out of the Orchid Room. He was calling the waiters goatherds."

Peacock looked up at them all and stood, collected, assembled, whole at last, among their shouts of laughter. One man who did not laugh, and who asked what the Orchid Room was, was put in his place. And in a moment, a voice bawled from the door, "Gentlemen. Dinner is served." The crowd moved through two ante-rooms into the Great Hall where, from their portraits on the wall, Mayors, Presidents and Justices looked down with the complacent rosiness of those who have dined and died. It was gratifying to Peacock that the President rested his arm on his shoulder for a few steps as they went into the hall.

Shel often cropped up in Peacock's life, especially in clubs and at dinners. It was pleasing. There was always praise; there were always questions. He had seen the posters about Shel's film during the week on his way to his office. They pleased, but they also troubled. Peacock stood at his place at table in the Great Hall and paused to look around, in case there was one more glance of vicarious fame to be collected. He was enjoying one of those pauses of self-possession in which, for a few seconds, he could feel the sensations Shel must feel when he stepped before the curtain to receive the applause of some great audience in London or New York. Then Peacock sat down. More than two hundred soup spoons scraped.

"Sherry, sir?" said the waiter.

Peacock sipped.

He meant no harm to Shel, of course. But in a city like this, with Shel appearing in a big picture, with his name fifteen feet long on the hoardings, talked about by girls in offices, the universal instinct of family disparagement was naturally tickled into life. The President might laugh and the crowd admire, but it was not always agreeable for the family to have Shel roaming loose—and often very loose—in the world. One had to assert the modesty, the anonymity of the ordinary assiduous Peacocks. One way of doing this was to add a touch or two to famous scandals: to enlarge the drunken scrimmages and add to the divorces and the breaches of contract, increase the overdoses taken by flighty girls. One was entitled to a little rake off—an accountant's charges—from the fame that so often annoyed. One was entitled, above all, because one loved Shel.

"Hock, sir?" said the waiter.

Peacock drank. Yes, he loved Shel. Peacock put down his glass and the man opposite to him spoke across the table, a man with an amused mouth, who turned his sallow face sideways so that one had the impression of being inquired into under a loose lock of black hair by one sharp, serious eye only.

"An actor's life is a struggle," the man said. Peacock recognised him: it was the man who had not laughed at his story and who had asked what the Orchid Room was, in a voice that had a sad and puncturing feeling for information sought for its own sake.

Peacock knew this kind of admirer of Shel's and feared him. They were not content to admire, they wanted to advance into intimacy, and collect facts on behalf of some general view of life's mysteriousness. As an accountant Peacock rejected mystery.

"I don't think l'il ole brudder Shel has struggled much," said Peacock, wagging his head from side to side carelessly.

"I mean he has to dedicate himself," said the man.

Peacock looked back mistrustfully.

"I remember some interview he gave about his schooldays—in this city," said the man. "It interested me. I do the books for the Hippodrome."

Peacock stopped wagging his head from side to side. He was alert. What Shel had said about his early life had been damned tactless.

"Shel had a good time," said Peacock sharply. "He always got his own way."

Peacock put on his face of stone. He dared the man to say out loud, in that company, three simple English words. He dared him. The man smiled and did not say them.

"Volnay, sir?" said the waiter as the pheasant was brought. Peacock drank.

Fried Fish Shop, Peacock said to himself as he drank. Those were the words. Shel could have kept his mouth shut about that. I'm not a snob, but why mention it? Why, after they were all doing well, bring ridicule upon the family? Why not say, simply, "Shop." Why not say, if he had to, "Fishmonger?" Why mention "Frying"? Why add "*Bankrupt* Fried Fish Shop"?

It was swinish, disloyal, ungrateful. Bankrupt—all right; but some of that money (Peacock said, hectoring the pheasant on his plate) paid for Shel's years at the Dramatic School. It was unforgiveable.

Peacock looked across at the man opposite, but the man had turned to talk to a neighbour. Peacock finished his glass and chatted with the man sitting to his right, but he felt like telling the whole table a few facts about dedication.

Dedication—he would have said. Let us take a look at the figures. An example of Shel's dedication in those Fried Fish Shop days he is so fond of remembering to make fools of us. Saturday afternoon. Father asleep in the back room. Shel says, "Come down the High Street with me, Tom. I want to get a record." Classical, of course. Usual swindle. If we get into the shop he won't have the money and will try and borrow from me. "No," I say. "I haven't got any money." "Well, let's get out of this stink of lard and fish." He wears me down. He wore us all down, the whole family. He would be sixteen, two years older than me. And so we go out and at once I know there is going to be trouble. "I saw the Devil in Cramers," he says. We go down the High Street to Cramers, it's a music shop, and he goes up to the girl to ask if they sell bicycle pumps or rubber heels. When the girl says "No," he makes a terrible face at her and shouts out "Bah." At Hooks, the stationers, he stands at the door, and calls to the girl at the cash desk: "You've got the Devil in here. I've reported it," and slams the door. We go on to Bonds, the grocers, and he pretends to be sick when he sees the bacon. Goes out. "Rehearsing," he says. The Bonds are friends of Father's. There is a row. Shel swears he was never anywhere near the place and goes back the following Saturday and falls flat on the floor in front of the Bond daughter groaning, "I've been poisoned. I'm dying. Water! Water!" Falls flat on his back ...

"Caught his foot in a grating, he told me, and fell," the man opposite was saying. "Isn't that what he told you, Peacock?"

Peacock's imaginary speech came suddenly to an end. The man was smiling as if he had heard every word.

"Who?" said Peacock.

"The President," said the man. "My friend, Mr. McAlister is asking me what happened to the President. Did he fall in the street?"

Peacock collected himself quickly and to hide his nakedness became Scottish.

"Ay, mon," he nodded across the table. "A wee bit of a tumble in the street."

Peacock took up his glass and drank.

"He's a heavy man to fall," said the man called McAlister.

"He carries a lot of weight," said his neighbour. Peacock eyed him. The impression was growing that this man knew too much, too quietly. It struck him that the man was one of those who ask what they know already, a deeply unbelieving man. They have to be crushed.

"Weight makes no difference," said Peacock firmly.

"It's weight and distance," said the Scotsman. "Look at children."

Peacock felt a smile coming over his body from the feet upwards.

"Weight and distance make no difference," Peacock repeated.

"How can you say that?"

An enormous voice, hanging brutally on the air like a sergeant's, suddenly shouted in the hall. It was odd to see the men in the portraits on the wall still sitting down after the voice sounded. It was the voice of the toastmaster.

"Gen—tle—men," it shouted. "I ask you. To rise to. The Toast of Her. Maj—es—ty. The Queen."

Two hundred or more accountants pushed back their chairs and stood up.

"The Queen," they growled. And one or two, Peacock among them, fervently added, "God bless her," and drained his glass.

Two hundred or more accountants sat down. It was the moment Peacock loved. And he loved the Queen.

"Port or brandy, sir?" the waiter asked.

"Brandy," said Peacock.

"You were saying that weight and distance make no difference. How do you make that out?" the sidelong man opposite said in a sympathetic and curious voice that came softly and lazily out.

Peacock felt the brandy burn. The question floated by, answerable if seized as it went and yet, suddenly, unanswerable for the moment. Peacock stared at the question keenly as if it were a fly that he was waiting to swat when it came round again. Ah, there it came. Now! But no, it had gone by once more. It was answerable. He knew the answer. Peacock smiled loosely biding his time. He felt the flame of authority, of absolute knowledge burn in him.

There was a hammering at the President's table, there was handclapping. The President was on his feet and his beard had begun to move up and down.

"I'll tell you later," said Peacock curtly across the table. The interest went out of the man's eye.

"Once more," the President's beard was saying and it seemed sometimes that he had two beards. "Honour," said one beard. "Privilege," said the other. "Old friends," said both beards together. "Speeches ... brief ... reminded of story ... shortest marriage service in the world ... Tennessee ..."

"Hah! Hah! Hah!" shouted a pack of wolves, hyenas, hounds in dinner jackets.

Peacock looked across at the unbeliever who sat opposite. The interest in weight and distance had died away in his face.

"Englishman ... Irishman ... Scotsman ... train ... Englishman said ... Scotsman said ... Och, says Paddy ..."

"Hah! Hah! Hah!" from the pack.

Over the carnations in the silver-plated vases on the table, over the heads of the diners, the cigar smoke was rising sweetly and the first level indigo shafts of it were tipping across the middle air and turning the portraits of the Past Masters into day dreams. Peacock gazed at it. Then a bell rang in his ear, so loudly that he looked shyly to see if anyone else had heard it. The voice of Shel was on some line of his memory, a voice richer, more insinuating than the toastmaster's or the President's, a voice utterly flooring.

"Abel?" Shel was saying. "Is that you Abel? This is Cain speaking. How's the smoke? Is it still going up straight to heaven? Not blowing about all over the place ..."

The man opposite caught Peacock's eye for a second, as if he too had heard the voice and then turned his head away. And, just at the very moment, when once more Peacock could have answered that question about the effect of weight and distance, the man opposite stood up, all the accountants stood up. Peacock was the last. There was another toast to drink. And immediately there was more hammering and another speaker. Peacock's opportunity was lost. The man who sat opposite had moved his chair back from the table and was sitting sideways to the table, listening, his interest in Peacock gone for good.

Peacock became lonely. Sulkily he played with matchsticks and arranged them in patterns on the tablecloth. There was a point at Annual Dinners when he always did this. It was at that point when one saw the function had become fixed by a flash photograph in the gloss of celebration and when everyone looked sickly and old. Eyes became hollow, temples sank, teeth loosened. Shortly the diners would be carried out in coffins. One waited restlessly for the thing to be over. Ten years of life went by and then, it seemed, there were no more speeches. There was some business talk in groups; then twos and threes left the table. Others filed off into a large chamber next door. Peacock's neighbours got up. He, who feared occasions, feared even more their dissolution. It was like that frightening ten minutes in a theatre when the audience slowly moves out, leaving a hollow stage and row after row, always increasing, of empty seats behind them. In a panic Peacock got up. He was losing all acquaintance. He had even let the man opposite slip away, for that man was walking down the hall with some friends. Peacock hurried down his side of the long table to meet them at the bottom and when he got there he turned and barred their way.

"What we were talking about," he said. "It's an art. Simply a matter of letting the breath go, relaxing the muscles. Any actor can do it. It's the first thing they learn."

"I'm out of my depth," said the Scotsman.

"Falling," said Peacock. "The stage fall." He looked at them with dignity, then he let the expression die on his face. He fell quietly full length to the floor. Before they could speak he was up on his feet.

"My brother weighs two hundred and twenty pounds," he said with condescension to the man opposite. "The ordinary person falls and breaks an arm or a foot, because he doesn't know. It's an art."

His eyes conveyed that if the Peacocks had kept a fried fish shop years ago, they had an art.

"Simple," said Peacock.

And down he went, thump, on the carpet again and lying at their feet he said:

"Painless. Nothing broken. Not a bruise. I said 'an art.' Really one might call it a science. Do you see how I'm lying?"

"What's happened to Peacock?" said two or three men joining the group.

"He's showing us the stage fall."

"Nothing," said Peacock, getting up and brushing his coat sleeve and smoothing back his hair. "It is just a stage trick."

"I wouldn't do it," said a large man, patting his stomach.

"I've just been telling them—weight is nothing. Look." Peacock fell down and got up at once.

"You turn. You crumple. You can go flat on your back. I mean, that is what it looks like," he said.

And Peacock fell.

"Shel and I used to practise it in the bedroom. Father thought the ceiling was coming down," he said.

"Good God, has Peacock passed out?" a group standing by the fireplace in the hall called across. Peacock got up and brushing his jacket again walked up to them. The group he had left watched him. There was a thump.

"He's done it again," the man opposite said. "Once more. There he goes. Look, he's going to show the President. He's going after him. No, he's missed him. The old boy has slipped out of the door."

Peacock was staring with annoyance at the door. He looked at other groups of twos and threes.

"Who was the casualty over there?" someone said to him as he walked past.

Peacock went over to them and explained.

"Like judo," said a man.

"No!" said Peacock indignantly, even grandly. And in Shel's manner. Anyone who had seen Shelmerdine Peacock affronted knew what he looked like. That large white face trod on you. "Nothing to do with judo. This is the theatre . . ."

"Shelmerdine Peacock's brother," a man whispered to a friend.

"Is that so?"

"It's in the blood," someone said.

To the man who had said "judo," Peacock said, "No throwing, no wrestling, no somersaulting or fancy tricks. That is not theatre. Just . . . simply . . ." said Peacock. And crumpling, as Shel might have done in *Macbeth* or *Hamlet*, or like some gangster shot in the stomach, Peacock once more let his body go down with the cynicism of the skilful corpse. This time he did not get up at once. He looked up at their knees, their waists, at their goggling faces, saw under their double chins and under their hairy eyebrows. He grinned at their absurdity. He saw that he held them. They were obliged to look at him. Shel must always have had this sensation of hundreds of astonished eyes watching him lie, waiting for him to move. Their gaze would never leave the body. He never felt less at a loss, never felt more completely himself. Even the air was better at carpet level; it was certainly cooler and he was glad of that. Then he saw two pairs of feet advancing from another group. He saw two faces peep over the shoulders of the others, and heard one of them say:

"It's Peacock—still at it."

He saw the two pairs of boots and trousers go off. Peacock got to his feet at once and resentfully stared after them. He knew something, as they went, that Shel must have known: the desperation, the contempt for the audience that is thinning out. He was still brushing his sleeve and trouser legs when he saw everyone moving away out of the hall. Peacock moved after them into the chamber.

A voice spoke behind him. It was the quiet, intimate voice of the man with the loose lock of black hair who had sat opposite to him.

"You need a drink," the man said.

They were standing in the chamber where the buffet table was. The man had gone into the chamber and, clearly, he had waited for Peacock. A question was going round as fast as a catherine wheel in Peacock's head and there was no need to ask it: it must be so blindingly obvious. He looked for someone to put it to, on the quiet, but there were only three men at the buffet table with their backs turned to him. Why (the question ran) at the end of a bloody good dinner is one always left with some awful drunk, a man you've never liked—an unbeliever?

Peacock mopped his face. The unbeliever was having a short disgusting laugh with the men at the bar and now was coming back with a glass of whisky.

"Sit down. You must be tired," said the unbeliever.

They sat down. The man spoke of the dinner and the speeches. Peacock did not listen. He had just noticed a door leading into a small ante-room and he was wondering how he could get into it.

"There was one thing I don't quite get," the man said. "Perhaps it was the quickness of the hand deceiving the eye. I should say feet. What I mean is—do you first take a step, I mean like in dancing: I mean is the art of falling really a paradox—I mean the art of keeping your balance all the time?"

The word "paradox" sounded offensive to Peacock.

The man looked too damn clever, in Peacock's opinion, and didn't sit still. Wearily Peacock got up.

"Hold my drink," he said. "You are standing like this, or facing sideways—on a level floor, of course. On a slope like this . . ."

The man nodded.

"I mean—well, now, watch carefully. Are you watching?"

"Yes," said the man.

"Look at my feet," said Peacock.

"No," said the man, hastily, putting out a free hand and catching Peacock by the arm. "I see what you mean. I was just interested in the theory."

Peacock halted. He was offended. He shook the man's arm off.

"Nothing theoretical about it," he said, and shaking his sleeves added: "No paradox."

"No," said the man standing up and grabbing Peacock so that he could not fall. "I've got the idea." He looked at his watch. "Which way are you going? Can I give you a lift?"

Peacock was greatly offended. To be turned down! He nodded to the door of the ante-room: "Thanks," he said. "The President's waiting for me."

"The President's gone," said the man. "Oh well, good night." And he went away. Peacock watched him go. Even the men at the bar had gone. He was alone.

"But thanks," he called after him. "Thanks."

Cautiously Peacock sketched a course into the ante-room. It was a small, high room, quite empty and yet (one would have said), packed

with voices, chattering, laughing and mixed with music along the pan-
elled walls, but chiefly coming from behind the heavy green velvet
curtains that were drawn across the window at one end. There were no
mirrors, but Peacock had no need of them. The effect was ornate—
gilded pillars at the corners, a small chandelier rising and falling
gracefully from a carven ceiling. On the wall hung what, at first sight,
seemed to be two large oil paintings of Queens of England but, on
going closer, Peacock saw there was only one oil painting—of Queen
Victoria. Peacock considered it. The opportunity was enormous. Loyally; his face went blank. He swayed, loyally fell, and loyally got to his
feet. The Queen might or might not have clapped her little hands. So
encouraged, he fell again and got up. She was still sitting there.

Shel, said Peacock, aloud to the Queen, has often acted before roy-
alty. He's in Hollywood now, having left me to settle all his tax affairs.
Hundreds of documents. All lies, of course. And there is this case for
alimony going on. He's had four wives, he said to Queen Victoria.
That's the side of theatre life I couldn't stand, even when we were boys.
I could see it coming. But—watch me, he said.

And delightfully he crumpled, the perfect backwards spin. Leaning
up on his elbow from where he was lying he waited for her to speak.

She did not speak, but two or three other queens joined her, all
crowding and gossiping together, as Peacock got up. The Royal Box!
It was full. Cars hooting outside the window behind the velvet curtains had the effect of an orchestra and then, inevitably, those heavy
green curtains were drawn up. A dark, packed and restless auditorium
opened itself to him. There was dense applause.

Peacock stepped forward in awe and wholeness. Not to fall, not to
fall, this time, he murmured. To bow. One must bow and bow and bow
and not fall, to the applause. He set out. It was a strangely long up-hill
journey towards the footlights and not until he got there did it occur to
him that he did not know how to bow. Shel had never taught him. Indeed, at the first attempt the floor came up and hit him in the face.

WHEN MY GIRL COMES HOME

She was kissing them all, hugging them, her arms bare in her summer dress, laughing and taking in a big draught of breath after every kiss, nearly knocking old Mrs. Draper off her feet, almost wrestling with Mrs. Fulmino, who was large and tall. Then Hilda broke off to give another foreign-sounding laugh and plunged at Jack Draper ("the baby") and his wife, at Mr. Fulmino, who cried out "What again?" and at Constance, who did not like emotion; and after every kiss, Hilda drew back, getting her breath and making this sound like "Hah!"

"Who is this?" she said, looking at me.

"Harry Fraser," Mr. Fulmino said. "You remember Harry?"

"You worked at the grocer's," she said. "I remember you."

"No," I said, "that was my brother."

"This is the little one," said Mrs. Fulmino.

"Who won the scholarship," said Constance.

"We couldn't have done anything without him," said Mr. Fulmino, expanding with extravagance as he always did about everything. "He wrote to the War Office, the Red Cross, the Prisoners of War, the American Government, all the letters. He's going to be our Head Librarian."

Mr. Fulmino loved whatever had not happened yet. His forecasts were always wrong. I left the library years ago and never fulfilled the future he had planned for me. Obviously Hilda did not remember me.

Thirteen years before, when she married Mr. Singh and left home, I was no more than a boy.

"Well, I'll kiss him too," she said. "And another for your brother."

That was the first thing to happen, the first of many signs of how her life had had no contact with ourselves.

"He was killed in the war, dear," said Mrs. Fulmino.

"She couldn't know," said Constance.

"I'm sorry," said Hilda.

We all stood silent, and Hilda turned to hold on to her mother, little Mrs. Johnson, whose face was coquettish with tears and who came only up to Hilda's shoulder. The old lady was bewildered. She was trembling as though she were going to shake to pieces like a tree in the autumn. Hilda stood still, touching her tinted brown hair which was done in a tight high style and still unloosened, despite all the hugs and kissings. Her arms looked as dry as sand, her breasts were full in her green, flowered dress and she was gazing over our heads now from large yellow eyes which had almost closed into two blind, blissful curving lines. Her eyebrows seemed to be lacquered. How Oriental she looked on that first day! She was looking above our heads at old Mrs. Draper's shabby room and going over the odd things she remembered, and while she stood like that, the women were studying her clothes. A boy's memory is all wrong. Naturally, when I was a boy I had thought of her as tall. She was really short. But I did remember her bold nose—it was like her mother's and old Mrs. Draper's; those two were sisters. Otherwise I wouldn't have known her. And that is what Mr. Fulmino said when we were all silent and incredulous again. We had Hilda back. Not just "back" either, but "back from the dead," reborn.

"She was in the last coach of the train, wasn't she, Mother?" Mr. Fulmino said to Mrs. Johnson. He called her "mother" for the occasion, celebrating her joy.

"Yes," said Mrs. Johnson. "Yes." Her voice scraped and trembled.

"In the last coach, next the van. We went right up the platform, we thought we'd missed her, didn't we? She was," he exclaimed with acquisitive pride, "in the First Class."

"Like you missed me coming from Penzance," said Mrs. Fulmino swelling powerfully and going that thundery violet colour which old wrongs gave her.

"Posh!" said Hilda. And we all smiled in a sickly way.

"Don't you ever do it again, my girl! Don't you ever do it again," said her mother, old Mrs. Johnson, clinging to her daughter's arm and shaking it as if it were a bellrope.

"I was keeping an eye on my luggage," Hilda laughed.

Ah! That was a point! There was not only Hilda, there was her luggage. Some of it was in the room, but the bigger things were outside on the landing, piled up, looking very new, with the fantastic labels of hotels in Tokyo, San Francisco, and New York on it, and a beautiful jewel box in white leather on top like a crown. Old Mrs. Draper did not like the luggage being outside the room in case it was in the way of the people upstairs. Constance went out and fetched the jewel box in. We had all seen it. We were as astonished by all these cases as we were by Hilda herself. After thirteen years, six of them war, we recognised that the poor ruined woman we had prepared for had not arrived. She shone with money. Later on, one after the other of us, except old Mrs. Draper who could not walk far, went out and looked at the luggage and came back to study Hilda in a new way.

We had all had a shock. She had been nearly two years coming home from Tokyo. Before that there was the occupation, before that the war itself. Before that there were the years in Bombay and Singapore, when she was married to an Indian they always called Mr. Singh. All those years were lost to us. None of us had been to India. What happened there to Mr. Singh? We knew he had died—but how? Even if we had known, we couldn't have imagined it. None of us had been to Singapore, none of us to Japan. People from streets like Hincham Street do go to such places—it is not past belief. Knock on the doors of half the houses in London and you will find people with relations all over the world—but none of us had. Mention these places to us, we look at our grey skies and see boiling sun. Our one certainty about Hilda was what, in fact, the newspaper said the next day, with her photograph and the headline: *A Mother's Faith. Four Years in Japanese Torture Camp. London Girl's Ordeal.* Hilda was a terrible item of news, a gash in our lives, and we looked for the signs of it on her body, in the way she stood, in the lines on her face, as if we were expecting a scream from her mouth like the screams we were told Bill Williams gave out at night in his sleep, after he had been flown back home when the war ended. We had had to wait and wait for Hilda. At one time—there was a postcard from Hawaii—she was pinned like a butterfly in the middle of the Pacific Ocean; soon after there was a letter from Tokyo saying she couldn't get a passage. Confusing. She was travelling backwards. Letters from Tokyo were still coming after her letters from San Francisco.

We were still standing, waiting for Constance to bring in the teapot, for the tea was already laid. The trolley buses go down Hincham Street. It is a mere one hundred and fifty yards of a few little houses and a few little shops, which has a sudden charmed importance because the main road has petered out at our end by the Lord Nelson and an enormous public lavatory, and the trolley buses have to run down Hincham Street before picking up the main road again, after a sharp turn at the convent. Hincham Street is less a street than an interval, a disheartened connection. While we stood in one of those silences that follow excitement, a trolley bus came by and Hilda exclaimed:

"You've still got the old trams. Bump! Bump! Bump!" Hilda was ecstatic about the sound. "Do you remember I used to be frightened the spark from the pole would set the lace curtains on fire when I was little?"

For, as the buses turned, the trolley arms would come swooping with two or three loud bumps and a spit of blue electricity, almost hitting Mrs. Draper's sitting-room window which was on the first floor.

"It's trolleys now, my girl," said old Mrs. Draper, whose voice was like the voice of time itself chewing away at life. "The trams went years ago, before the war."

Old Mrs. Draper had sat down in her chair again by the fire which always burned winter and summer in this room; she could not stand for long. It was the first remark that had given us any sense of what was bewildering all of us, the passing of time, the growing of a soft girl into a grown, hard-hipped woman. For old Mrs. Draper's mind was detached from events around her and moved only among the signal facts and conclusions of history.

Presently we were, as the saying is, "at our teas." Mr. Fulmino, less puzzled than the rest of us, expanded in his chair with the contentment of one who had personally operated a deeply British miracle. It was he who had got Hilda home.

"We've got all the correspondence, haven't we, Harry?" he said. "We kept it—the War Office, Red Cross, Prisoner of War Commission, everything, Hilda. I'll show it to you."

His task had transformed him and his language. Identification, registration, accommodation, communication, rehabilitation, hospitalisation, administration, investigation, transportation—well we had all dreamed of Hilda in our different ways.

"They always said the same thing," Mrs. Fulmino said reproachfully. "No one of the name of Mrs. Singh on the lists."

"I wrote to Bombay," said Mr. Fulmino.

"He wrote to Singapore," said Mrs. Fulmino.

Mr. Fulmino drank some tea, wiped his lips and became geography.

"All British subjects were rounded up, they said," Mrs. Fulmino said.

We nodded. We had made our stand, of course, on the law. Mrs. Fulmino was authority.

"But Hilda was married to an Indian," said Constance.

We glanced with a tolerance we did not usually feel for Constance. She was always trying to drag politics in.

"She's a British subject by birth," said Mrs. Fulmino firmly.

"Mum," Hilda whispered, squeezing her mother's arm hard, and then looked up to listen, as if she were listening to talk about a faraway stranger.

"I was in Tokyo when the war started," she said. "Not Singapore."

"Oh Tokyo!" exclaimed Mr. Fulmino, feeling in his waistcoat for a pencil to make a note of it and, suddenly, realising that his note-taking days were over.

"Whatever the girl has done she has been punished for it," came old Mrs. Draper's mournful voice from the chair by the fire, but in the clatter no one heard her, except old Mrs. Johnson, who squeezed her daughter's arm and said:

"My girl is a jewel."

Still, Hilda's words surprised us. We had worked it out that after she and Mr. Singh were married and went to Bombay he had heard of a better job in the state railway medical service and had gone to Singapore where the war had caught her. Mrs. Fulmino looked affronted. If Mr. Fulmino expanded into geography and the language of state—he worked for the Borough Council—Mrs. Fulmino liked a fact to be a fact.

"We got the postcards," said Mrs. Fulmino sticking to chronology.

"Hawaii," Mr. Fulmino said. "How'd you get there? Swim, I suppose." He added, "A sweet spot, it looks, suit us for a holiday—palms."

"Coconuts," said young Jack Draper, who worked in a pipe factory, speaking for the first time.

"Be quiet," said his wife.

"It's an American base now," said Constance with her politically sugared smile.

We hesitated but let her observation pass. It was simple to ignore her. We were happy.

"I suppose they paid your fare," said Jack Draper's wife, a north-country woman.

"Accommodation, transportation," said Mr. Fulmino. "Food, clothing. Everything. Financed by the international commission."

This remark made old Mrs. Johnson cry a little. In those years none of us had deeply believed that Hilda was alive. The silence was too long; too much time had gone by. Others had come home by the thousand with stories of thousands who had died. Only old Mrs. Johnson had been convinced that Hilda was safe. The landlord at the Lord Nelson, the butcher, anyone who met old Mrs. Johnson as she walked by like a poor, decent ghost with her sewing bundles, in those last two years, all said in war-staled voices:

"It's a mother's faith, that's what it is. A mother's faith's a funny thing."

She would walk along, with a cough like someone driving tacks. Her chest had sunk and under her brown coat her shoulder blades seemed to have sharpened into a single hump. Her faith gave her a bright, yet also a sly, dishonest look.

"I'm taking this sewing up to Mrs. Tracy's. She wants it in a hurry," she might say.

"You ought to rest, Mrs. Johnson, like the doctor said."

"I want a bit of money for when my girl comes home," she said. "She'll want feeding up."

And she would look around perhaps, for a clock, in case she ought, by this time, to have put a pot on the stove.

146 · *Essential Stories*

She had been too ill, in hospital, during the war, to speak about what might have happened to Hilda. Her own pain and fear of dying deafened her to what could be guessed. Mrs. Johnson's faith had been born out of pain, out of the inability—within her prison of aching bones and crushed breathing—to identify herself with her daughter. Her faith grew out of her very self-centredness. And when she came out from the post office every week, where she put her savings, she looked demure, holy and secretive. If people were too kind and too sympathetic with her, she shuffled and looked mockingly. Seven hospitals, she said, had not killed *her*.

Now, when she heard Mr. Fulmino's words about the fare, the clothes, the food, the expense of it all, she was troubled. What had she worked for—even at one time scrubbing in a canteen—but to save Hilda from a charity so vast in its humiliation, from so blank a herding mercy. Hilda was hers, not theirs. Hilda kept her arm on her mother's waist and while Mr. Fulmino carried on with the marvels of international organisation (which moved Mrs. Fulmino to say hungrily, "It takes a war to bring it out"), Hilda ignored them and whispered to comfort her mother. At last the old lady dried her eyes and smiled at her daughter. The smile grew to a small laugh, she gave a proud jerk to her head, conveying that she and her Hil were not going to kowtow in gratitude to anyone, and Hilda, at last, said out loud to her mother what, no doubt, she had been whispering:

"He wouldn't let me pay anything, Mum. Faulkner his name was. Very highly educated. He came from California. We had a fancy dress dance on the ship and he made me go as a geisha . . . He gave me these . . ." And she raised her hand to show her mother the bracelets on it.

Mrs. Johnson laughed wickedly.

"Did he . . . ? Was he . . . ?" said Mrs. Johnson.

"No. Well, I don't know," said Hilda. "But I kept his address."

Mrs. Johnson smiled round at all of us, to show that in spite of all, being the poorest in the family and the ones that had suffered most, she and Hilda knew how to look after themselves.

This was the moment when there was that knock on the door. Everyone was startled and looked at it.

"A knock!" said Mr. Fulmino.

"A knock, Constance," said young Mrs. Draper who had busy north-country ears.

"A knock," several said.

Old Mrs. Draper made one of her fundamental utterances again, one of her growls from the belly of the history of human indignation.

"We are," she said, "in the middle of our teas. Constance, go and see and tell them."

But before Constance got to the door, two young men, one with a camera, came right into the room, without asking. Some of us lowered our heads and then, just as one young man said, "I'm from the *News*," the other clicked his camera.

Jack Draper said, nearly choking:

"He's taken a snap of us eating."

While we were all staring at them, old Mrs. Draper chewed out grandly:

"Who may they be?"

But Hilda stood up and got her mother to her feet, too. "Stand up all of us," she said eagerly. "It's for the papers."

It was the Press. We were in confusion. Mrs. Fulmino pushed Mr. Fulmino forward towards the reporter and then pulled him back. The reporter stood asking questions and everyone answered at once. The photographer kept on taking photographs and, when he was not doing that, started picking up vases and putting them down and one moment was trying the drawer of a little table by the window. They pushed Hilda and her mother into a corner and took a picture of them, Hilda calling to us all to "come in" and Mr. Fulmino explaining to the reporters. Then they went, leaving a cigarette burning on one of old Mrs. Draper's lace doyleys under the fern and two more butts on the floor. "What did they say? What did they say?" we all asked one another, but no one could remember. We were all talking at once, arguing about who had heard the knock first. Young Mrs. Draper said her tea was spoiled and Constance opened the window to let the cigarette smoke out and then got the kettle. Mr. Fulmino put his hand on his wife's knee because she was upset and she shook it off. When we had calmed down Hilda said:

"The young one was a nice-looking boy, wasn't he, Mum?" and Mr. Fulmino, who almost never voiced the common opinion about anything but who had perhaps noticed how the eyes of all the women went larger at this remark, laughed loudly and said:

"We've got the old Hilda back!"

I mention this because of the item in the papers next day: A Mother's Faith. Four Years in Japanese Torture Camp. London Girl's Ordeal.

Wonderful, as Mr. Fulmino said.

———

To be truthful, I felt uncomfortable at old Mrs. Draper's. They were not my family. I had been dragged there by Mr. Fulmino, and by a look now and then from young Mrs. Draper and from Constance I had the feeling that they thought it was indecent for me to be there when I had only been going with Iris, Mr. Fulmino's daughter, for two or three months. I had to be tolerated as one more example of Mr. Fulmino's uncontrollable gifts—the gift for colonising.

Mr. Fulmino had shot up from nothing during the war. It had given him personality. He was a short, talkative, heavy man of forty-five with a wet gold tooth and glossy black hair that streamlined back across his head from an arrow point, getting thin in front. His eyes were anxious, overworked and puddled, indeed if you had not known him you would have thought he had had a couple of black eyes that had never got right. He bowled along as he walked like someone absorbed by fondness for his own body. He had been in many things before he got to work for the Council—the army (but not a fighting soldier) in the war, in auctions and the bar of a club. He was very active, confiding and enquiring.

When I first met him I was working at the counter of the Public Library, during the war, and one day he came over from the Council Offices and said, importantly:

"Friend, we've got a bit of a headache. We've got an enquiry from the War Office. Have you got anything about Malaya—with maps?"

In the next breath he was deflating himself:

"It's a personal thing. They never tell you anything. I've got a niece out there."

Honesty made him sound underhand. His manner suggested that his niece was a secret fortification somewhere east of Suez. Soon he was showing me the questionnaire from the Red Cross. Then he was telling me that his wife, like the rest of the Drapers, was very handsome—

"a lovely woman" in more ways, his manner suggested, than one—but that since Hilda had gone, she had become a different woman. The transition from handsome to different was, he suggested, a catastrophe which he was obliged to share with the public. He would come in from fire-watching, he said, and find her demented. In bed, he would add. He and I found ourselves fire-watching together, and from that time he started facetiously calling me "my secretary."

"I asked my secretary to get the sand and shovel out," he would say about our correspondence. "And he wrote the letter."

So I was half a stranger at Hilda's homecoming. I looked round the room or out at the shops opposite and, when I looked back at the family several times, I caught Hilda's eyes wandering too. She also was out of it. I studied her. I hadn't expected her to come back in rags, as old Mrs. Draper had, but it was a surprise to see she was the best-dressed woman in the room and the only one who looked as if she had ever been to a hairdresser. And there was another way in which I could not match her with the person Mr. Fulmino and I had conjured. When we thought of everything that must have happened to her it was strange to see that her strong face was smooth and blank. Except for the few minutes of arrival and the time the reporters came, her face was vacant and plain. It was as vacant as a stone that has been smoothed for centuries in the sand of some hot country. It was the face of someone to whom nothing had happened; or, perhaps, so much had happened to her that each event wiped out what had happened before. I was disturbed by something in her—the lack of history, I think. We were worm-eaten by it. And that suddenly brought her back to me as she had been when she was a schoolgirl and when my older brother got into trouble for chasing after her. She was now sharper in the shoulders and elbows, no longer the swollen schoolgirl but, even as a girl, her face had the same quality of having been fixed and unchangeable between its high cheek bones. It was disturbing, in a face so anonymous, to see the eyes move, especially since she blinked very little; and if she smiled it was less a smile than an alteration of the two lines at the corners of her lips.

The party did not settle down quite in the same way after the reporters had been and there was talk of not tiring Hilda after her long journey. The family would all be meeting tomorrow, the Sunday, as they always did, when young Mrs. Jack Draper brought her children. Jack Draper was thinking of the pub which was open now and asking if anyone was going over. And then, something happened. Hilda walked over to the window to Mr. Fulmino and said, just as if she had not been there at the time:

"Ted—what did that man from the *News* ask you—about the food?"

"No," said Mr. Fulmino widening to a splendid chance of not giving the facts. "No—he said something about starving the prisoners. I was telling him that in my opinion the deterioration in conditions was inevitable after the disorganisation in the camps resulting from air operations . . ."

"Oh, I thought you said we starved. We had enough."

"What?" said Mr. Fulmino.

"Bill Williams was a skeleton when he came back. Nothing but a bowl of rice a day. Rice!" said Mrs. Fulmino. "And torture."

"Bill Williams must have been in one of those labour camps," said Hilda. "Being Japanese I was all right."

"Japanese!" said Mr. Fulmino. "You?"

"Shinji was a Japanese," said Hilda. "He was in the army."

"You married a Japanese!" said Mrs. Fulmino, marching forward.

"That's why I was put in the American camp, when they came. They questioned every one, not only me. That's what I said to the reporter. It wasn't the food, it was the questions. What was his regiment? When did you hear from him? What was his number? They kept on. Didn't they, Mum?"

She turned to her mother who had taken the chance to cut herself another piece of cake and was about to slip it into her handkerchief, I think, to carry to her own room. We were all flabbergasted. A trolley bus went by and took a swipe at the wall. Young Mrs. Draper murmured something and her young husband Jack said loudly, hearing his wife:

"Hilda married a Nip!"

And he looked at Hilda with astonishment. He had very blue eyes.

"You weren't a prisoner!" said Mrs. Fulmino.

"Not of the Japanese," said Hilda. "They couldn't touch me. My husband was Japanese."

"I'm not stupid. I can hear," said young Mrs. Draper to her husband. She was a plain-spoken woman from the Yorkshire coalfields, one of a family of twelve.

"I've nowt to say about who you married, but where is he? Haven't you brought him?" she said.

"You were married to Mr. Singh," said Mrs. Fulmino.

"They're both dead," said Hilda, her vacant yellow eyes becoming suddenly brilliant like a cat's at night. An animal sound, like the noise of an old dog at a bone, came out of old Mrs. Draper by the fire.

"Two," she moaned.

No more than that. Simply, again: "Two."

Hilda was holding her handbag and she lifted it in both hands and covered her bosom with it. Perhaps she thought we were going to hit her. Perhaps she was going to open the bag and get out something extraordinary—documents, letters, or a handkerchief to weep into. But no—she held it there very tight. It was an American handbag—we hadn't seen one like that before, cream-coloured, like the luggage. Old Mrs. Johnson hesitated at the table, tipped the piece of cake back out of her handkerchief on to a plate, and stepped to Hilda's side and stood, very straight for once, beside her, the old blue lips very still.

"Ted," accused Hilda. "Didn't you get my letters? Mother," she stepped away from her mother, "didn't you tell them?"

"What, dear?" said old Mrs. Johnson.

"About Shinji. I wrote you. Did Mum tell you?" Hilda appealed to us and now looked fiercely at her mother.

Mrs. Johnson smiled and retired into her look of faith and modesty. She feigned deafness.

"I put it all in the post office," she said. "Every week," she said. "Until my girl comes home, I said. She'll need it."

"Mother!" said Hilda, giving the old lady a small shake. "I wrote to you. I told you. Didn't you tell them?"

"What did Hilda say?" said Mr. Fulmino gently, bending down to the old lady.

"Sh! Don't worry her. She's had enough for today. What did you tell the papers, Ted?" said Mrs. Fulmino, turning on her husband. "You can't ever keep your big mouth shut, can you? You never let me see the correspondence."

"I married Shinji when the war came up," Hilda said.

And then old Mrs. Draper spoke from her armchair by the fire. She had her bad leg propped up on a hassock.

"Two," said Mrs. Draper savagely again.

Mr. Fulmino, in his defeat, lost his nerve and let slip a remark quite casually, as he thought, under his voice, but everyone heard it—a remark that Mrs. Fulmino was to remind him of in months to come.

"She strikes like a clock," he said.

We were stupefied by Mr. Fulmino's remark. Perhaps it was a relief.

"Mr. Fraser!" Hilda said to me. And now her vacant face had become dramatic and she stepped towards me, appealing outside the family. "You knew, you and Ted knew. You've got all the letters . . ."

If ever a man looked like the Captain going down with his ship and suddenly conscious, at the last heroic moment, that he is not on a ship at all, but standing on nothing and had hopelessly blundered, it was Mr. Fulmino. But we didn't go down, either of us. For suddenly old Mrs. Johnson couldn't stand straight any longer, her head wagged and drooped forward and, but for a chair, she would have fallen to the ground.

"Quick! Constance! Open the window," Mrs. Fulmino said. Hilda was on her knees by her mother.

"Are you there, Hilly?" said her mother.

"Yes, I'm here, Mum," said Hilda. "Get some water—some brandy." They took the old lady next door to the little room Hilda was sharing with her that night.

———

"What I can't fathom is your aunt not telling me, keeping it to herself," said Mr. Fulmino to his wife as we walked home that evening from Mrs. Draper's, and we had said "Good-bye" to Jack Draper and his wife.

He was not hurt by Mrs. Johnson's secretiveness but by an extraordinary failure of co-operation.

It was unwise of him to criticise Mrs. Fulmino's family.

"Don't be so smug," said Mrs. Fulmino. "What's it got to do with you? She was keeping it from Gran, you know Gran's tongue. She's her sister." They called old Mrs. Draper Gran or Grandma sometimes.

But when Mr. Fulmino got home he asked me in so that we could search the correspondence together. Almost at once we discovered his blunder. There it was in the letter saying a Mrs. Singh or Shinji Kobayashi had been identified.

"Shinji!" exclaimed Mrs. Fulmino, putting her big index finger on the page. "There you are, plain as dirt."

"Singh," said Mr. Fulmino. "Singh, Shinji, the same name. Some Indians write Singh, some Shinji."

"And what is Kobayashi? Indian too? Don't be a fool."

"It's the family name or Christian name of Singh," said Mr. Fulmino, doing the best he could.

Singh, Shinji, Shinji, Singh, he murmured to himself and he walked about trying to convince himself by incantation and hypnosis. He lashed himself with Kobayashi. He remembered the names of other Indians, Indian cities, mentioned the Ganges and the Himalayas; had a brief, brilliant couple of minutes when he argued that Shinji was Hindu for Singh. Mrs. Fulmino watched him with the detachment of one waiting for a bluebottle to settle so that she could swat it.

"*You* thought Kobayashi was Indian, didn't you, Harry?" he appealed to me. I did my best.

"I thought," I said weakly, "it was the address."

"Ah, the address!" Mr. Fulmino clutched at this, but he knew he was done for. Mrs. Fulmino struck.

"And what about the Sunday papers, the man from the *News*?" she said. "You open your big mouth too soon."

"Christ!" said Mr. Fulmino. It was the sound of a man who has gone to the floor.

I will come to that matter of the papers later on. It is not very important.

When we went to bed that night we must all have known in our different ways that we had been disturbed in a very long dream. We had been living on inner visions for years. It was an effect of the long war. England had been a prison. Even the sky was closed and, like convicts, we had been driven to dwelling on fancies in our dreary minds. In the cinema the camera sucks some person forward into an enormous close-up and holds a face there yards wide, filling the whole screen, all holes and pores, like some sucking octopus that might eat up an audience many rows at a time. I don't say these pictures aren't beautiful sometimes, but afterwards I get the horrors. Hilda had been a close-up like this for us when she was lost and far away. For myself, I could hardly remember Hilda. She was a collection of fragments of my childhood and I suppose I had expected a girl to return.

My father and mother looked down on the Drapers and the Johnsons. Hincham Street was "dirty" and my mother once whispered that Mr. Johnson had worked "on the line," as if that were a smell. I remember the old man's huge crinkled white beard when I was a child. It was horribly soft and like pubic hair. So I had always thought of Hilda as a railway girl, in and out of tunnels, signal boxes and main line stations, and when my older brother was "chasing" her as they said, I admired him. I listened to the quarrels that went on in our family—how she had gone to the convent school and the nuns had complained about her; and was it she or some other girl who went for car rides with a married man who waited round the corner of Hincham Street for her? The sinister phrase "The nuns have been to see her mother" stuck in my memory. It astonished me to see Hilda alive, calm, fat and walking after that, as composed as a railway engine. When I grew up and Mr. Fulmino came to the library, I was drawn into his search because she brought back those days with my brother, those clouts on the head from some friend of his, saying, "Buzz off. Little pigs have big ears," when my brother and he were whispering about her.

To Mrs. Fulmino, a woman whose feelings were in her rolling arms, flying out from one extreme to another as she talked, as if she were doing exercises, Hilda appeared in her wedding clothes and all the sexuality of an open flower, standing beside her young Indian husband who was about to become a doctor. There was trouble about the wedding, for Mr. Singh spoke a glittering and palatial English—the beautiful English a snake might speak, it seemed to the family—that made a few pock marks on his face somehow more noticeable. Old Mrs. Draper alone, against all evidence—Mr. Singh had had a red racing car—stuck to it that he was "a common lascar off a ship." Mrs. Fulmino had been terrified of Mr. Singh—she often conveyed—and had "refused to be in a room alone with him." Or "How can she let him touch her?" she would murmur, thinking about that, above all. Then whatever vision was in her mind would jump forward to Hilda, captured, raped, tortured, murdered in front of her eyes. Mrs. Fulmino's mind was voluptuous. When I first went to Mr. Fulmino's house and met Iris and we talked about Hilda, Mrs. Fulmino once or twice left the room and he lowered his voice. "The wife's upset," he said. "She's easily upset."

We had not all been under a spell. Not young Jack Draper nor his wife, for example. Jack Draper had fought in the war and where we thought of the war as something done to us and our side, Jack thought of it as something done to everybody. I remember what he said to his wife before the Fulminos and I said "Good night" to them on the Saturday Hilda came home.

"It's a shame," said Jack, "she couldn't bring the Nip with her."

"He was killed," said his wife.

"That's what I mean," said Jack. "It's a bleeding shame she couldn't."

We walked on and then young Mrs. Draper said, in her flat, northern laconic voice:

"Well, Jack, for all the to-do, you might just as well have gone to your fishing."

For Jack had made a sacrifice in coming to welcome Hilda. He went fishing up the Thames on Saturdays. The war for him was something that spoiled fishing. In the Normandy landing he had thought mostly of that. He dreamed of the time when his two boys would be old enough to fish. It was what he had had children for.

"There's always Sunday," said his wife, tempting him. Jack nodded. She knew he would not fall. He was the youngest of old Mrs. Draper's family, the baby, as they said. He never missed old Mrs. Draper's Sundays.

———

It was a good thing he did not, a good thing for all of us that we didn't miss, for we would have missed Hilda's second announcement.

Young Mrs. Draper provoked it. These Sunday visits to Hincham Street were a ritual in the family. It was a duty to old Mrs. Draper. We went there for our tea. She provided, though Constance prepared for it as if we were a school, for she kept house there. We recognised our obligation by paying sixpence into the green pot on the chiffonier when we left. The custom had started in the bad times when money was short; but now the money was regarded as capital and Jack Draper used to joke and say, "Who are you going to leave the green pot to, Mum?" Some of Hilda's luggage had been moved by the afternoon into her mother's little room at the back and how those two could sleep in a bed so small was a question raised by Mrs. Fulmino whose night with Mr. Fulmino required room for struggle, as I know, for this colonising man often dropped hints about how she swung her legs over in the night.

"Have you unpacked yet, Hilda?" Mrs. Fulmino was asking.

"Unpacked!" said Constance. "Where would she put all that?"

"I've been lazy," said Hilda. "I've just hung up a few things because of the creases."

"Things do crease," said Mrs. Fulmino.

"Bill Williams said he would drop in later," said Constance.

"That man suffered," said Mrs. Fulmino, with meaning.

"He heard you were back," said Constance.

Hilda had told us about Shinji. Jack Draper listened with wonder. Shinji had been in the jute business and when the war came he was called up to the army. He was in "Stores." Jack scratched with delight when he heard this. "Same as I tried to work it," Jack said. Shinji had been killed in an air raid. Jack's wife said, to change the subject, she liked that idea, the idea of Jack "working" anything, he always let everyone climb up on his shoulders. "First man to get wounded. I knew he would be," she said. "He never looks where he's going."

"Is that the Bill Williams who worked for Ryan, the builder?" said Hilda.

"He lives in the Culverwell Road," young Mrs. Draper said.

Old Mrs. Draper, speaking from the bowels of history, said:

"He got that Sellers girl into trouble."

"Yes," exclaimed Hilda, "I remember."

"It was proved in court that he didn't," said Constance briskly to Hilda. "You weren't here."

We were all silent. One could hear only the sounds of our cups on the saucers and Mrs. Fulmino's murmur, "More bread and butter?" Constance's face had its neat, pink, enamelled smile and one saw the truthful blue of her small eyes become purer in colour. Iris was next to me and she said afterwards something I hadn't noticed, that Constance hated Hilda. It is one of the difficulties I have in writing, that, all along, I was slow to see what was really happening, not having a woman's eye or ear. And being young. Old Mrs. Draper spoke again, her mind moving from the past to the present with that suddenness old people have.

"If Bill Williams is coming, he knows the way," she said.

Hilda understood that remark for she smiled and Constance flushed. (Of course, I see it now: two women in a house! Constance had ruled old Mrs. Draper and Mrs. Johnson for years and her money had made a big difference.) They knew that one could, as the saying is, "trust Gran to put her oar in."

Again young Mrs. Draper changed the subject. She was a nimble, tarry-haired woman, impatient of fancies, excitements and disasters. She liked things flat and factual. While the family gaped at Hilda's clothes and luggage, young Mrs. Draper had reckoned up the cost of them. She was not avaricious or mean, but she knew that money is money. You know that if you have done without. So she went straight into the important question being (as she would say), not like people in the South, double-faced Wesleyans, but honest, plain and straight out with it, what are they ashamed of? Jack, her husband, was frightened by her bluntness, and had the nervous habit of folding his arms across his chest and scratching fast under his armpits when his wife spoke out about money; some view of the river, with his bait and line and the evening flies, came into his panicking mind. Mr. Fulmino once said that Jack scratched because the happiest moments of his life, the moments of escape, had been passed in clouds of gnats.

"I suppose, Hilda, you'll be thinking of what you're going to do?" young Mrs. Draper said. "Did they give you a pension?"

I was stroking Iris's knee but she stopped me, alerted like the rest of them. The word "pension" is a very powerful word. In this neighbourhood one could divide the world into those who had pensions and those who hadn't. The phrase "the old pensioner" was one of envy, abuse and admiration. My father, for example, spoke contemptuously of pensioners. Old Mrs. Draper's husband had had a pension, but my father would never have one. As a librarian (Mr. Fulmino pointed out), I would have a pension and thereby I had overcome the first obstacle in being allowed to go out with his daughter.

"No," said Hilda. "Nothing."

"But he was your husband, you said," said Constance.

"He was in the army, you say," said young Mrs. Draper.

"Inflation," said Mr. Fulmino grandly. "The financial situation."

He was stopped.

"Then," said young Mrs. Draper, "you'll have to go to work."

"My girl won't want for money," said old Mrs. Johnson, sitting beside her daughter as she had done the day before.

"No," said young Mrs. Draper. "That she won't while you're alive, Mrs. Johnson. We all know that, and the way you slaved for her. But Hilda wants to look after you, I'm sure."

It was, of course, the question in everyone's mind. Did all those clothes and cases mean money or was it all show? That is what we all wanted to know. We would not have raised it at that time and in that way. It wasn't our way—we would have drifted into finding out—Hilda was scarcely home. But young Mrs. Draper had been brought up hard, as she said, twelve mouths to feed.

"*I'm* looking after *you,* Mum," said Hilda, smiling at her mother.

Mrs. Johnson was like a wizened little girl gazing up at a taller sister.

"I'll take you to Monte Carlo, Mum," Hilda said.

The old lady tittered. We all laughed loudly. Hilda laughed with us.

"That gambling place!" the old lady giggled.

"That's it," laughed Hilda. "Break the bank."

"Is it across water?" said the old lady, playing up. "I couldn't go on a boat. I was so sick at Southend when I was a girl."

"Then we'll fly."

"Oh!" the old lady cried. "Don't, Hil—I'll have a fit."

" 'The Man Who Broke the Bank at Monte Carlo,' " Mr. Fulmino sang. "You might find a boy friend, Mrs. Johnson."

Young Mrs. Draper did not laugh at this game; she still wanted to know; but she did smile. She was worried by laughter. Constance did not laugh but she showed her pretty white teeth.

"Oh, she's got one for me," said Mrs. Johnson. "So she says."

"Of course I have. Haven't I, Harry?" said Hilda, talking across the table to me.

"Me? What?" I said completely startled.

"You can't take Harry," said Iris, half frightened.

"Did you post the letter?" said Hilda to me.

"What letter?" said Iris to me. "Did she give you a letter?"

Now there is a thing I ought to have mentioned! I had forgotten all about the letter. When we were leaving the evening before, Hilda had called me quietly to the door and said:

"Please post this for me. Tonight."

"Hilda gave me a letter to post," I said.

"You did post it?" Hilda said.

"Yes," I said.

She looked contentedly round at everyone.

"I wrote to Mr. Gloster, the gentleman I told you about, on the boat. He's in Paris. He's coming over at the end of the week to get a car. He's taking Mother and me to France. Mr. Gloster, Mum, I told you. No, not Mr. Faulkner. That was the other boat. He was in San Francisco."

"Oh," said Mrs. Johnson, a very long "oh," and wriggling like a child listening to a story. She was beginning to look pale, as she had the evening before when she had the turn.

"France!" said Constance in a peremptory voice.

"Who is Mr. Gloster—you never said anything," said Mrs. Fulmino.

"What about the currency regulations?" said Mr. Fulmino.

Young Mrs. Draper said, "France! He must have money."

"Dollars," said Hilda to Mr. Fulmino.

Dollars! There was a word!

"The almighty dollar," said Constance, in the cleansed and uncorrupted voice of one who has mentioned one of the commandments. Constance had principles; we had the confusion of our passions.

And from sixteen years or more back in time or perhaps it was from some point in history hundreds of years back and forgotten, old Mrs. Draper said: "And is this Indian married?"

Hilda—to whom no events, I believe, had ever happened—replied: "Mr. Gloster's an American, Gran."

"He wants to marry her," said old Mrs. Johnson proudly.

"If I'll have him!" said Hilda.

"Well, he can't if you won't have him, can he, Hilda?" said Mrs. Fulmino.

"Gloster. G-L-O-S-T-E-R?" asked Mr. Fulmino.

"Is he in a good job?" asked young Mrs. Draper.

Hilda pointed to a brooch on her blouse.

"He gave me this," she said.

She spoke in her harsh voice and with a movement of her face that in anyone else one would have called excited, but in her it had a disturbing lack of meaning. It was as if Hilda had been hooked into the air by invisible wires and was then swept out into the air and back to Japan, thousands of miles away again, and while she was on her way, she turned and knocked us flat with the next item.

"He's a writer," she said. "He's going to write a book about me. He's very interested in me . . ."

Mrs. Johnson nodded.

"He's coming to fetch us, Mum and me, and take us to France to write this book. He's going to write my life."

Her life! Here was a woman who had, on top of everything else, a life.

"Coming *here?*" said Mrs. Fulmino with a grinding look at old Mrs. Draper and then at Constance, trying to catch their eyes and failing; in despair she looked at the shabby room, to see what must be put straight, or needed cleaning or painting. Nothing had been done to it for years for Constance, teaching at her school all day, and very clean in her person, let things go in the house and young Mrs. Draper said old Mrs. Draper smelled. All the command in Mrs. Fulmino's face collapsed as rapidly, on her own, she looked at the carpets, the lino, the curtains.

"What's he putting in this book?" said young Mrs. Draper cannily.

"Yes," said Jack Draper, backing up his wife.

"What I tell him," Hilda said.

"What she tells him," said old Mrs. Johnson sparkling. Constance looked thoughtfully at Hilda.

"Is it a biography?" Constance asked coldly. There were times when we respected Constance and forgot to murmur "Go back to Russia" every time she spoke. I knew what a biography was and so did Mr. Fulmino, but no one else did.

"It's going to be made into a film," Hilda replied.

"A film," cried Iris.

Constance gleamed.

"You watch for American propaganda," said Constance. There you are, you see: Constance was back on it!

"Oh, it's about me," said Hilda. "My experience."

"Very interesting," said Mr. Fulmino, preparing to take over. "A Hollywood production, I expect. Publication first and then they go into production."

He spread his legs.

None of us had believed, or even understood what we heard, but we looked with gratitude to Mr. Fulmino for making the world steady again.

Jack Draper's eyes filled with tears because a question was working in him but he could not get it out.

"Will you be in this film?" asked Iris.

"I'll wait till he's written it," said Hilda with that lack of interest we had often noticed in her, after she had made some dramatic statement.

Mrs. Fulmino breathed out heavily with relief and after that her body seemed to become larger. She touched her hair at the back and straightened her dress, as if preparing to offer herself for the part. She said indeed:

"I used to act at school."

"She's still good at it," said Mr. Fulmino with daring to Jack Draper who always appreciated Mr. Fulmino, but seeing the danger of the moment hugged himself and scratched excitedly under both armpits, laughing.

"You shouldn't have let this Mr. Gloster go," said Constance.

Hilda was startled by this remark and looked lost. Then she shrugged her shoulders and gave a low laugh, as if to herself.

Mr. Fulmino's joke had eased our bewilderment. Hilda had been our dream but now she was home she changed as fast as dreams change. She was now, as we looked at her, far more remote to us than she had been all the years when she was away. The idea was so far beyond us. It was like some story of a bomb explosion or an elopement or a picture of bathing girls one sees in the newspapers—unreal and, in a way, insulting to being alive in the ordinary daily sense of the word. Or, she was like a picture that one sees in an art gallery, that makes you feel sad because it is painted.

After tea when Hilda took her mother to the lavatory, Constance beckoned to Iris and let her peep into the room Hilda was sharing, and young Mrs. Draper, not to be kept out of things, followed. They were back in half a minute:

"Six evening dresses," Iris said to me.

"She said it was Mr. Faulkner who gave her the luggage, not this one who was going to get her into pictures," said Mrs. Fulmino.

"Mr. Gloster, you mean," said Constance.

Young Mrs. Draper was watching the door, listening for Hilda's return.

"Ssh," she said, at the sound of footsteps on the stairs and, to look at us, the men on one side of the room and the women on the other, silent, standing at attention, facing each other, we looked like soldiers.

"Oh," said Constance. The steps we had heard were not Hilda's. It was Bill Williams who came in.

"Good afternoon one and all," he said. The words came from the corner of a mouth that had slipped down at one side. Constance drew herself up, her eyes softened. She had exact, small, round breasts. Looking around, he said to Constance: "Where is she?"

Constance lowered her head when she spoke to him, though she held it up shining, admiring him, when he spoke to us, as if she were displaying him to us.

"She'll be here in a minute," she said. "She's going into films."

"I'll take a seat in the two and fourpennies," said Bill Williams and he sat down at his ease and lit a cigarette.

Bill Williams was a very tall, sick-faced man who stooped his shoulders as if he were used to ducking under doors. His dry black hair, not oiled like Mr. Fulmino's, bushed over his forehead and he had the shoulders, arms and hands of a lorry driver. In fact, he drove a light van for a textile firm. His hazel eyes were always watching and wandering and we used to say he looked as though he was going to snaffle something but that may simply have been due to the restlessness of a man with a poor stomach. Laziness, cunning and aches and pains were suggested by him. He was a man taking his time. His eyebrows grew thick and the way one brow was raised, combined with the side-slip of his mouth, made him look like some shrewd man about to pick up a faulty rifle, hit the bull's eye five times running at a fair and moan afterwards. He glanced a good deal at Constance. He was afraid of his manners before her, we thought, because he was a rough type.

"Put it here," said Constance, bringing him an ashtray. That was what he was waiting for, for he did not look at her again.

Bill Williams brought discomfort with him whenever he came on Sundays and we were always happier when he failed to come. If there was anything private to say we tried to get it over before he came. How a woman like Constance, a true, clean, settled schoolteacher who even spoke in the clear, practical and superior manner of someone used to the voice of reason, who kept her nails so beautifully, could have taken up with him, baffled us. He was very often at Mrs. Draper's in the week, eating with them, and Constance, who was thirty-five, quarrelled like a girl when she was getting things ready for him. Mrs. Fulmino could not bear the way he ate, with his elbows out and his face close to the plate. The only good thing about the affair was that, for once, Constance was overruled.

"Listen to her," Bill Williams would say with a nod of his head. "A rank red Communist. Tell us about Holy Russia, Connie."

"Constance is my correct name, not Connie," she said.

Their bickering made us die. But we respected Constance even when she was a trial. She had been twice to Russia before the war and though we argued violently with her, especially Mr. Fulmino who tried to take over Russia, and populate it with explanations, we always boasted to other people that she'd been there.

"On delegations," Mr. Fulmino would say.

But we could *not* boast that she had taken up with Bill Williams. He had been a hero when he came back from Japan, but he had never kept a job since, he was rough and his lazy zigzagging habits in his work made even Constance impatient. He had for her the fascination a teacher feels for a bad pupil. Lately their love affair had been going better because he was working outside London and sometimes he worked at week-ends; this added to the sense of something vague and secretive in his life that had attracted Constance. For there was much that was secret in her or so she liked to hint—it was political. Again, it was the secretiveness of those who like power; she was the school-mistress who has the threat of inside knowledge locked up in the cup-board. Once Mrs. Fulmino went purple and said to her husband—who told me, he always told me such things—that she believed Constance had lately started sleeping with Bill Williams. That was because Con-stance had once said to her:

"Bill and I are individuals."

Mrs. Fulmino had a row with Iris after this and stopped me seeing her for a month.

Hilda came back into the room alone. Bill Williams let his mouth slip sideways and spoke a strange word to her, saying jauntily to us: "That's Japanese."

Hilda wasn't surprised. She replied with a whole sentence in Japan-ese.

"That means"—but Bill Williams was beaten, but he passed it off. "Well, I'd best not tell them what it means," he said.

"East meets East," Mr. Fulmino said.

"It means," said Hilda, "you were on the other side of the fence but now the gate is open."

Bill Williams studied her inch by inch. He scratched his head.

"Straight?" he said.

"Yes," she said.

"Stone me, it was bloody closed when we were there," said Bill Williams offensively, but then said: "They fed her well, didn't they, Constance? Sit down." Hilda sat down beside him.

"Connie!" he called. "Seen these? Just the job, eh?" He was nodding at Hilda's stockings. Nylons. "Now," he said to Hilda, looking closely at her. "Where were you? It got a bit rough at the finish, didn't it?"

Jack Draper came close to them to hear, hoping that Hilda would say something about what moved him the most: the enemy. Bill Williams gave him a wink and Hilda saw it. She looked placidly at Bill Williams, considering his face, his neck, his shoulders and his hands that were resting on his knees.

"I was okey doke," she said.

Bill Williams dropped his mouth open and waggled the top of his tongue in a back tooth in his knowing manner. To our astonishment Hilda opened her mouth and gave a neat twist to her tongue in her cheek in the same way.

Bill Williams slapped his knee and, to cover his defeat in this little duel, said to all of us:

"This little girl's got yellow eyes."

All the colour had gone from Connie's face as she watched the meeting.

"They say you're going to be in pictures," said Bill Williams.

And then we had Hilda's story over again. Constance asked what papers Mr. Gloster wrote for.

"I don't know. A big paper," said Hilda.

"You ought to find out," Constance said. "I'll find out."

"Um," said Hilda with a nod of not being interested.

"I could give him some of my experience," said Bill Williams. "Couldn't I, Connie? Things I've told you—you could write a ruddy book."

He looked with challenge at Hilda. He was a rival.

"Gawd!" he exclaimed. "The things."

We heard it again, how he was captured, where his battery was, the long march, Sergeant Harris who was hanged, Corporal Rowley bayo-neted and left to die in the sun, the starvation, the work on the road that killed half of them. But there was one difference between this story and the ones he had told before. The sight of Hilda altered it.

"You had to get round the guards," he said with a wink. "If you used your loaf a bit, eh? Scrounge around, do a bit of trade. One or two had Japanese girls. Corporal Jones went back afterwards trying to trace his, wanted to marry her."

Hilda listened and talked about places she had lived in, how she had worked in a factory.

"That's it," said Bill Williams, "you had to know your way around and talk a bit of the lingo."

Jack Draper looked with affection and wonder at the talk, lowering his eyes if her eyes caught his. Every word entered him. The heat! she said. The rain. The flowers. The telegraph poles! Jack nodded.

"They got telegraph poles," he nodded to us.

You sleep on the floor. Shinji's mother, she mentioned. She could have skinned her. Jack, brought up among so many women, lost inter-est, but it revived when she talked of Shinji. You could see him mouth-ing his early marvelling sentence: "She married a Nip," but not saying it. She was confirming something he had often thought of in Nor-mandy; the men on the other side were married too. A bloody marvel. Why hadn't she brought him home? He would have had a friend.

"Who looked after the garden when Shinji was called up?" he asked. "Were they goldfish, ordinary goldfish, in the pond?"

Young Mrs. Draper shook her head.

"Eh," she said. "If he'd a known he'd have come over to change the water. Next time we have a war you just let him know."

Mrs. Fulmino who was throbbing like a volcano said:

"We better all go next time by the sound of it."

At the end, Bill Williams said:

"I suppose you're going to be staying here."

"No," said Constance quickly, "she isn't. She's going to France. When is it, Hilda? When is Mr. Gloster coming?"

"Next week, I don't know," said Hilda.

"You shouldn't have let him go!" laughed Bill Williams. "Those French girls will get him in Paree."

"That is what I have been saying," said Constance. "He gave her that brooch."

"Oh ah! It's the stockings I'm looking at," said Bill Williams. "How did you get all that stuff through the customs? Twenty cases, Connie told me."

"Twelve," said Hilda.

Bill Williams did not move her at all. Presently she got up and started clearing away the tea things. I will say this for her, she didn't let herself be waited on.

Iris, Mr. and Mrs. Fulmino and the young Drapers and their children and myself left Hincham Street together.

"You walk in front with the children, Iris," said Mrs. Fulmino. Then they turned on me. What was this letter, they wanted to know. Anyone would have thought by their questions that I ought to have opened it and read it.

"I just posted it at the corner." I pointed to the pillar box. Mrs. Fulmino stopped to look at the pillar box and I believe was turning over in her mind the possibility of getting inside it. Then she turned on her husband and said with contemptuous suspicion: "Monte Carlo!" As if he had worked the whole thing in order to go there himself.

"Two dead," she added in her mother's voice, the voice of one who would have been more than satisfied with the death of one.

"Not having a pension hasn't hurt her," said Mrs. Draper.

"Not a tear," said Mrs. Fulmino.

Jack and Mr. Fulmino glanced at each other. It was a glance of surreptitious gratitude: tears—they had escaped that.

Mr. Fulmino said: "The Japanese don't cry."

Mrs. Fulmino stepped out, a bad sign; her temper was rising.

"Who was the letter to?" she asked me. "Was the name Gloster?"

"I didn't look," I said.

Mrs. Fulmino looked at her husband and me and rolled her eyes. Another of our blunders!

"I don't believe it," she said.

———

But Mrs. Fulmino *did* believe it. We all believed and disbelieved everything at once.

I said I would come to the report in the *News*. It was in thick lettering like mourning, with Hilda's picture: A Mother's Faith. Four Years in Japanese Torture Camp. London Girl's Ordeal. And then an account of how Hilda had starved and suffered and been brain-washed by questioners. Even Hilda was awed when she read it, feeling herself drain away, perhaps, and being replaced by this fantasy; and for the rest of us, we had become used to living in a period when events reduced us to beings so trivial that we had no strong feeling of our own existence in relation to the world around us. We had been bashed first one way, then the other, by propaganda, until we were indifferent. At one time people like my parents or old Mrs. Draper could at least trust the sky and feel that it was certain and before it they could have at least the importance of being something in the eye of heaven.

Constance read the newspaper report and it fulfilled her.

"Propaganda," she said. "Press lies."

"All lies," Mr. Fulmino agreed with wonder. The notion that the untrue was as effective as the true opened to him vast areas to his powers. It was like a temptation.

It did not occur to us that we might be in a difficult situation in the neighbourhood when the truth came out, until we heard Constance and Bill Williams had gone over to the Lord Nelson with the paper and Constance had said, "You can't believe a word you read in the capitalist press."

Alfred Levy, the proprietor and a strong Tory, agreed with her. But was Hilda criticised for marrying an enemy? The hatred of the Japanese was strong at this time. She was not. Constance may not have had the best motives for spreading the news, we said, but it did no harm at all. That habit of double vision affected every one publicly. We lived in the true and the untrue, comfortably and without trouble. People picked up the paper, looked at her picture and said, "That's a shocking thing. A British subject," and even when they knew, even from Hilda's own lips the true story, they said, congratulating themselves on their cunning, "The papers make it all up."

Of course, we were all in that stage where the forces of life, the desire to live, were coming back, and although it was not yet openly expressed, we felt that curiosity about the enemy that ex-soldiers like Jack Draper felt when he wondered if some Japanese or some Germans were as fed up as he was on Saturdays by missing a day's fishing. When people shook Hilda's hand they felt they gave her life. I do not say there were not one or two mutterings afterwards, for people always went off from the Lord Nelson when it closed in a state of moralisation: beer must talk; the louts singing and the couples saying this or that "wasn't right." But this gossip came to nothing because, sooner or later, it came to a closed door in everybody's conscience. There were the men who had shot off trigger fingers, who had got false medical certificates, deserters, ration frauds, black marketeers, the pilferers of army stores. And the women said a woman is right to stand by her husband and, looking at Hilda's fine clothes, pointed out to their husbands that that kind of loyalty was sometimes rewarded; indeed, Mrs. Fulmino asserted, by law.

We had been waiting for Hilda; now, by a strange turn, we were waiting for Hilda's Mr. Gloster. We waited for a fortnight and it ran on into three weeks. George Hartman Gloster. I looked up the name on our cards at the library, but we had no books of his. I looked up one or two catalogues. Still nothing. It was not surprising. He was an American who was not published in this country. Constance came in and looked too.

"It is one of those names the Americans don't list," she said. Constance smiled with the cool air of keeping a world of meaningful secrets on ice.

"They don't list everything," she said.

She brought Bill Williams with her. I don't think he had ever been in a public library before, because his knowing manner went and he was overawed. He said to me:

"Have you read all these books? Do you buy them secondhand? What's this lot worth?"

He was a man always on the look-out for a deal; it was typical of him that he had come with Constance in his firm's light-green van. It was not like Constance to travel in that way. "Come on," he said roughly.

The weather was hot; we had the sun blinds down in the Library. We were in the middle of one of those brassy fortnights of the London summer when English life, as we usually know it, is at a standstill, and everyone changes. A new grinning healthy race with long red necks sticking out of open shirts and blouses appears, and the sun brings out the variety of faces and bodies. Constance might have been some trim nurse marching at the head of an official procession. People looked calm, happy and open. There was hardly ever a cloud in the sky, the slate roofs looked like steel with the sun's rays hitting them, and the side streets were cool in sharp shadow. It was a pleasant time for walking, especially when the sky went whitish in the distances of the city in the evening and when the streets had a dry pleasant smell and the glass of millions of windows had a motionless but not excluding stare. Even a tailor working late above a closed shop looked pleased to be going on working, while everyone else was out, wearing out their clothes.

Iris and I used to go to the park on some evenings and there every blade of grass had been wire-brushed by sunlight; the trees were heavy with still leaves and when darkness came they gathered into soft black walls and their edges were cut out against the nail varnish of the city's night. During the day the park was crowded. All over the long sweeps of grass the couples were lying, their legs at careless angles, their bottoms restless as they turned to the horseplay of love in the open. Girls were leaning over the men rumpling their hair, men were tickling the girls' chins with stalks of grass. Occasionally they would knock the wind out of each other with plunging kisses; and every now and then a girl would sit up and straighten her skirt at the waist, narrowing her eyes in a pretence of looking at some refining sight in the distance, until she was pulled down again and, keeping her knees together, was caught again. Lying down you smelt the grass and listened to the pleasant rumble of the distant traffic going round like a wheel that never stopped.

I was glad to know the Fulminos and to go out with Iris. We had both been gayer before we met each other, but seriousness, glumness, a sadness came over us when we became friends—that eager sadness that begins with thoughts of love. We encouraged and discouraged these thoughts in each other yet were always hinting and the sight of so much love around us turned us naturally away from it to think about it privately the more. She was a beautifully-formed girl as her mother must have once been, but slender. She had a wide laugh that shook the curls of her thick black hair. She was being trained at a typing school.

One day when I was sitting in the park and Iris was lying beside me, we had a quarrel. I asked her if there was any news of Mr. Gloster—for she heard everything. She had said there was none and I said, sucking a piece of grass:

"That's what I would like to do. Go round the world. Anywhere. America, Africa, China."

"A chance is a fine thing," said Iris, day dreaming.

"I could get a job," I said.

Iris sat up.

"Leave the Library?" she said.

"Yes," I said. "If I stay there I won't see anything." I saw Iris's face change and become very like her mother's. Mrs. Fulmino could make her face go larger and her mouth go very small. Iris did not answer. I went on talking. I asked her what she thought. She still did not answer.

"Anything the matter?" She was sulking. Then she said, flashing at me:

"You're potty on that woman too. You all are. Dad is, Jack is; and look at Bill Williams. Round at Hincham Street every day. He'll be having his breakfast there soon. Fascinated."

"He goes to see Constance."

"Have you seen Constance's face?" she jeered. "Constance could kill her."

"She came to the Library."

"Ah," she turned to me. "You didn't tell me that."

"She came in for a book, I told you. For Mr. Gloster's books. Bill Williams came with her."

Iris's sulk changed into satisfaction at this piece of news.

"Mother says if Constance's going to marry a man like Mr. Williams," she said, "she'll be a fool to let him out of her sight."

"I'll believe in Mr. Gloster when I see him," Iris said. It was, of course, what we were all thinking. We made up our quarrel and I took Iris home. Mrs. Fulmino was dressed up, just putting the key in the door of her house. Iris was astonished to see her mother had been out and asked where she had been.

"Out," said Mrs. Fulmino. "Have I got to stay in and cook and clean for you all day?"

Mrs. Fulmino was even wearing gloves, as if she had been to church. And she was wearing a new pair of shoes. Iris went pale at the sight of them. Mrs. Fulmino put her gloves down on the sitting-room table and said:

"I've got a right to live, I suppose?"

We were silenced.

One thing we all agreed on while we waited for Mr. Gloster was that Hilda had the money and knew how to spend it. The first time she asked the Fulminos and young Drapers to the cinema, Mrs. Fulmino said to her husband:

"You go. I've got one of my heads."

"Take Jack," young Mrs. Draper said. "I've got the children."

They were daring their husbands to go with her. But the second time, there was a party. Hilda took some of them down to Kew. She took old Mrs. Johnson down to Southend—and who should they meet there but Bill Williams who was delivering some goods there, spoiling their day because old Mrs. Johnson did not like his ways. And Hilda had given them all presents. And two or three nights a week she was out at the Lord Nelson.

It was a good time. If anyone asked, "Have you heard from Mr. Gloster yet?" Hilda answered that it was not time yet and, as a dig at Constance that we all admired, she said once: "He has business at the American Embassy." And old Mrs. Johnson held her head high and nodded.

At the end of three weeks we became restless. We noticed old Mrs. Johnson looked poorly. She said she was tired. Old Mrs. Draper became morose. She had been taught to call Mr. Gloster by his correct name, but now she relapsed.

"Where is this Indian?" she uttered.

And another day, she said, without explanation:

"Three."

"Three what, Gran?"

"There've been two, that's enough."

No one liked this, but Mrs. Johnson understood.

"Mr. Gloster's very well, isn't he, Hil? You heard from him yesterday?" she said.

"I wasn't shown the letter," said old Mrs. Draper. "We don't want a third."

"We don't," said Mrs. Fulmino. With her joining in "on Gran's side," the situation changed. Mrs. Fulmino had a low voice and the sound of it often sank to the floor of any room she was in, travelling under chairs and tables, curling round your feet and filling the place from the bottom as if it were a cistern. Even when the trolley bus went by Mrs. Fulmino's low voice prevailed. It was an undermining voice, breaking up one's uppermost thoughts and stirring up what was underneath them. It stirred us all now. Yes, we wanted to say, indeed, we wanted to shout, where is this Mr. Gloster, why hasn't he come, did you invent him? He's alive, we hope? Or is he also—as Gran suggests—dead?

Even Mr. Fulmino was worried.

"Have you got his address?" he asked.

"Yes, Uncle dear," said Hilda. "He'll be staying at the Savoy. He always does."

Mr. Fulmino had not taken out his notebook for a long time but he did so now. He wrote down the name.

"Has he made a reservation?" said Mr. Fulmino. "I'll find out if he's booked."

"He hasn't," said Bill Williams. "I had a job down there and I asked. Didn't I, Connie?"

Mrs. Fulmino went a very dark colour. She wished she had thought of doing this. Hilda was not offended, but a small smile clipped her lips as she glanced at Connie:

"I asked Bill to do it," she said.

And then Hilda in that harsh lazy voice which she had always used for announcements: "If he doesn't come by Wednesday you'll have to speak for me at your factory, Mr. Williams. I don't know why he hasn't come, but I can't wait any more."

"Bill can't get you a job. You have to register," said Constance.

"Yes, she'll have to do that," said Mr. Fulmino.

"I'll fix it. Leave it to me," said Bill Williams.

"I expect," said young Mrs. Draper, "his business has kept him." She was sorry for Hilda.

"Perhaps he's gone fishing," said Jack Draper, laughing loudly in a kind way. No one joined in.

"Fishing for orders," said Bill Williams.

Hilda shrugged her shoulders and then she made one of those remarks that Grandma Draper usually made—I suppose the gift really ran through the family.

"Perhaps it was a case," she said, "of ships that pass in the night."

"Oh no, dear," said Mrs. Johnson trembling, "not ships." We went to the bus stop afterwards with the Fulminos and the young Drapers. Mrs. Fulmino's calm had gone. She marched out first, her temper rising.

"Ships!" she said. "When you think of what we went through during the war. Did you hear her? Straight out?"

"My brother Herbert's wife was like that. She's a widow. Take away the pension and they'll work like the rest of us. I had to."

"Job! Work! I know what sort of work she's been doing. Frank, walk ahead with Iris."

"Well," said young Mrs. Draper, "she won't be able to go to work in those clothes and that's a fact."

"All show," said Mrs. Fulmino triumphantly. "And I'll tell you something else—she hasn't a penny. She's run through her poor mother's money."

"Ay, I don't doubt," said young Mrs. Draper, who had often worked out how much the old lady had saved.

Mr. Gloster did not come on Wednesday or on any other day, but Hilda did not get a job either, not at once. And old Mrs. Johnson did not go to Monte Carlo. She died. This was the third, we understood, that old Mrs. Draper had foreseen.

———

Mrs. Johnson died at half past eight in the morning just after Constance had gone off to school, the last day of the term, and before old Mrs. Draper had got up. Hilda was in the kitchen wearing her blue Japanese wrap when she heard her mother's loud shout, like a man selling papers, she said, and when Hilda rushed in her mother was sitting up in bed. She gripped Hilda with the ferocity of the dying, as if all the strength of her whole life had come back and she was going to throw her daughter to the ground. Then she died. In an hour she looked like a white leaf that has been found after a lifetime pressed between the pages of a book and as delicate as a saint. The death was not only a shock: from the grief that spread from it staining all of us, I trace the ugly events that followed. Only the frail figure of old Mrs. Johnson, with her faith and her sly smile, had protected us from them until then, and when she went, all defence went with her.

I need not describe her funeral—it was done by Bickersons: Mr. Fulmino arranged it. But one thing astonished us: not only our families but the whole neighbourhood was affected by the death of this woman who, in our carelessness, we thought could hardly be known to anyone. She had lived there all her life, of course, but people come and go in London, only a sluggish residue stay still; and I believe it was just because a large number of passing people knew just a little about her, because she was a fragment in their minds, that her death affected them.

They recognised that they themselves were not people but fragments. People remembered her going into shops now and then, or going down to the bus stop, passing down a street. They remembered the bag of American cloth she used to carry containing her sewing—they spoke for a long time afterwards about this bag, more about it, indeed, than about herself.

Bickersons is a few doors from the Lord Nelson, so that when the hearse stood there covered with flowers everyone noticed it, and although the old lady had not been in that public house for years since the death of her husband, all the customers came out to look. And they looked at Hilda sitting in her black in the car when the hearse moved slowly off and all who knew her story must have felt that the dream was burying the dreamer. Hilda's face was dirty with grief and she did not turn her head to right or left as they drove off. I remember a small thing that happened when we were all together at old Mrs. Draper's, after we had got her back with difficulty up the stairs.

"Bickersons did it very well," said Mr. Fulmino, seeking to distract the old lady who, swollen with sadness, was uncomfortable in her best clothes. "They organise everything so well. They gave me this."

He held up a small brass disc on a little chain. It was one of those identity discs people used to wear on their wrists in the war.

"She had never taken it off," he said. It swung feebly on its chain. Suddenly, with a sound like a shout Mr. Fulmino broke into tears. His face caved in and he apologised: "It's the feeling," he said. "You have the feeling. You feel." And he looked at us with panic, astonished by this discovery of an unknown self, spongy with tears, that had burst out and against whom he was helpless.

Mrs. Fulmino said gently:

"I expect Hilda would like to have it."

"Yes, yes. It's for her," he said, drying his eyes and Hilda took it from him and carried it to her room. While she was there (and perhaps she was weeping too), Mr. Fulmino looked out from his handkerchief and said, still sobbing:

"I see that the luggage has gone."

None of us had noticed this and we looked at Constance who said in a whisper: "She is leaving us. She has found a room of her own." That knocked us back. "Leaving!" we exclaimed. It told against Hilda for, although we talked of death being a release for the dead person we did not like to think of it as a release for the living; grief ought to hold people together and it seemed too brisk to have started a new life so soon. Constance alone looked pleased by this. We were whispering but stopped when we heard Hilda coming back.

Black had changed her. It set off her figure and although crying had hardened her, the skin of her neck and her arms and the swell of her breasts seemed more living than they had before. She looked stronger in body perhaps because she was shaken in mind. She looked very real, very present, more alive than ourselves. She had not heard us whispering, but she said, to all of us, but particularly to Mr. Fulmino:

"I have found a room for myself. Constance spoke to Bill Williams for me, he's good at getting things. He found me a place and he took the luggage round yesterday. I couldn't sleep in that bed alone any more."

Her voice was shaky.

"She didn't take up much room. She was tiny and we managed. It was like sleeping with a little child."

Hilda smiled and laughed a little.

"She even used to kick like a kid."

———

Ten minutes on the bus from Hincham Street and close to the centre of London is a dance hall called "The Temple Rooms." It has two bands, a low gallery where you can sit and a soft drink bar. Quite a few West Indians go there, mainly students. It is a respectable place; it closes at eleven and there is never any trouble. Iris and I went there once or twice. One evening we were surprised to see Constance and Bill Williams dancing there. Iris pointed to them. The rest of the people were jiving, but Bill Williams and Constance were dancing in the old-fashioned way.

"Look at his feet!" Iris laughed.

Bill Williams was paying no attention to Constance, but looking around the room over her head as he stumbled along. He was tall.

"Fancy Auntie Constance!" said Iris. "She's getting fed up because he won't listen."

Constance Draper dancing! At her age! Thirty-eight!

"It's since the funeral," said Mr. Fulmino over our usual cup of tea. "She was fond of the old lady. It's upset her."

Even I knew Mr. Fulmino was wrong about this. The madness of

Constance dated from the time Bill Williams had taken Hilda's luggage round to her room and got her a job at the reception desk in the factory at Laxton. It dated from the time, a week later, when standing at old Mrs. Draper's early one evening, Constance had seen Hilda get out of Bill Williams's van. He had given her a lift home. It dated from words that passed between Hilda and Constance soon afterwards. Hilda said Williams hung around for her at the factory and wanted her to go to a dance. She did not want to go, she said—and here came the fatal sentences—both of her husbands had been educated men. Constance kept her temper but said coldly:

"Bill Williams is politically educated."

Hilda had her vacant look.

"Not his hands aren't," she said.

The next thing, Constance—who hardly went into a pub in her life—was in the Lord Nelson night after night, playing bar billiards with Bill Williams. She never let him out of her sight. She came out of school and instead of going home, marking papers and getting a meal for herself and old Mrs. Draper, she took the bus out to the factory and waited for him to come out. Sometimes he had left on some job by the time she got there and she came home, beside herself, questioning everybody. It had been her habit to come twice a week to change her library books. Now she did not come. She stopped reading. At The Temple Rooms, when Iris and I saw her, she sat out holding hands with Bill Williams and rubbing her head into his shoulder, her eyes watching him the whole time. We went to speak to them and Constance asked:

"Is Hilda here tonight?"

"I haven't seen her."

"She's a whore," said Constance in a loud voice. We thought she was drunk.

It was a funny thing, Mr. Fulmino said to me, to call a woman a whore. He spoke as one opposed to funny things.

"If they'd listened to me," he said, "I could have stopped all this trouble. I offered to get her a job in the Council Offices but," he rolled his eyes, "Mrs. F. wouldn't have it and while we were arguing about it, Bill Williams acts double quick. It's all because this Mr. Gloster didn't turn up."

Mr. Fulmino spoke wistfully. He was, he conveyed, in the middle of a family battle; indeed, he had a genuine black eye the day we talked about this. Mrs. Fulmino's emotions were in her arms.

This was a bad period for Mr. Fulmino because he had committed a folly. He had chosen this moment to make a personal triumph. He had got himself promoted to a much better job at the Council Offices and one entitling him to a pension. He had become a genuine official. To have promoted a man who had the folly to bring home a rich whore with two names, so causing the robbery and death of her mother, and to have let her break Constance's heart, was, in Mrs. Fulmino's words, a crime. Naturally, Mr. Fulmino regarded his mistakes as mere errors of routine and even part of his training for his new position.

"Oh well," he said when we finished our tea and got up to pay the bill, "it's the British taxpayer that pays." He was heading for politics. I have heard it said, years later, that if he had had a better start in life he would have gone to the top of the administration. It is a tragic calling.

If Hilda was sinister to Constance and Mrs. Fulmino, she made a different impression on young Mrs. Draper. To call a woman a whore was neither here nor there to her. Up North where she came from people were saying that sort of thing all day long as they scrubbed floors or cleaned windows or did the washing. The word gave them energy and made things come up cleaner and whiter. Good money was earned hard; easy money went easy. To young Mrs. Draper Hilda seemed "a bit simple," but she had gone to work, she earned her living. Cut off from the rest of the Draper family, Hilda made friends with this couple. Hilda went with them on Saturday to the Zoo with the children. They were looking at a pair of monkeys. One of them was dozing and its companion was awake, pestering and annoying it. The children laughed. But when they moved on to another cage, Hilda said, sulkily:

"That's one thing. Bill Williams won't be here. He pesters me all the time."

"He won't if you don't let him," said young Mrs. Draper.

"I'm going to give my notice if he doesn't stop," said Hilda. She hunched a shoulder and looked around at the animals.

"I can't understand a girl like Constance taking up with him. He's not on her level. And he's mean. He doesn't give her anything. I asked if he gave her that clip, but she said it was Gran's. Well, if a man doesn't give you anything he doesn't value you. I mean she's a well-read girl."

"There's more ways than one of being stupid," said young Mrs. Draper.

"I wonder she doesn't see," said Hilda. "He's not delivering for the firm. When he's got the van out, he's doing something on the side. When I came home with him there was stuff at the back. And he keeps on asking how much things cost. He offered to sell my bracelet."

"You'd get a better price in a shop if you're in need," said young Mrs. Draper.

"She'd better not be with him if he gets stopped on the road," said Jack, joining in. "You wouldn't sell that. Your husband gave it you."

"No. Mr. Faulkner," said Hilda, pulling out her arm and admiring it.

Jack was silent and disappointed; then he cheered up.

"You ought to have married that earl you were always talking about when you were a girl. Do you remember?" he said.

"Earls—they're a lazy lot," said young Mrs. Draper.

"I did, Jack," said Hilda. "They were as good as earls, both of them."

And to young Mrs. Draper she said: "They wouldn't let another man look at me. I felt like a woman with both of them."

"I've nowt against that if you've got the time," said young Mrs. Draper. She saw that Hilda was glum.

"Let's go back and look at the giraffes. Perhaps Mr. Faulkner will come for you now Mr. Gloster hasn't," young Mrs. Draper said.

"They were friends," said Hilda.

"Oh, they knew each other!" said young Mrs. Draper. "I thought you just . . . met them . . ."

"No, I didn't meet them together, but they were friends."

"Yes. Jack had a friend, didn't you?" said Mrs. Draper, remembering.

"That's right," said Jack. He winked at Hilda. "Neck and neck, it was." And then he laughed outright.

"I remember something about Bill Williams. He came out with us one Saturday and you should have seen his face when we threw the fish back in the water."

"We always throw them back," said young Mrs. Draper taking her husband's arm, proudly.

"Wanted to sell them or something. Black market perch!"

"He thinks I've got dollars," said Hilda.

"No, fancy that, Jack—Mr. Gloster and Mr. Faulkner being friends. Well, that's nice." And she looked sentimentally at Hilda.

"She's brooding," young Mrs. Draper said to Mrs. Fulmino after this visit to the Zoo. "She won't say anything." Mrs. Fulmino said she had better not or *she* might say something. "She knows what I think. I never thought much of Bill Williams, but he served his country. She didn't."

"She earns her living," said Mrs. Draper.

"Like we all do," said Mrs. Fulmino. "And it's not men, men, men all day long with you and me."

"One's enough," said young Mrs. Draper, "with two children round your feet."

"She doesn't come near me," said Mrs. Fulmino.

"No," Mr. Fulmino said sadly, "after all we've done."

———

They used to laugh at me when I went dancing with Iris at The Temple Rooms. We had not been there for more than a month and Iris said: "He can't stop staring at the band."

She was right. The beams of the spotlights put red, green, violet and orange tents on the hundreds of dancers. It was like the Arabian Nights. When we got there, Ted Coster's band was already at it like cats on dustbins and tearing their guts out. The pianist had a very thin neck and kept wagging his head as if he were ga-ga; if his head had fallen off he would have caught it in one of his crazy hands and popped it on again without losing a note; the trumpet player had thick eyebrows that went higher and higher as he tried and failed to burst; the drummers looked doped; the saxophone went at it like a man in bed with a girl who had purposely left the door open. I remember them all, especially the thin-lipped man, very white-faced, with the double bass drawing his bow at knee level, to and fro, slowly, sinful. They all whispered, nodded and rocked together, telling dirty stories until bang, bang, bang, the dancers went faster and faster, the row hit the ceiling or died out with the wheeze of a balloon. I was entranced.

"Don't look as though you're going to kill someone," Iris said.

That shows how wrong people are. I was full of love and wanted to cry.

After four dances I went off to the soft drink bar and there the first person I saw was Bill Williams. He was wearing a plum-coloured suit and a red and silver tie and he stood, with his dark hair dusty-looking and sprouting forward as if he had just got out of bed and was ducking his head on the way to the bathroom.

"All the family here?" he asked, looking all round.

"No," I said. "Just Iris and me."

He went on looking around him.

"I thought you only came Saturdays," he said suspiciously. He had a couple of friends with him, two men who became restless on their feet, as if they were dancing, when I came up.

"Oh," said Bill Williams. Then he said, "Nicky pokey doda—that's Japanese, pal, for keep your mouth shut. Anyone say anything, you never see me. I'm at Laxton, get me? Bill Williams? He's on night shift. You must be barmy. OK? Seeing you," he said. "No sign of Constance."

And he walked off. His new friends went a step or two after him, dancing on their pointed shoes, and then stopped. They twizzled round, tapping their feet, looking all round the room until he had got to the carpeted stairs at the end of the hall. I got my squash and when I turned round, the two men had gone too.

But before Bill Williams had got to the top of the stairs he turned round to look at the dancers in one corner. There was Hilda. She was dancing with a young West Indian. When I got back to our table she was very near.

I have said that Hilda's face was eventless. It was now in a tranced state, looking from side to side, to the floor, in the quick turns of the dance, swinging round, stepping back, stepping forward. The West Indian had a long jacket on. His knees were often nearly bent double as though he were going to do some trick of crawling towards her, then he recovered himself and turned his back as if he had never met her and was dancing with someone else. If Hilda's face was eventless, it was the event itself, it was the dance.

She saw us when the dance was over and came to our table breathlessly. She was astonished to see us. To me she said, "And fancy you!" She did not laugh or even smile when she looked at me. I don't know how to describe her look. It was dead. It had no expression. It had nothing. Or rather, by the smallest twitch of a muscle, it became nothing. Her face had the nakedness of a body. She saw that I was deaf to what Iris was saying. Then she smiled and in doing that, she covered herself.

"I am with friends over there"—we could not tell who the friends were—then she leaned to us and whispered:

"Bill Williams is here too."

Iris exclaimed.

"He's watching me," Hilda said.

"I saw him," I said. "He's gone."

Hilda stood up frowning.

"Are you sure? Did you see him? How long ago?"

I said it was about five minutes before.

She stood as I remember her standing in Mrs. Draper's room on the first day when she arrived and was kissing everyone. It was a peculiar stance because she usually stood so passively; a stance of action and, I now saw, a stance of plain fright. One leg was planted forward and bent at the knee like a runner at the start and one arm was raised and bent at the elbow, the elbow pushed out beyond her body. Her mouth was open and her deep-set yellow eyes seemed to darken and look tired.

"He was with some friends," I said and, looking back at the bar, "They've gone now."

"Hah!" It was the sound of a gasp of breath. Then suddenly the fright went and she shrugged her shoulders and talked and laughed to all of us. Soon she went over to her friends, the coloured man and a white couple; she must have got some money or the ticket for her handbag from one of them, for presently we saw her walking quickly to the cloak-room.

Iris went on dancing. We must have stayed another half an hour and when we were leaving we were surprised to see Hilda waiting in the foyer. She said to me:

"His car has gone."

"Whose?"

"Bill Williams's car."

"Has he got a car?" Iris said.

"Oh, it's not his," said Hilda. "It's gone. That's something. Will you take me home? I don't want to go alone. They followed me here."

She looked at all of us. She was frightened.

I said, "Iris and I will take you on our way."

"Don't make me late," said Iris crossly. "You know what Mum is." I promised. "Did you come with him?"

"No, with someone else," Hilda said, looking nervously at the glass swing door. "Are you sure his friends went too? What did they look like?"

I tried to describe them.

"I've seen the short one," she said, frowning, "somewhere."

It was only a quarter of an hour's ride at that hour of the night. We walked out of The Temple Rooms and across the main road to the bus stop and waited under the lights that made our faces corpse-like. I have always liked the hard and sequinned sheen of London streets at night, their empty dockyard look. The cars come down them like rats. The red trolley bus came up at last and when we got in Hilda sat between us. The bus-load of people stared at her and I am not surprised. I have said what she looked like—the hair built up high, her bright green wrap and red dress. I don't know how you would describe such clothes. But the people were not staring at her clothes. They were staring at her eyebrows. I said before that her face was an extension of her nudity and I say it again. Those eyebrows of hers were painted and looked like the only things she had on—they were like a pair of beetles with turned-up tails that had settled on her forehead. People laughed under their hands and two or three youths at the front of the bus turned round and guffawed and jostled and whistled; but Hilda, remember, was not a girl of sixteen gone silly, but a woman, hard rather than soft in the face, and the effect was one of exposure, just as a mask has the effect of exposing.

We did not talk but when the trolley arm thumped two or three times at a street junction, Hilda said with a sigh, "Bump! Bump! Bump!" She was thinking of her childhood in old Mrs. Draper's room at Hincham Street. We got off the bus a quarter of a mile further on and, as she was stepping off, Hilda said, speaking of what was in her mind, I suppose, during the ride:

"Shinji had a gold wrist-watch with a gold strap and a golden pen. They had gone when he was killed. They must have cost him a hundred pounds. Someone must have stolen them and sold them.

"I reported it," Hilda said. "I needed the money. That is what you had to do—sell something. I had to eat."

And the stare from her mask of a face stated something of her life that her strangeness had concealed from us. We walked up the street.

She went on talking about that watch and how particular Shinji was about his clothes, especially his shirts. All his collars had to be starched, she said. Those had gone too, she said. And his glasses. And his two gold rings. She walked very quickly between us. We got to the corner of her street. She stopped and looked down it.

"Bill Williams's van!" she said.

About thirty houses down the street we could indeed see a small van standing.

"He's waiting for me," she said.

It was hard to know whether she was frightened or whether she was reckoning, but my heart jumped. She made us stand still and watch. "My room's in the front," she said. I crossed over to the other side of the street and then came back.

"The light is on," I said.

"He's inside," she said.

"Shall I go and see?" I said.

"Go," said Iris to me.

Hilda held my wrist.

"No," she said.

"There are two people, I think, in the front garden," I said.

"I'm going home with you," Hilda said to Iris decisively. She rushed off and we had to race after her. We crossed two or three streets to the Fulminos' house. Mrs. Fulmino let us in.

"Now, now, Hilda, keep your hair on. Kill you? Why should he? This is England, this isn't China . . ."

Mr. Fulmino's face showed his agony. His mouth collapsed, his eyes went hard. He looked frantic with appeal. Then he turned his back on us, marched into the parlour and shouted as if he were calling across four lines of traffic:

"Turn the wireless off."

We followed him into the room. Mrs. Fulmino, in the suddenly silent room, looked like a fortress waiting for a flag to fall.

We all started talking at once.

"Can I stay with you tonight?" she said. "Bill Williams has broken into my house. I can't go there. He'll kill me." The flag fell.

"Japan," said Mrs. Fulmino disposing of her husband with her first shot. Then she turned to Hilda; her voice was coldly rich and rumbling. "You've always a home here, as you well know, Hilda," she went on, giving a very unhomely sound to the word. "And," she said, glancing at her neat curtains to anyone who might be in ambush outside the window, "if anyone tries to kill you, they will have to kill," she nodded to her husband, "Ted and me first. What have you been doing?"

"I was down at The Temple. Not with Bill Williams," said Hilda. "He was watching me. He's always watching me."

"Now look here, Hilda, why should Bill Williams want to kill you? Have you encouraged him?"

"Don't be a fool!" shouted Mrs. Fulmino.

"She knows what I mean. Listen to me, Hilda. What's going on between you and Bill Williams? Constance is upset, we all know."

"Oh keep your big mouth shut," said Mrs. Fulmino. "Of course she's encouraged him. Hilda's a woman, isn't she? I encouraged you, didn't I?"

"I know how to look after myself," said Hilda, "but I don't like that van outside the house at this hour of night, I didn't speak to him at the dance."

"Hilda's thinking of the police," ventured Mr. Fulmino.

"Police!" said Mrs. Fulmino. "Do you know what's in the van?"

"No," said Hilda. "And that's what I don't want to know. I don't want him on my doorstep. Or his friends. He had two with him. Harry saw them."

Mrs. Fulmino considered.

"I'm glad you've come to us. I wish you'd come to us in the first place," she said. Then she commanded Mr. Fulmino: "You go up there at once with Harry," she said to him, "and tell that man to leave Hilda alone. Go on, now. I can't understand you"—she indicated me—"running off like that, leaving a van there. If you don't go I'll go myself. I'm not afraid of a paltry . . . a paltry . . . what does he call himself? You go up."

Mrs. Fulmino was as good a judge of the possibilities of an emotional situation as any woman on earth: this was her moment. She wanted us out of the house and Hilda to herself.

We obeyed.

Mr. Fulmino and I left the house. He looked tired. He was too tired to put on his jacket. He went out in his shirt sleeves.

"Up and down we go, in and out, up and down," said Mr. Fulmino. "First it's Constance, now it's Hilda. And the pubs are closed."

"There you are, what did I tell you?" said Mr. Fulmino when we got to Hilda's street. "No van, no sign of it, is there? You're a witness. We'll go up and see all the same."

Mr. Fulmino had been alarmed but now his confidence came back. He gave me a wink and a nod when we got to the house.

"Leave it to me," he said. "You wait here."

I heard him knock at the door and after a time knock again. Then I heard a woman's voice. He was talking a long time. He came away.

He was silent for a long time as we walked. At last he said:

"That beats all. I didn't say anything. I didn't say who I was. I didn't let on. I just asked to see Hilda. 'Oh,' says the landlady, 'she's out.' 'Oh,' I said, 'that's a surprise.' I didn't give a name—'Out you say? When will she be back?' 'I don't know,' said the landlady, and this is it, Harry—'she's paid her rent and given her notice. She's leaving first thing in the morning,' the landlady said. 'They came for the luggage this evening.' Harry," said Mr. Fulmino, "did Hilda say anything about leaving?"

"No."

"Bill Williams came for her luggage."

We marched on. Or rather we went stealthily along like two men walking a steel wire of suspicion. We almost lost our balance when two cats ran across the street and set up howls in a garden, as if they were howling us down. Mr. Fulmino stopped.

"Harry!" he said. "She's playing us up. She's going off with Bill Williams."

"But she's frightened of him. She said he was going to kill her."

"I'm not surprised," said Mr. Fulmino. "She's been playing him up. Who was she with at the dance hall? She's played everyone up. Of course she's frightened of him. You bet. I'm sorry for anyone getting mixed up with Bill Williams—he'll knock some sense into her. He's rough. So was her father."

"Bill Williams might have just dropped by to have a word," I said.

"Funny word at half past eleven at night," said Mr. Fulmino. "When I think of all that correspondence, all those forms—War Office, State Department, United Nations—we did, it's been a poor turn-out. You might say," he paused for an image sufficiently devastating, "a waste of paper, a ruddy wanton waste of precious paper."

We got back to his house. I have never mentioned, I believe, that it had an iron gate that howled, a noise that always brought Mrs. Fulmino to her curtains, and a clipped privet hedge, like a moustache, to the tiny garden.

We opened the gate, the gate howled, Mrs. Fulmino's nose appeared at the curtains.

"Don't say a word," said Mr. Fulmino.

Tea—the room smelled of that, of course. Mrs. Fulmino had made some while we were out. She looked as though she had eaten something too. A titbit. They all looked sorry for Mr. Fulmino and me. And Mrs. Fulmino *had* had a titbit! In fact I know from Iris that the only thing Mrs. Fulmino had got out of Hilda was the news that she had had a postcard from Mr. Faulkner from Chicago. He was on the move.

"Well?" said Mrs. Fulmino.

"It's all right, Hilda," said Mr. Fulmino coldly. "They've gone."

"There," said Mrs. Fulmino, patting Hilda's hand.

"Hilda," said Mr. Fulmino, "I've been straight with you. I want you to be straight with me. What's going on between you and Bill Williams . . . ?"

"Hilda's told me . . ." Mrs. Fulmino said.

"I asked Hilda, not you," said Mr. Fulmino to his wife, who was so surprised that she went very white instead of her usual purple.

"Hilda, come on. You come round here saying he's going to kill you. Then they tell me you've given your notice up there."

"She told me that. I think she's done the right thing."

"And did you tell her why you gave your notice?" asked Mr. Fulmino.

"She's given her notice at the factory too," said Mrs. Fulmino.

"Why?" said Mr. Fulmino.

Hilda did not answer.

"You are going off with Bill Williams, aren't you?"

"Ted!" Hilda gave one of her rare laughs.

"What's this?" cried Mrs. Fulmino. "Have you been deceiving me? Deceit I can't stand, Hilda."

"Of course she is," said Mr. Fulmino. "She's paid her rent. He's collected her luggage this evening—where is it to be? Monte Carlo? Oh, it's all right, sit down," Mr. Fulmino waved Mrs. Fulmino back. "They had a row at the dance this evening."

But Hilda was on her feet.

"My luggage," she cried, holding her bag with both hands to her bosom as we had seen her do once before when she was cornered. "Who has touched my luggage?"

I thought she was going to strike Mr. Fulmino.

"The dirty thief. Who let him in? Who let him take it? Where's he gone?"

She was moving to the door. We were stupefied.

"Bill Williams!" she shouted. Her rage made those artificial eyebrows look comical and I expected her to pick them off and throw them at us. "Bill Williams I'm talking about. Who let that bloody war hero in? That bitch up there . . ."

"Hilda," said Mr. Fulmino. "We don't want language."

"You fool," said Mrs. Fulmino in her lowest, most floor-pervading voice to her husband. "What have you been and done? You've let Bill Williams get away with all those cases, all her clothes, everything. You let that spiv strip her."

"Go off with Bill Williams!" Hilda laughed. "My husband was an officer."

"I knew he was after something. I thought it was dollars," she said suddenly.

She came back from the door and sat down at the table and sobbed.

"Two hundred and fifty pounds, he's got," she sobbed. It was a sight to see Hilda weeping. We could not speak.

"It's all I had," she said.

We watched Hilda. The painted eyebrows made the grimace of her weeping horrible. There was not one of us who was not shocked. There was in all of us a sympathy we knew how to express but which was halted—as by a fascination—with the sight of her ruin. We could not help contrasting her triumphant arrival with her state at this moment. It was as if we had at last got her with us as we had, months before, expected her to be. Perhaps she read our thoughts. She looked up at us and she had the expression of a person seeing us for the first time. It was like an inspection.

"You're a mean lot, a mean respectable lot," she said. "I remember you. I remember when I was a girl. What was it Mr. Singh said, I can't remember—he was clever—oh well, leave it, leave it. When I saw that little room they put my poor mother in, I could have cried. No sun. No warmth in it. You just wanted someone to pity. I remember it. And your faces. The only thing that was nice was," she sobbed and laughed for a moment, "was bump, bump, bump, the trolley." She said loudly: "There's only one human being in the whole crew—Jack Draper. I don't wonder he sees more in fish."

She looked at me scornfully. "Your brother—he was nice," she said. "Round the park at night! That was love."

"Hilda," said Mrs. Fulmino without anger. "We've done our best for you. If we've made mistakes I hope you haven't. We haven't had your life. You talk about ships that pass in the night, I don't know what you mean, but I can tell you there are no ships in this house. Only Ted."

"That's right," said Mr. Fulmino quietly too. "You're overwrought."

"Father," said Mrs. Fulmino, "hadn't you better tell the police?"

"Yes, yes, dear," agreed Mr. Fulmino. "We'd better get in touch with the authorities."

"Police," said Hilda, laughing in their faces. "Oh God! Don't worry about that. You've got one in every house in this country." She picked up her bag, still laughing, and went to the door.

"Police," she was saying, "that's ripe."

"Hilda, you're not to go out in the street looking like that," said Mrs. Fulmino.

"I'd better go with her," said Mr. Fulmino.

"I'll go," I said. They were glad to let me.

———

It is ten years since I walked with Hilda to her lodgings. I shall not forget it, and the warm, dead, rubbery city night. It is frightening to walk with a woman who has been robbed and wronged. Her eyes were half-closed as though she was reckoning as she walked. I had to pull her back on to the pavement or she would have gone flat into a passing car. The only thing she said to me was:

"They took Shinji's rings as well."

Her room was on the ground floor. It had a divan and a not very clean dark green cover on it. A pair of shoes were sticking out from under it. There was a plain deal cupboard and she went straight to it. Two dresses were left. The rest had gone. She went to a table and opened the drawer. It was empty except for some letters.

I stood not knowing what to say. She seemed surprised to see me there still.

"He's cleared the lot," she said vacantly. Then she seemed to realise that she was staring at me without seeing me for she lowered her angry shoulders.

"We'll get them back," I said.

"How?" she said, mocking me, but not unkindly.

"I will," I said. "Don't be upset."

"You!" she said.

"Yes, I will," I said.

I wanted to say more. I wanted to touch her. But I couldn't. The ruin had made her untouchable.

"What are you going to do?" I said.

"Don't worry about me," she said. "I'm okey-doke. You're different from your brother. You don't remember those days. I told Mr. Gloster about him. Come to that, Mr. Faulkner too. They took it naturally. That was a fault of Mr. Singh"—she never called him by his Christian name—"jealousy."

She kicked off her shoes and sat down on the cheap divan and frowned at the noise it made and she laughed.

"One day in Bombay I got homesick and he asked me what I was thinking about and I was green, I just said 'Sid Fraser's neck. It had a mole on it'—you should have seen his face. He wouldn't talk to me for a week. It's a funny thing about those countries. Some people might rave about them, I didn't see anything to them."

She got up.

"You go now," she said laughing. "I must have been in love."

I dreamed about Hilda's face all night and in the morning I wouldn't have been surprised to see London had been burned out to a cinder. But the next night her face did not come and I had to think about it. Further and further it went, a little less every day and night, and I did not seem to notice when someone said Bill Williams had been picked up by the police, or when Constance had been found half dead with aspirins and when, in both cases, Mr. Fulmino told me he had to "give assistance in the identification," for Hilda had gone. She left the day after I took her to her room. Where she went no one knew. We guessed. We imagined. Across water, I thought, getting further and further away, in very fine clothes and very beautiful. France, Mr. Fulmino thought, or possibly Italy. Africa, even. New York, San Francisco, Tokyo, Bombay, Singapore. Where? Even one day six months after she had left when he came to the library and showed me a postcard he had had from her, the first message, it did not say where she was and someone in the post office had pulled off the stamp. It was a picture of Hilda herself on a seat in a park, sitting with Mr. Faulkner and Mr. Gloster. You wouldn't recognise her.

But Mr. Gloster's book came out. Oh yes. It wasn't about Japan or India or anything like that. It was about us.

Just a Little More

They were speaking in low voices in the kitchen.

"How is he? Has he said what he is going to do?" she asked her husband. "Is there any news?"

"None at all," her husband whispered. "He's coming down now. He says he just wants a house by the sea, in a place where the air is bracing and the water's soft and there's a good variety of fish."

"Sh-h-h! Why do we whisper like this? Here he comes. Get the plates."

A moment later, the very old gentleman, her father-in-law, was standing in the doorway, staring and smiling. He was short and very fat, and one of the things he liked to do was to pause in the doorway of a room and look it over from ceiling to floor. In the old days, his family or his workers at the factory used to stiffen nervously when he did this, wondering where his eye would stop.

"Excuse me being rude," he said at last. "What a lovely smell."

"Take your father in," the wife said. "These plates are hot. Go into the dining-room, Grandpa."

"I'm just looking at your refrigerator, darling," the old gentleman said. "Very nice. It's a Pidex, I see. Is that a good make? I mean is it good—does it work well? . . . I'm glad to hear that. Did you get it from the Pidex people? . . . Ah, I thought you did. Good people."

The son, who was in his fifties, took the old gentleman by the elbow and moved him slowly into the dining-room. The old gentleman blew his nose.

"No. Your mother's hands were as cold as ice when I got to her," said the old gentleman, astonished by a memory. "But she had gone. Where do I go? Do I sit here?"

He sat down very suddenly at the table. Although he weighed close to two hundred pounds, his clothes hung loosely on him, for he had once weighed much more. His nostrils had spread and reddened over a skin that was greenish and violet on the cheeks but as pale and stringy as a chicken's at the neck.

His daughter-in-law and two grandchildren brought in the joint and the vegetables. The grandchildren were called Richard and Helen. They were in their teens. Their mouths watered when they saw the food on the table, and they leaned towards it, but kept their eyes politely on the old man, like elderly listeners.

"I hope you haven't cooked anything special for me," the old man said. "I was just saying I talk too much when I come for a week-end here, and I eat too much. It's living alone—having no one to talk to, and so forth, and you can't be bothered to eat—that's the point. What a lovely piece of beef that is! Wonderful. I haven't seen a joint of beef like that for centuries. A small bit of loin of lamb we might have, but my wife can't digest it." He often forgot that his wife was dead. "And it doesn't keep. I put it in the larder and I forget and it goes wrong." His big face suddenly crinkled like an apple, with disgust.

"Well, well, I don't know, I'm sure," he went on, gazing at the beef his son was now carving. "I suppose it's all right. What do you call a joint like that?" He pointed across the table to his grandson. "We used to have beef when your father was a boy, Richard. Your father was a boy once. You can't imagine that, can you? Aitchbone, was it? I can't remember. I don't know where your mother used to get it. Bell's, I suppose. I don't know what we paid for it. Sixpence a pound, perhaps. We can't do it now; it's the price."

His son passed him a plate. The old man hesitated not knowing whether to pass it on and not wanting to. "If this is for me, don't give me any more," he said. "I hardly eat anything nowadays. If I could have just a little fat . . ." Relieved, he kept the plate.

"Pass the vegetables to Grandpa," said his daughter-in-law to Helen.

"Grandpa, vegetables?" Helen said, looking younger now as she spoke.

"Oh," said the old gentleman. He had gone into a dream. "I was just watching you carving," he said to his son. "I was looking at your face. You've got just the expression of your great-grandfather Harry. I remember him when I was a little boy. Father took me to see him—it was one morning. He took me down to a warehouse, would it be?—in the docks or harbour—a factory, perhaps—and he lifted me up to a window and I saw him, just his face, it was only a minute. He was slitting up herrings; it was a curing place."

"Fish! I knew it." His daughter-in-law laughed.

"The sea is in our blood," said her husband. Everyone was laughing.

"What is this? What are you laughing at? What have I said?" the old gentleman asked, smiling. "Are you getting at me?"

"That is where you get your taste for kippers," said his daughter-in-law to her husband.

"Ah, kippers!" said the old gentleman, delighted by his strange success. "How are you for fish in this neighbourhood? Do you get good fish? I sometimes feel like a piece of fish. But there doesn't seem to be the fish about, these days. I don't know why that is. No, I went up to the fishmonger on Tuesday and I looked. He came up to me, and I said 'Good morning,' 'Good morning, Mr. Hopkins,' he said. 'What can I do for you?' 'Do for me?' I said. 'Give me a fortnight in Monte Carlo.' He exploded. I said, 'What's happened to you? What's wrong?' 'What do you mean, Mr. Hopkins?' he said. 'I mean, where's your fish?' I said. 'That's not what I call fish. Not f-i-s-h.' He knew what I meant. 'Sole,' he said. 'Dover sole,' I said. 'Mr. Hopkins,' he said, 'I haven't had a Dover sole for a fortnight. Not one I'd sell *you*. Lemon sole,' he said, and something—grayling did he say? Well, that's the way it is. And so we go on.

"No," the old man said after a moment. "Kitty, your mother, my wife, was very fond of fish. When we were first married, and so forth, we came down from the north—How old are you, my boy? Fifty-seven? You're not fifty-seven!—it was just before you were born, and my wife said, 'I'd give anything for an oyster.' The train didn't get in till eight, but we were young and reckless in those days. I didn't care a damn for anyone. I was ready to knock the world over. I was in a good crib, five pounds a week at Weekley's—before Hollins took them over.

All expenses. I thought I was Julius Caesar—marvellous, isn't it? Do I mean him? And we went across the road and your mother said, 'Come on—' "

The son interrupted, picking up the story. "And a bus driver leaned out of his cab and said, 'Watch out, lady. Babies are scarce this year.' Mother told me."

"I'm sure she didn't," said the old gentleman, blushing a little. "Your father's imagination, Richard!"

"Yes, but what happened?" asked his daughter-in-law.

"And there was a little place, a real old London fish place—sawdust on the floor, I suppose they had in those days. Crossfield . . . Cross . . . Crofty—I forget the name—and we had a dozen oysters each, maybe I had a couple of dozen; I don't remember now, I couldn't say. Frederick's—that was the name of the place. Frederick's. And I suppose we must have followed it with Dover sole. They used to do a wonderful Welsh rabbit."

"And that is how I was born," said the son. "Let me give you some more beef, Father."

"Me? Oh, no. I don't eat what I used to. It's living alone, and these new teeth of mine—I've had a lot of trouble with them. Don't give me any more. I don't mind a couple of slices—well, just another. And some fat. I like a piece of fat. That's what I feel. You go home and you get to the house, and it's dark. And it's empty. You go in and the boiler's low—I don't seem to get the right coke. Do you get good coke here? You look at it all and you look in the larder and you can't be bothered. There's a chop, a bit of bread and cheese, perhaps. And you think, well, if this is all there is in life, you may as well finish it. I'm in a rut down in that place. I've got to get away. I can't breathe there. I'd like to get down to the sea."

"I think you ought to go where you have friends," said his daughter-in-law.

The old gentleman put his knife and fork down. "Friends?" he said, in a stern voice, raising his chin. "I have no friends. All my friends are dead." He said this with indignation and contempt.

"But what about your friend Rogers, in Devonshire?" said his son.

"Rogers? I was disappointed in Rogers. He's aged. He's let himself go. I hadn't seen him for twenty-five years. When I saw him, I said to him, 'Why, what's the matter with you? Trying to pretend you are an old man?' He looked at me. He'd let his moustache go long and grey. I wouldn't have known him. And there was something else. A funny thing. It upset me." The old gentleman's jolly face shrivelled up again, with horror. "The hairs in his nose had gone grey!" he said. "I couldn't bear it. He was very kind, and his wife was. We had lunch. Soup of some kind—tomato, or maybe oxtail—and then a piece of lamb, potatoes, and cauliflower. Oh, very nice. I've forgotten what the dessert was—some cream, I suppose, they have good cream there—and coffee, of course. Cheese . . . I don't remember. Afterwards—and this is what upset me about old people—they wanted a rest. Every day, after lunch, they go off and have a sleep—every day. Can you imagine that? I couldn't stand that. Terrible."

"It's good to have a siesta," said the son.

"I couldn't. I never have. I just can't," said the old gentleman, in a panic. "The other afternoon after lunch, I forget what I had, a chop, I think—I couldn't be bothered to cook vegetables, well, on your own you don't, that's the point—I dropped off. I don't know for how long, and when I woke up it was dark. I couldn't see anything. I didn't know where I was. 'Where am I?' I said. 'What day is it?' And I reached out for my wife. I thought I was in bed, and I called out, 'Kitty, Kitty, where are you?' and then I said, 'Oh.' It came back to me. I'm here. In this room. I couldn't move. I got up and put on the light. I was done up. I poured myself out a small glass of port. I felt I had to. It was shocking. And shocking dreams."

He stared and then suddenly he turned to his daughter-in-law and said, in another voice, "Those sandwiches I shan't forget. Egg, wasn't it? You remember?" He wagged a finger at Helen. "Helen, your mother is a wonder at egg sandwiches. It was the first time in my life I'd ever eaten them. The day we put Kitty away, you remember she came down and made egg sandwiches. What is the secret of it? She won't tell. Butter, I suppose? Richard, what is the word I want? You know— 'smashing,' I suppose you'd call them."

He paused, and his eyes grew vaguer. "No," he went on, "I don't know what I'll do. I think I shall go to the sea and look around. I shall get a list of houses, and put my furniture in store. I could live with your brother John, or you. I know I could, but it would be wrong. You have your own lives. I want my independence. Life is beginning for me— that is what I feel. I feel I would like to go on a cruise round the world.

There was a house at Bexhill I saw. They wanted seven thousand for it. I felt it would suit me."

"Seven thousand!" said his son, in alarm. "Where would you get seven thousand from?"

"Oh," said the old gentleman sharply, "I should raise it."

"Raise it!" exclaimed the son. "How?"

"That's just it," said the old gentleman cheerfully. "I don't know. The way will open up. You perhaps, or John."

Husband and wife looked down the table at each other in consternation.

"Shall we go upstairs and have some coffee?" she said.

"That son of yours, that Richard—did you see what he ate?" said the old gentleman as he got up from the table. "Marvellous, isn't it? Of course, things are better than when I was a boy. I feel everything is better. We used to go to school with twopence for a pie. Not every day—twice a week. The other days, we just looked at the shop window. Pies piled up. And once a week—Friday, I expect—it was herrings in the evening. The fisherwoman came calling them in the street, eighteen a shilling, fresh fish out of the sea. Salmon I used to be fond of. D'you ever have salmon?"

He paused in the doorway and looked at the carpet on the stairs and at the wallpaper. "I like rich things," he said, nodding to the carpet. "That gravy was good. Luscious grapes, pears, all large fruits I like. Those Christmas displays at the meat market—turkeys and geese by the thousand there used to be. I always used to bring your mother something. A few chops, two or three pairs of kippers. And so forth. I don't know what."

"Upstairs to the sitting-room, Father," said the son. "I'm coming in a minute with the coffee."

The son went into the kitchen, and the whispering began again.

"Seven thousand!" he said. "Seven million wouldn't keep him!"

"Sh-h-h," said his wife. "It's a day-dream."

"But what are we going to do?"

In a few minutes, he took the coffee upstairs. The old gentleman was sitting down, with his waistcoat undone and his thumbs twiddling on his stomach.

"I've been thinking about you," the old gentleman said rebukingly.

"You've lost weight. You don't eat. You worry too much. My wife used to worry."

The son passed a coffee cup to him.

"Is there a lot of sugar in it? Thank you," the old man said. He gave it a stir, took a sip, and then held the cup out. "I think I'll have a couple of spoonfuls more."

Our Oldest Friend

"Look out!" someone said. "Here comes Saxon."

It was too late. Moving off the dance floor and pausing at the door with the blatant long sight of the stalker, Saxon saw us all in our quiet corner of the lounge and came over. He stopped and stood with his hands on his hips and his legs apart, like a goalkeeper. Then he came forward.

"Ah! This *is* nice!" he crowed, in the cockerel voice that took us back to the Oxford years. He pulled up a chair and placed it so that none of us could easily get out. It passed through our heads that we had seen that dinner-jacket of his before. He must have had it since the last term at school. It was short, eager and juvenile in the sleeves and now his chest had bolstered it, he seemed to be bursting with buns and toffee. A piece of stiff fair hair stuck up boyishly at the back. He crossed his short legs and squeezed them with satisfaction as his sharp blue eyes looked around our circle over his strong glasses.

"How awfully nice." For niceness was everything for him. "Everyone is here," he said and nodded back to the people on the dance floor. "Jane Fawcett, Sanderson-Brown, Tony Jameson and Eileen—I just missed them in Brussels, they'd just left for Munich—very nice catching them here. With the Williamsons!"

He ran off a list of names, looking over one lens of the glasses that were not quite straight on his young enthusiastic nose as he spoke them, and marking each name with a sly look of private knowledge. We were the accused—accused not so much of leaving him out of things, as of thinking, by so doing, that he *was* out of them. His short, trotting legs infallibly took him to old acquaintance. Names from the past, names that we had forgotten from school and then Oxford came out, and made our wives look across at us at first with bewilderment and then set them to whispering and giggling.

"What are you doing, Saxon?" someone said. "Are you still on the Commission?"

"In principle yes, in practice," said Saxon, uttering his favourite words, "I'm the liaison between Ways and Means and the Working Party."

"The liaison!" one of the wives said.

"Yes. It's awfully nice. It works very well. We have to keep in touch with the sub-committees. I saw the Dustman the other day. He's a Trustee now, he came in from Arbitration."

"The Dustman?" Mrs. Selby said to her husband.

"Oxford," said Selby. "Lattersmith. Economist. Very old. He was called the Dustman because he was very dirty."

"Tessa's father," Saxon said. And as he shot the name of Tessa at us, he grinned at each one of us in turn to see what could be found in our faces. There are things in the past that become geological. Selby's face became as red as Aberdeen marble; some of us turned to sandstone; one or two to millstone grit or granite; that was how alarm and disclaimer took us.

"Your oldest friend," said Mrs. Selby to her husband, grinding out the phrase.

"In principle yes, in practice no," said Selby bitterly mocking Saxon's well-known phrase.

"*My* oldest friend, if you please," said Thomas, always a rescuer.

"And mine!" two of us said together, backing him up.

"Is she yours?" said kind Jenny Fox to me.

"She is the 'oldest friend' of all of us."

We laughed together loudly, but not in unity of tone. Hargreaves was too loud, Fox was too frivolous, Selby was frightened and two or three laughs were groans. There was something haphazard, hollow, insincere and unlasting about our laughter, but Day saved us by saying in his deep grave voice to Saxon:

"We ought to settle this. Who *is* Tessa's oldest friend? When did *you* meet Tessa, Saxon?"

"Selby and I were at school with her, at Asaph's."

"You didn't tell me that," said Selby's wife to her husband.

"I tried to get her to come tonight," said Saxon. "She's gone out with the Dustman. He said they might drop in later."

Our wives put on stiff faces: one or two picked up their handbags and looked at the door on to the dance floor, as if they were going to search it, and even the building. The incident was one of Saxon's always unanswerable successes but once more Thomas saved us. He said to Saxon:

"So *you're* her oldest friend."

And Selby said grimly: "Yes, you were at Asaph's a year before me."

"Saxon! You've been holding out on us," we said with false jollity.

One of the ladies nodded at us and said to her neighbour: "They seem to be a club."

The pious pretence on the part of our wives that they did not know Tessa Lattersmith was, in its way, brilliant in our embarrassed state. It brought out the hypocrisy in Harry James who said in a light-headed way:

"She's married now, I suppose?"

"Oh no," said Saxon. "She's carrying on." And he meant carrying on, as it were, in the sense of working hard on the joint committee, himself informed because he was, after all, the liaison.

"You mean," said Mrs. Selby, "she hasn't found anyone's husband willing?"

"Shame!" said Saxon as at an annual general meeting. "Shame."

"Perhaps," said the kind young Jenny Fox, "she doesn't want to be married."

"She's very rich," said James.

"Very attractive," said Day.

"Big gobbling eyes."

"Lovely voice."

"I don't agree," said Fox. "It bodes. It comes creeping into you. It gets under your shirt. It seems to come up from the floor. Expensive clothes, though."

"Not like the Dustman's!" shouted Thomas, rescuing us again. "D'you remember? I used to see him at the station waiting for the

Oxford train. He used to walk up to the very last bench on the platform, and flop down. I thought he was a tramp kipping down for the night, the first time. His clothes were creased as though he'd slept in them. He had that old suitcase, made of cardboard I should say, tied with string—and parcels of books tied up. Like Herbert Spencer. You know Herbert Spencer had to have everything tied to him? He sat there looking wretched and worn out, with his mouth open and his thick hair full of dust—a real layabout from the British Museum. He hardly got his feet off the ground when he walked, but sort of trudged, as if he was wading through sand. He must be well past seventy."

"No, he's barely sixty. Tessa's only thirty-two."

"Thirty-seven," said Mrs. Selby.

"He's sixty-two," said Saxon. "Tessa is a year younger than me."

"The Lattersmiths were rich," said James again. "I mean compared with the rest of us."

"The Dustman's wife had the money," said Thomas. "She belonged to one of those big shipping families. Did you ever see her? She's like Tessa—oh, she comes after you with those big solemn eyes."

"We went to see her, didn't we?" Day said to his wife. "She saw Diana's necklace, her eyes were fixed on it . . ."

"*And* my rings!"

"She just wanted them. Greedy. She couldn't bear it that Diana had something that she hadn't got."

"She wanted you as well," said Diana.

"Oh," said Tom, the rescuer. "There's nothing in that. Old Ma Dustman wanted me too, in fact she wanted all of us. 'I am so worried about Tessa, I wish she'd settle down. I wish she'd find a nice husband—now *you,* you're fond of Tessa, I'm sure.' "

"Shame!" called Saxon again.

We had forgotten about him; he was sweating as he watched us with delight.

"No, it's true," I said to Saxon.

"And she couldn't have them, poor things," one of the wives said and the others joined in laughing at us.

James once more pushed us into trouble.

"Did you ever go on a picnic with them? I mean when they came down to School? No? Saxon, didn't you and Selby? Didn't you? None of your camp fires with damp sticks, thermos bottles and tea slopping over the tomato sandwiches. Oh no! And it never rained: old Ma Dustman had ordered sun down from Fortnum and Mason's. They brought the Daimler and the butler came—how did they fit him in, I wonder? I bet he went ahead in the Rolls. He set tables and chairs. Silver teapot, the best Rockingham . . ."

"Not Rockingham, it can't have been."

"Well old Spode. Something posh. The butler handed round the stuff. I only just knew Tessa then. I had brought a girl called Sadie and Tessa brought a girl called Adelaide with her and Tessa said 'I want you to meet Harry James. He's my oldest friend.' Sadie looked sick."

"It had started then?" some of our wives cried out.

"Long before that," I said. "In the cradle."

"Exactly what she said just before we were married when you introduced me," said Mrs. Day to her husband.

"She said it to me at our wedding," said Mrs. Selby and, glaring at her husband, "I don't know *why.*"

"I don't get what her fascination for you all was!" said sly Mrs. James.

"Oh," we all said largely, in a variety of voices, "I don't know . . . She was about . . ."

"You know, I think it was sex," said Jenny Fox.

"Was it sex?" we looked at each other, putting as much impartiality as we could into the enquiry.

"Sex! Of course it was sex," said Mrs. Selby, putting her chin up and gripping her handbag on her knee.

"Not for me," said Harry James.

"Nor me." One wife squeezed her husband's hand. "Why not?"

This dumbfounded us. We huddled together. Why had none of us made a pass? Were we frightened?

"You took her to picture galleries," said Mrs. Selby.

"Yes," said Selby. "She did nothing but talk about a man called Cézanne."

"That's it. A whole party of us went to Parma and she did nothing but talk of a man called Fabrice," said Tom.

"Fabrice?"

"Stendhal," said Saxon.

"I had Lawrence in Rome."

"There was always another man. Anyone have Picasso? Or Giacometti?" said James.

"Who did you have, Selby? Russell? Einstein?"

Selby had had enough. With the treachery of the desperate, he said: "She talked of nothing but you, James."

"No," said Tom the rescuer. "You can't have had. *I* had you, James."

"I had Tom."

"Day was my trouble."

"With me it was Bill."

"What a lovely daisy chain," one of the wives said. "The whole distinguished lot of you. Who's missing?"

"Saxon," Jenny Fox said.

We all stared accusingly at him. Saxon went on squeezing himself. He looked archly over his glasses.

"I had the Dustman," he said complacently.

We laughed but Mrs. Selby silenced us and said to Saxon: "Go on. You're the only one who's telling the truth."

"She was always very worried about the Dustman," he said. "They're a wretched family. He scarcely ever goes home."

And at this, the band started again and Saxon got up and asked my wife to dance. We were left with Saxon's picture of that rich girl alone in the world. Before the evening was out he had danced with each one of our wives. We all grinned and said "Look at old Saxon at the end of term dance."

If there was one non-dancer on the floor it was he. His feet, rather like the Dustman's, trudged, in straight, fated lines, deep in sand; enthusiastically deep. He danced, as it were, in committee. Our wives found themselves in the grip of one who pushed them around, all the time looking askance from side to side as if they were sections or sub-sections for which he was trying to find a place in some majority report. They lost their power to dance. The matter had become desperately topographical to them; while he, as he toiled on, was running off the names of people.

"I saw him in Paris on the second day of the conference." Or "They were in New York when Foreign Relations met the working party."

Or "They ran into one another in Piccadilly when the delegation met the Trustees. Thompson, Johnson, Hobson, Timson, Richardson, Wilkinson"—our wives returned to us like new editions of *Who's Who*.

Except Mrs. Selby. She was much taller than he and on the floor she had the prosecuting look of one who was going to wring what she wanted out of Saxon. She did not look down at him but over his head at the piece of fair hair that stuck up at the back of his head. He soon had to give up his committee style. She got a grip of him, got him into corners, carried him off to the middle, turned savagely near the band and in this spot, she shouted to him:

"What's all this stuff about Tessa and the Dustman?"

And as she said it, seeing him turn to the right, she swung him round to the left and when the dancers were thinning on the floor she planted him in a quiet spot in the middle.

"Tessa's slept with all of you, hasn't she?" she said.

"Shame!" Saxon said, stopping dead. He took off his glasses and there was a sudden change in him. Often since, seeing that naked look on his face, I have thought: "How he must have hated us." I remember at school how we stuffed sausage down his neck and how he just let us do it. Sausage after sausage went down. Then off came the glasses and he backed to an open window. Now, on the dance floor, with his glasses off, Saxon suddenly began to dance—if that is the word for it—as if he had been stung. Where had he learned these extraordinary steps?— that sudden flinging wide of his short legs and arms, that strange buckling and straightening of the body, the thrusting forward and back of his punch-ball head, those sudden wrenchings of Mrs. Selby back and forth, and spinning her round, that general air of looking for a knock-out in the rebound off the ropes. Mrs. Selby's firm eyes were disordered as she tried to foresee his movements, and amid the disorder, she was magnetised by the fiendish rhythm of his feet and by the austere look of his unforgiving face.

"Hasn't she?" called Mrs. Selby, in a last piteous attempt. The band stopped and she stood there getting her breath in the middle of the floor. Saxon, without music, dropped back into the goalkeeper stance we knew so well, with his hands on his hips and short legs apart. She was staring at Saxon, he was staring at her. It was a long stare. Selby and his partner passed them and he saw what Mrs. Selby saw: obstinate tears were forming in Saxon's naked eyes; water filled them; it dropped on his pink cheeks. He took out his glasses and pretended to wipe them with his handkerchief and put them on. He was sternly, silently, crying. Mrs. Selby put out her hand repentantly; no doubt he did not see her hand but walked with her off the floor. We were clapping in the silly way people do and someone called out:

"Where did you learn that one, Saxon?"

He looked with bewilderment at us.

"I'll be back in a minute," he said and walked across the room to the outer hall of the hotel.

Mrs. Selby put herself with kind Jenny Fox and whispered to her for a long time and Mrs. Fox said:

"It's not your fault. How could you know?"

"I only *said* it," Mrs. Selby said wretchedly, looking at the swing door that let cold air in from the outer hall when it flashed round and where Saxon had gone.

"What was the matter with Saxon?" Selby accused.

"He's upset—nothing," said Mrs. Fox turning to Selby as she patted Mrs. Selby's hand. And then, arguing for herself, Mrs. Selby told us.

Presently the swing door flashed and Saxon came back and three of us got up to offer him a chair. We gave him the best one, beside a low table which had a brilliant lamp on it. Instantly it threw his shadow on the white wall—a shadow that caricatured his face—the long nose, the chin that receded, the glasses tilted as he looked askance at us, the sprig of schoolboy hair.

"They haven't turned up yet," he said.

We looked at our Saxon with awe. It was obvious he was in love with that rich, beautiful woman. He must always have been in love with her. We had pulled her to pieces in front of him. What he must have been feeling as he pretended and as he submitted to our joke. And, after all this, she had not come. Where was she? One or two of us wanted to get up and find her. Where would she be? We could not guess. We had to admit that Tessa merely slummed with us. She would never think of coming to a second-rate hotel like this or to an old Asaphians' reunion. She'd be at some smart dinner party, something very grand—she certainly had "oldest friends" in very grand circles. One could imagine her long neck creeping up close to the conscience of an Archbishop. Or disturbing the shirt of an Ambassador, or her boding voice creeping up the sleeve of a banker who would be saying: "Young lady, what are all your hippie friends up to nowadays?" at one of old Ma Dustman's dinner parties. *She* would be stripping the jewellery off the women and telling Sir Somebody Something that one would be a fool to sell one's Matisses yet. The Dustman would not be there. We tried not to look at the unmarriageable silhouette of Saxon's head on the wall.

"Where did you pick up that wonderful step, Saxon?" Mrs. Selby said gaily, to make amends.

Saxon gave a forgiving glance. He had recovered.

"At the Cool It," he said.

"What's the Cool It?" Thomas said.

"A club," said Saxon.

"Never heard of it."

"In the docks," said Saxon.

"The docks?"

Saxon in the docks! The liaison committees in the docks! Saxon in low life! Saxon a libertine!

"What on earth takes you to the docks? Research? Come clean. Having fun?"

In our repentance, we made a hero of him. The old sly Saxon, pleased and pink, was with us again.

"In principle, yes," said Saxon. "I sometimes go with the Dustman."

We could not speak. Saxon and the Dustman in the docks!

"What is it—a cellar?"

"It's a sewer," said Saxon complacently. "Tessa goes there with her father."

"The Dustman takes his daughter to a place like that!"

"He says it will loosen her up," said Saxon, looking for hope in our eyes. "You see he wants her to get married."

Saxon settled back, impudently, comfortably, in the chair. The brocade enriched him and he maliciously considered us one by one.

"To a stoker?" said Selby.

"No," said Saxon. "To me—in principle. That's why I go down there. You see, she's worried about him. We go down to see he doesn't get into trouble. I had to pull him out of a nasty fight last week. We got him out. We got him home. To her place. He hates going to his."

The notion of Saxon fighting was as startling as his dance.

"She must be very grateful to you," we said politely.

"Why do you say 'marry in principle?'" said Selby.

"He means," Mrs. Selby explained sharply to her husband, disliking the mockery, "the Dustman is her oldest friend, older even than Saxon is. Isn't that so, Saxon?"

"In practice, yes," said Saxon, entirely forgiving her. "I'll go and have another look for them. They promised to come. The Dustman said it would be awfully nice to see us all again. I'll just go and see."

And he got up and trotted across the yards of hotel carpet that had a pattern of enormous roses. It seemed that their petals were caressing him on his way to the door. The door spun round and Saxon vanished.

Our wives said: "What a sad story!" and "What a bitch that girl is." But we thought: "Good old Saxon." And "He's suffering for us." Selby put it crudely saying: "That lets us off the hooks." And then our feelings changed. There was Saxon sitting like a committee on his own feelings, delegating them incurably to sub-committees, and sitting back doing nothing, relying on an amendment. He must have been doing this for the last eight years. But this led us to another feeling. *We* would never have behaved as Saxon behaved. Each of us saw that beautiful girl in our minds and thought we would have soon pulled her out of this ridiculous obsession with the Dustman and his low life. And how often we had heard of coquettes like Tessa settling down at last in their thirties with faithful bores like Saxon, men they had snubbed over and over again before that alarming age caught them out.

We kept our eyes on the main door of the hotel and were so fixed on it that we did not notice, at once, a figure crossing the dance floor at our side and looking in at us.

"Well!" we heard Tessa's slow, only too well-known voice, dwelling raffishly on the word so that it meant "What are you up to? You didn't think you could keep me out of this." Her large solemn eyes, as forcefully short-sighted as Saxon's were, put their warning innuendo to each of us in turn and the mouth of a beautiful Persian cat possessed us one by one. The spell was on us. A comfortable mew to each of our wives indicated that she had known us years before they had.

We were nearly screaming for help. It was for Thomas, the rescuer, to save us.

"Saxon has just gone out looking for your father."

She was up from her chair at once and making for the main door. She had fine legs, a fast passionate step, and Mrs. Selby said of her dress:

"It's expensive, but pink is hopeless if you're putting on weight."

But Selby, over-eager for any hope that could be got out of the situation, said:

"Did you see her when she came in? It was exactly like Saxon. Hunting. You know—in principle yes, but in practice—well. She's a liaison too. I think the Dustman's loosened her up and found the man for her."

But no one paid much attention to Selby for the swing doors flashed and across the hall came the Dustman, Saxon and Tessa together.

"Look, daddy," she said to the old man. He had not, of course, changed into a dinner-jacket and his tweed jacket was done up on the wrong button. His trudging step, I now thought, was not so much a trudge as a scraping caused by the probability that he was swinging by an invisible rope hooked to the seat of his learned trousers.

"Look," she said, "all my oldest friends!"

And Saxon stood apart with his hands on his hips, watching, his legs apart, keeping goal, wistful, admiring, triumphant.

"Who's dancing?" piped the old man. And soon all of us were on the floor, the Dustman shoving Mrs. Selby along as if to her doom, and Tessa following him with her eyes all the time, as Saxon leapt into his passionate, dreadful and unavailing antics all round her. Once in a while she would note where he was, open her mouth to say something pleasant, and then coldly change her mind.

ON THE EDGE OF THE CLIFF

The sea fog began to lift towards noon. It had been blowing in, thin and loose for two days, smudging the tops of the trees up the ravine where the house stood. "Like the cold breath of old men," Rowena wrote in an attempt at a poem, but changed the line, out of kindness, to "the breath of ghosts," because Harry might take it personally. The truth was that his breath was not foggy at all, but smelt of the dozens of cigarettes he smoked all day. He would walk about, taking little steps, with his hand outstretched, tapping the ash off as he talked. This gave an abstracted searching elegance which his heavy face and long sentences needed. In her dressing gown Rowena went to his room. His glasses were off and he had finished shaving and he turned a face savaged to the point of saintliness by age, but with a heavy underlip that made him look helplessly brutal. She laughed at the soap in his ears.

"The ghosts have gone," she said poetically. "We can go to Withy Hole! I'll drive by the Guilleth road, there's a fair there. They'll tell our fortunes."

"Dull place," he said. "It used to be full of witches in the sixteenth century."

"I'm a witch," she said. "I want to go to the fair. I saw the poster. It starts today."

"We'll go," he said, suspicious, but giving in.

He was seventyish, and with a young girl of twenty-five one had, of course, to pretend to be suspicious. There are rules for old men who are in love with young girls, all the stricter when the young girls are in love with them. It has to be played as a game.

"The sea pinks will be out on the cliffs," he said.

"You old botanist!" she said.

He was about to say "I know that" and go on to say that girls were like flowers with voices and that he had spent a lot of his life collecting both, but he had said these things to her often before and at his age one had to avoid repeating oneself, if possible. Anyway, it was more effective as a compliment when other people were there and they would turn to look at her. When young girls turned into women they lost his interest: he had always lived for reverie.

"So it's settled," she said.

Now he looked tragic as he gazed at her. Waving his razor, he began his nervous trick of taking a few dance-like steps and she gave him one of her light hugs and ran out of the room.

What with his organising fusses and her habit of vanishing to do something to a drawing she was working on, the start was late.

"We'll have to eat something," she said, giving an order.

But it was his house, not hers. He'd lived alone long enough not to be able to stand a woman in his kitchen, could not bear to see her cut a loaf or muddle the knives and forks or choke the sink with tea leaves.

"Rowena and I," he said to people who came to see them, in his military voice, "eat very little. We see no one."

This was not true, but like a general with a literary turn, he organised his imagination. He was much guided by literature. His wife had gone mad and had killed herself. So in the house he saw himself as a Mr. Rochester, or in the car as Count Mosca with the young duchess in *La Chartreuse de Parme*; if they met people, as Tolstoy's worldly aunt. This was another game: it educated the girl.

While he fussed between the kitchen and the room they ate in, she came down late and idled, throwing back her long black hair, lassoing him with smiles and side glances thrown out and rushed at him while he had a butter plate in his hand and gave him another of her light engulfing hugs and laughed at the plate he waved in the air.

"Rowena!" he shouted, for she had gone off again. "Get the car out."

The house was halfway up the long ravine, backed and faced by an army of ash trees and beeches. There was the terrace and the ingenious steep garden and the plants that occupied him most of the day, and down from the terrace he had had to cut the twenty or thirty steps himself, heaving his pickaxe. Rowena had watched his thick stack of coarse grey hair and his really rather brutal face and his pushed-out lips, as he hacked and the pick hit the stones. He worked with such anger and pride, but he looked up at her sometimes with appealing, brilliant eyes. His furious ancient's face contained pain naturally.

She knew he hated to be told to be careful when he came down the steps. She knew the ceremony of getting him into the car, for he was a tall, angular man and had to fold himself in, his knees nearly touching his chin, to which the long deep despondent lines of his face ran heavily down. It was exciting for her to drive the old man dangerously fast down the long circling lane through the trees, to show how dangerous she could be, while he talked. He would talk nonstop for the next hour, beginning, of course, with the country fair.

"It's no good. Plastic, like cheap food. Not worth seeing. The twentieth century has packaged everything."

And he was on to the pre-Roman times, the ancient spirit of carnival, Celtic gods and devils, as they drove out of the ravine into deep lanes, where he could name the ferns in the stone walls, and the twisting hills and corners that shook the teeth and the spine. Historical instances poured out of him. He was, she said, Old Father Time himself, but he did not take that as a joke, though he humoured her with a small laugh. It was part of the game. He was not Father Time, for in one's seventies, one is a miser of time, putting it by, hiding the minutes, while she spent fast, not knowing she was living in time at all.

Guilleth was a dull, dusty, Methodistical little town with geraniums in the windows of the houses. Sammy's Fair was in a rough field just outside it, where dogs and children ran about. There was only one shooting gallery; they were still putting up the back canvas of the coconut shy. There were hoopla stalls, a lot of shouting and few customers. But the small roundabout gave out its engine whistle and the children packed the vulgar circle of spotted cows with huge pink udders, the rocking horses, the pigs, the tigers and a pair of giraffes.

The professor regarded it as a cultural pathos. He feared Rowena. She was quite childishly cruel to him. With a beautiful arrogance that mocked him, she got out of the car and headed for ice cream. He had to head her off the goldfish in their bowls. She'd probably want to bring one home.

"Give me some money," she said, going to the roundabout. There was a small crowd near that. "I'm going on the giraffe. Come on."

"I'll watch you," he complained and cleaned his glasses.

There she was, riding a giraffe already, tall and like a schoolmistress among the town children, with her long hair, which she kept on throwing back as she whirled round, a young miracle, getting younger and younger. There were other girls. There were town youths and there was an idiotic young man riding backwards on a cow, kicking out his legs and every now and then waving to the crowd. Rowena on her giraffe did not smile, but as she came round sedately, waved to the old man as she sailed by.

He looked at his watch. How much longer?

"I'm going on again," she called, and did not get off.

He found himself absurdly among the other patient watchers, older than all, better dressed too, on his dignity, all curiosity gone. He moved away to separate himself from his bunch of them, but he had the impression they all moved with him. There was a young woman in a bright-red coat who always seemed to be in the next bunch he joined. Round came the giraffe: round came the young man on the cow. The young woman in red waved. Seeing that to wave was the correct thing, the old man too waved at the giraffe. The woman waved again a moment later and stared at him as if annoyed. He moved a yard from her, then five yards, then to the other side of the roundabout. Here he could wave without being conspicuous, yet the woman was standing close to him once more. She was small with reddish hair, her chin up, looking at him.

"You don't remember me," she accused him in a high voice. Her small eyes were impudent. He stepped back, gaping.

"Daisy Pyke," she said.

Pyke? Pyke? He gaped at her briefly, his mind was sailing round with Rowena.

"George's wife," she said, challenging his stupidity.

"George . . ." But he stopped. George Pyke's wife must be fifty by now. This woman could not be more than thirty. Her daughter—had they had a daughter?

"Have I changed as much as that?" she said. Her manner was urchin-like and she grinned with pleasure at his confusion and then her mouth drooped at the corners plaintively, begging. Nowadays he thought only of Rowena's wide mouth, which made all other women vague to him. And then the hard little begging, pushing mouth and its high voice broke into his memory. He stepped back with embarrassment and a short stare of horror which he covered quickly, his feet dancing a few steps, and saying with foolish smiles, "Daisy! I thought . . . I was watching that thing. What are you doing here?"

Now that he remembered, he could not conceal a note of indignation and he stood still, his eyes peered coldly. He could see this had its effect on her.

"The same as you," she said in that curt off-hand voice. "Waiting. Waiting for them to come off." And she turned away from him, offended, waved wildly at the roundabout and shouted, "Stephen, you fool!" The young man riding backwards on the cow waved back and shouted to her.

What an appalling thing! But there it is—one must expect it when one is old: the map in one's head, indeed the literal map of the country empties and loses its contours, towns and villages, and people sink out of sight. The protective faces of friends vanish and one is suddenly alone, naked and exposed. The population ranked between oneself and old enemies suddenly dissolves and the enemy stands before one. Daisy Pyke!

The old man could not get away. He said as politely as he could manage, "I thought you went abroad. How is George?"

"We did. George," she said, "died in Spain." And added briskly, "On a golf course."

"I'm sorry. I didn't know."

She looked back at the roundabout and turned again to say to him, "I know all about you. You've got a new house at Colfe. I've still got the old house, though actually it's let."

Forty miles lay between Colfe and Daisy Pyke—but no people in between! Now the roundabout stopped. There was a scramble of children getting on and getting off, and the local watchers moved forward too.

"I must get Rowena," he said ruthlessly and he hurried off, calling out in his peremptory voice, "Rowena!"

He knew that Daisy Pyke was watching him as he held out a hand to help Rowena off, but Rowena ignored it and jumped off herself.

"Rowena. We must go."

"Why? It was lovely. Did you see that ridiculous young man?"

"No, Rowena," he said. "Where?"

"Over there," she said, "with the girl in red, the one you were chatting up, you old rip. I saw you!" She laughed and took his arm. "You're blushing."

"She's not a girl," he said. "She's a woman I used to know in London twenty years ago. It was rather awful! I didn't recognise her. I used to know her husband. She used to be a friend of Violet's."

"Violet's!" said Rowena. "But you *must* introduce me." She was always eager to know, as if to possess, everyone he had ever known, to have all of him, even the dead. Above all Violet, his wife. Rowena longed to be as old as that dead woman.

"Really, Harry, you are frightful with people."

"Oh, well . . . But she's appalling. We had a terrible row."

"One of your old loves," she teased.

"I had to throw her out of the house," he said. "She's a liar."

"Then I *must* see her," said Rowena. "How thrilling."

"I think they've gone," he said.

"No," said Rowena. "There they are. Take me over."

And she pulled him towards the hoopla stall where Daisy Pyke and the young man were standing. There lay the delightfulness of Rowena: she freed him from the boredom into which his memories had set and hardened. He had known many young girls who in this situation would be eagerly storing opportunities for jealousy of his past life. Rowena was not like that.

At the stall, with its cunningly arranged bowls, jugs, and toys, the young man with the yellow curling hair was pitching rings onto the table, telling Daisy to try and altering the angle of the ring in her hand.

"Choose what you want, hold the ring level and lightly, don't skim fast. Don't bowl it like that! Like this."

Daisy's boldness had gone. She was fond and serious, glancing at the young man before she threw.

"Daisy," said the old man, putting on a shady and formal manner as if he were at a party, "I have brought Rowena to meet you."

And Rowena stepped forward gushingly. "How d'you do! I was telling Harry about the young man on the cow."

"Here he is," said Daisy stiffly. "Stephen!"

The young man turned and said "Hello" and went on throwing rings. "Like that," he said.

Rowena watched him mockingly.

"We are just off," said Harry.

"I've heard a lot about you," said Daisy to Rowena.

"We're going to walk along the cliffs," said Harry.

"To Withy Hole," said Rowena.

"It was extraordinary meeting you here," said Harry.

"Perhaps," said Daisy, "we'll meet again."

"Oh, well—you know we hardly see anyone now," said Harry.

Daisy studied Rowena impudently and she laughed at the boy, who had failed again.

"I won a goldfish once," said Rowena, laughing. "It died on the way home."

"Extraordinary," the old man said as he and Rowena walked away. "That must be George's son, but taller. George was short."

When she got him back into the car she saw by his leaden look that the subject was closed. She had met one more of his friends—that was the main thing.

The hills seemed to pile up and the sea to get farther and farther away and then, suddenly, as they got over the last long hill, they passed the caravan sites that were empty at this time of the year and looked like those flat white Andalusian towns he remembered, from a distance. The old man was saying, "But we have this new rootless civilisation, anarchic but standardised"—suddenly the sea appeared between the dunes below, not grey and choppy, but deep blue, all candour, like a young mouth, between the dunes and beyond it, wide and still and sleepily serene. The old man was suddenly in command, fussing about the exact place where they could leave the car, struggling over the sand dunes dotted with last year's litter, on to the huge cliffs. At the top there they could look back and see on the wide bay the shallow sea breaking idly, in changing lines of surf, like lips speaking lines that broke unfinished and could not be heard. A long way off a dozen surfers were wading out, deeper and deeper, towards the bigger waves as if they were leaving the land for good and might be trying to reach the horizon. Rowena stopped to gaze at them, waiting for one of them to come in on a long glissade, but the old man urged her on to the close turf of the cliffs. That is what he had come for: boundlessness, distance. For thirty miles on a clear day in May like this, one could walk without meeting a soul, from headland to headland, gazing through the hum of the wind and under the cries of the dashing gulls, at what seemed to be an unending procession of fading promontories, each dropping to its sandy cove, yet still riding out into the water. The wind did not move the old man's tough thatch of hair but made his big ears stick out. Rowena bound her loose hair with a scarf. From low cliff to high cliff, over the cropped turf, which was like a carpet, where the millions of sea pinks and daisies were scattered, mile after mile in their colonies, the old man led the way, digging his knees into the air, gesticulating, talking, pointing to a kestrel above or a cormorant black as soot on a rock, while she followed lazily yards behind him. He stopped impatiently to show her some small cushioned plant or stood on the cliff's edge, like a prophet, pointing down to the falls of rock, the canyons, caverns, and tunnels into which the green water poured in black and was sucked out into green again and spilled in waterfalls down the outer rocks. The old man was a strong walker, bending to it, but when he stopped he straightened, and Rowena smiled at his air of detachment as he gazed at distant things as if he knew them. To her he looked like a frightening mixture of pagan saint and toiling animal. They would rest at the crest of a black cliff for a few minutes, feel the sun burn their skin, and then on they went.

"We can't see the bay any more," she said. She was thinking of the surf-riders.

"The cliff after the next is the Hole," he said and pulled her to her feet.

"Yes, the Hole," she said.

He had a kind of mania about the Hole. This was the walk he liked best and so did she, except for that ugly final horror. The sea had tunnelled under the rock in several places along this wild coast and had sucked out enormous slaty craters fifty yards across and this one a hundred and eighty feet deep, so that even at the edge one could not see the water pouring in. One stood listening for the bump of hidden water on a quiet day: on wild ones it seethed in the bottom of the pot. The place terrified Rowena and she held back, but he stumbled through the rough grasses to the edge, calling back bits of geology and navigation—and to amuse her, explained how smugglers had had to wait for the low wave to take them in.

Now, once more, they were looking at the great meaningless wound. As he stood at the edge he seemed to her to be at one with it. It reminded her of his mouth when she had once seen it (with a horror she tried to wipe from her mind) before he had put his dentures in. Of her father's too.

Well, the objective was achieved. They found a bank on the seaward side out of the wind where the sun burned and they rested.

"Heaven," she said and closed her eyes.

They sat in silence for a long time but he gazed at the rising floor of eventless water. Far out, from time to time, in some small eddy of the wind, little families of whitecaps would appear. They were like faces popping up or perhaps white hands shooting out and disappearing pointlessly. Yes, they were the pointless dead.

"What are you thinking about?" she asked without opening her eyes.

He was going to say "At my age one is always thinking about death," but he said "You."

"What about me?" she said with that shamelessness of girls.

"Your ears," he said.

"You are a liar," she said. "You're thinking about Daisy Pyke."

"Not now," he said.

"But you must be," she said. She pointed. "Isn't the cove just below where you all used to bathe with nothing on? Did she come?"

"Round the corner," he said, correcting her. "Violet and I used to bathe there. Everyone came. Daisy came once when George was on the golf course. She swam up and down, hour after hour, as cold as a fish. Hopeless on dry land. Gordon and Vera came, but Daisy only once. She didn't fit in—very conventional—sat telling dirty stories. Then she went swimming, to clean up. George was playing golf all day and bridge all evening; that didn't go down well. They had a dartboard in their house: the target was a naked woman. A pretty awful, jokey couple. You can guess the bull's-eye."

"What was this row?" she said.

"She told lies," he said, turning to her. And he said this with a hiss of finality which she knew. She waited for one of his stories, but it did not come.

"I want to swim in the cove," said Rowena.

"It's too cold this time of the year," he said.

"I want to go," she said.

"It's a long way down and hard coming back."

"Yes, but I want to go—where you all used to go."

She was obstinate about this, and of course he liked that.

"All right," he said, getting up. Like all girls she wanted to leave her mark on places. He noticed how she was impelled to touch pictures in galleries when he had taken her to Italy. Ownership! Power! He used to dislike that but now he did not; the change was a symptom of his adoration of her. And she did want to go. She did want to assert her presence on that empty sand, to make the sand feel her mark.

They scrambled the long way down the rocks until the torn cliffs were gigantic above them. On the smooth sand she ran barefoot to the edge of the sea rippling in.

"It's ice!" she screamed.

He stood there, hunched. There was a litter of last year's rags and cartons near the rocks. Summer crowds now swarmed into the place, which had been secret. He glowered with anger at the debris.

"I'm going to pee," he said.

She watched the sea, for he was a long time gone.

"That was a big one," she shouted.

But he was not there. He was out on the rocks, he had pulled off his clothes. He was standing there, his body furred with grey hair, his belly wrinkled, his thighs shrunk. Up went his bony arms.

"You're not to! It will kill you! Your heart!" she shouted.

He gave a wicked laugh, she saw his yellow teeth, and in he dived and was crawling and shouting in the water as he swam out farther, defying her, threshing the water, and then as she screamed at him, really frightened, he came crawling in like some ugly hairy sea animal, his skin reddened with cold, and stood dripping with his arms wide as if he was going to give a howl. He climbed over the rocks and back to the sand and got his clothes and was drying himself with his shirt.

"You're mad," she said. "You're not to put that wet thing on."

"It will dry in this sun," he said.

"What was all that for?" she said. "Did you find her?"

"Who?" he said, looking round in bewilderment. He had dived in boastfully and in a kind of rage, a rage against time, a rage against Daisy Pyke too. He did not answer, but looked at her with a glint of shrewdness in his eyes. She was flattered by the glitter in this look from a sometimes terrifying old man.

He was tired now and they took the short inland road to the car close to those awful caravans, and when she got him into the car again he fell asleep and snorted. He went to his room early but could not sleep; he had broken one of his rules for old men. For the first time he had let her see him naked. He was astounded when she came into his room and got into his bed: she had not done this before. "I've come to see the Ancient Mariner," she said.

———

How marvellous. She is jealous, after all. She loves me, he went about saying to himself in the next weeks. She drove to what they called "our town" to buy cakes. "I am so thin," she said.

The first time she returned saying she had seen his "dear friend Daisy." She was in the supermarket.

"What's she doing there?" he said. "She lives forty miles away. What did she say?"

"We did not speak. I mean, I don't think she saw me. Her son was with her. He said hello. He'd got the hood of the car up. She came out and gave me a nod—I don't think she likes me," she said with satisfaction.

The next week she went again to get petrol. The old man stayed at the house, shook one or two mats, and swept the sitting-room floor. It was his house and Rowena was untidy. Then he sat on the terrace, listening for her car, anxiously.

Presently he picked up the sound, much earlier than her usual time, and saw the distant glint in the trees as the car wound its way up. There she was, threading her beauty through the trees. He heard with alarm the sudden silences of the car at some turn in the hill, then heard it getting louder as it turned a corner, then passing into silence again. He put his book down and went inside in a dutiful panic to put the kettle on, and while he waited for it to boil he took the cups out pedantically, one by one, to the table on the terrace and stood listening again. Now it was on the last stretch, now he heard a crackling of wheels below. He ran in to heat the teapot and ran out with his usual phrase: "Did you get what you wanted?"

Then, puffing up the last steps, she came. But it was not she; it was a small woman, bare-legged and in sandals, with a swaggering urchin grin on her face, pulling a scarf off her head. Daisy!

"Gosh!" she said.

Harry skipped back a yard and stood, straightening and forbidding. "Daisy!" he said, annoyed, as if waving her off.

"Those steps! Harry!" she said. "Gosh, what a view."

She gave a dry dismissive laugh at it. She had, he remembered, always defied what she saw. The day when he had seen her at the fair seemed to slide away under his feet and years slid by, after that, following that day.

"What—" he began. Then in his military way, he jerked out, "Rowena's gone into town. I am waiting for her."

"I know," said Daisy. "Can I sit down and get my breath? I know. I saw her." And with a plotting satisfaction: "Not to speak to. She passed me. Ah, that's better."

"We never see people," said Harry sternly. "You see I am working. If the telephone rings, we don't answer it."

"The same with us. I hope I'm not interrupting. I thought—I'll dash up, just for a minute."

"And Rowena has her work . . ." he said. Daisy was always an interrupter.

"I gave you a surprise," said Daisy comfortably. "She is lovely. That's why I came. You're lucky—how d'you do it? Where did you find her? And what a place you've got here! I made Stephen go and see his friends. It was such a long time—years, isn't it? I had to come. You haven't changed, you know. But you didn't recognise me, did you? You were trying not to see me, weren't you?"

Her eyes and her nose were small. She is at her old game of shock tactics, he thought. He looked blankly at her.

"I explained that," he said nervously. "I must go and turn the kettle off," he said. He paused to listen for Rowena's car, but there was no sound.

"Well," she said. "There you are. Time goes on."

When he came back with a teapot and another cup, she said, "I knew you wouldn't come and see me, so I came to see you. Let me see," she said and took off the scarf from her head. "I told you George died, didn't I? Of course I did," she said briskly.

"Yes."

"Well . . ." she said. "Harry, I had to see you. You are the only wise man I know." She looked nervously at the garden and across to the army of trees stacked on the hill and then turned to him. "You're happy and I am happy, Harry. I didn't come to make a scene and drag it all up. I was in love with you, that was the trouble, but I'm not now. I was wrong about you, about you and Violet. I couldn't bear to see her suffer. I was out of my mind. I couldn't bear to see you grieving for her. I soon knew what it was when poor George died. Harry, I just don't want you to hate me any more. I mean, you're not still furious, are you? We do change. The past is past."

The little liar, he thought. What has she come up here for? To cause trouble between himself and Rowena as she had tried to do with his wife and himself. He remembered Daisy's favourite word: honesty. She was trying for some reason to confuse him about things he had settled a long time ago in his mind.

He changed the subject. "What is—"—he frowned—"I'm sorry, I can't remember names nowadays—your son doing?"

She was quick to notice the change, he saw. Nothing ever escaped Daisy.

"Oh, Tommy, the ridiculous Tommy. He's in Africa," she said, merrily dismissing him. "Well, it was better for him—problems. I'm a problem to him—George was so jealous too."

"He looks exactly like George," Harry said. "Taller, of course, the curly hair."

"What are you talking about? You haven't seen him since he was four." She laughed.

"Don't be stupid, Daisy, we saw him last week at that—what is the name of the place?—at the fair."

The blood went from Daisy's face. She raised her chin. "That's a nasty one," she said and gave her head a fierce shake. "You meant it to, didn't you? That was Stephen. I thought you'd be the last to think a thing like that, with your Rowena. I expect people say it and I don't care and if anyone said it to him he wouldn't know what they were talking about. Stephen's my lover."

The old sentimental wheedling Daisy was in the coy smile that quickly followed her sharpness. "He's mad about me," she said. "I may be old enough to be his mother, but he's sick of squealing, sulky girls of seventeen. If we had met years ago, he would have hated me. Seriously, Harry, I'd go down on my knees to him."

"I am sorry—I—that's why I didn't recognise you. You can ask Rowena. I said to her, 'That's Daisy Pyke's daughter,'" Harry said, "when I saw you."

Daisy gaped at him and slowly, her lips curled up with delight. "Oh, good! Is that true? Is it? You always told the truth. You really thought that! Thank you, Harry, that's the nicest thing you ever said to me. I love you for it."

She leaned forward, appealing to him quietly.

"George never slept with me for seven years before he died. Don't ask me about it, but that's the truth. I'd forgotten what it was. When Stephen asked me I thought it was an insult—you know, all this rape about. I got into the car and slammed the door in his face and left him on the road—well, not on the road, but wherever it was—and drove off. I looked back. He was still standing there. Well, I mean, at my age! That next day—*you* know what it is with women better than anyone— I was in such a mood. When I got back to the house I shouted for George, howled for him to come back and poured myself a tumblerful of whisky and wandered about the house slopping it on the carpet." She laughed. "George would have killed me for *that* if he had come— and I went out into the garden and there was Stephen, you won't believe it, walking bold as brass up from the gate. He came up quickly and just took the glass from me very politely—the stuff was pouring down my dress—and put it on the grass and he wiped my blouse. That's what did it."

She paused thoughtfully and frowned. "Not there," she said prudishly, "not at the house, of course. I wanted to get away from it. I can't bear it. We went to the caravan camp. That's where he was living. I don't know why I'm telling you this. I mean, there's a lot more."

She paused. "Love is something at our age, isn't it? I mean, when I saw you and Rowena at Guilleth—I thought I must go and talk to you. Being in the same boat."

"We're not," he said, annoyed. "I am twenty years older than you."

"Thirty, if you don't mind," she said, opening her bag and looking into her mirror. When she had put it away with a snap she looked over the flowers in the steep garden to the woods. She was listening for the sound of a car. He realised he had stopped listening for it. He found himself enjoying this hour, despite his suspicions of her. It drove away the terrors that seemed to dissolve even the trees of the ravine. With women, nature returned to its place, the trees became real trees. One lived in a long moment in which time had stopped. He did not care for Daisy, but she had that power of enticement which lay in stirring one with the illusion that she was defying one to put her right. With Rowena he had thrown away his vanity; with Daisy it returned.

"Where did you and Rowena go the day we saw you?" she asked suddenly.

"Along the cliffs," he said.

"You didn't go to the cove, did you? It's a long way. And you can't swim at this time of the year."

"We went to the cove and I *did* swim," he said. "I wouldn't let Rowena."

"I should hope not! You don't forget old times, do you?" She laughed coolly. "I hope you didn't tell Rowena—young girls can be so jealous. I *was*—d'you remember? Gosh, I'm glad I'm not young still, aren't you?"

"Stop being so romantic, Daisy," said the old man.

"Oh, I'm not romantic any more," she said. "It doesn't pay else one would pity *them*, Rowena and Stephen. So you did go to the cove—did you think of me?"

"I only think of death now," he said.

"You always were an interesting man, the type that goes on to his nineties, like they do now," she said. "I never think about it. Stephen would have a fit. He doesn't even know what he's going to do. Last week he thought he'd be a beach guard. Or teach tennis. Or a singer! He was surfing on the beach when I first saw him. He was living at the camp."

She paused, offended. "Did you know they switch off the electric light at ten o'clock at the office in those places? No one protests. Like sheep. It would make me furious to be treated like that. You could hear everyone snoring at once. Not that we joined in, I must say. Actually, we're staying in his mother's house now, the bunks are too narrow in those caravans, but she's come back. So we're looking for something— I've let my house. The money is useful."

The old man was alarmed. He was still trying to make out the real reason for her visit. He remembered the old Daisy—there was always a hidden motive, something she was trying out. And he started listening urgently again for Rowena's car. I know what it is, he thought; she wants to move in here!

"I'm afraid it would be impossible to have you here," he said.

"Here, Harry?" she said, astonished. "None of that! That's not what I came for. Anyway," she said archly, "I wouldn't trust you."

But she considered the windows and the doors of the house and then the view. She gave a business-like sniff and said seriously, "You can't keep her a prisoner here. It won't last."

"Rowena is not a prisoner. She can come and go when she likes. We understand that."

"It depends what you mean by coming and going," said Daisy shrewdly. "You mean you are the prisoner. That is it! So am I!"

"Oh," said Harry. "Love is always like that. I live only for her."

"That is it! I will tell you why I came to see you, Harry. When I saw Rowena in town I kept out of her way. You won't believe it—I can be tactful."

She became very serious. "Because I don't want us to meet again." It was an open declaration. "I mean not see you for a long time, I mean all of us. You see, Rowena is so beautiful and Stephen—well, you've seen him. You and I would start talking about old times and people, and they'd be left out and drawn together—now, wouldn't they? I just couldn't bear to see him talking to her, looking at her. I wish we had not met down at the fair. It's all right now, he's with his surfing friends, but you understand?"

She got up and said, "I mean it, Harry. I know what would happen and so do you and I don't want to *see* it happen."

She went up to him because he had stood up and she tapped him hard on the chest with her firm bold finger. He could feel it on his skin, a determined blow, after she had stepped away.

"I know it can't last," she said. "And you know it can't. But I don't want *you* to see it happen," she said in her old hard taunting style. "We never really use your town anyway. I'll see *he* doesn't. Give me your word. We've got to do this for each other. We've managed quite well all these years, haven't we? And it's not saying we'll *never* meet someday, is it?"

"You're a bitch, Daisy," he said, and he smiled.

"Yes, I'm a bitch still, Harry," she said. "But I'm not a fool."

She put out her hand again and he feared she was going to dig that hard finger in his chest again, but she didn't. She tied her scarf round her hair. "If anything happened I'd throw myself down Withy Hole."

"Stop being so melodramatic, Daisy," he said.

"Well, I don't want you conniving," she said coarsely. "I don't want any of your little arrangements."

And she turned to the ravine and listened. "Car coming up," she said.

"Rowena," he said.

"I'll be off. Remember."

"Be careful at the turns," he said helplessly. "She drives fast. You'll pass her on the road."

They did not kiss or even shake hands. He listened to her cursing the steps as she went down and calling out, "I bet you dug out these bloody steps yourself."

He listened to the two cars whining their way towards each other as they circled below, now Rowena's car glinted, now Daisy's. At last Rowena's slowed down at the steps, spitting stones.

Rowena came up and said, "I've just passed Daisy on the road."

"Yes, she's been here. What a tale!"

She looked at the empty cups. "And you didn't give your dearest friend any tea, you wretch."

"Oh, tea—no—er—she didn't want any," he stammered.

"As gripping as all that, was it?" she laughed.

"Very," he said. "She's talking of marrying that young man. Stephen's not her son."

"You can't mean that," she said, putting on a very proper air. "She's old enough—" but she stopped, and instead of giving him one of her light hugs, she rumpled his hair. "People do confide in you, I must say," she said. "I don't think I like her coming up here. Tell me what she said."

A NOTE ON THE TYPE

The principal text of this Modern Library edition
was set in a digitized version of Janson, a typeface that
dates from about 1690 and was cut by Nicholas Kis,
a Hungarian working in Amsterdam. The original matrices have
survived and are held by the Stempel foundry in Germany.
Hermann Zapf redesigned some of the weights and sizes for
Stempel, basing his revisions on the original design.

Modern Library is online at
www.modernlibrary.com

MODERN LIBRARY ONLINE IS YOUR GUIDE
TO CLASSIC LITERATURE ON THE WEB

THE MODERN LIBRARY E-NEWSLETTER

Our free e-mail newsletter is sent to subscribers, and features sample chapters, interviews with and essays by our authors, upcoming books, special promotions, announcements, and news.

To subscribe to the Modern Library e-newsletter, send a blank e-mail to: **sub_modernlibrary@info.randomhouse.com** or visit **www.modernlibrary.com**

THE MODERN LIBRARY WEBSITE

Check out the Modern Library website at
www.modernlibrary.com for:

- The Modern Library e-newsletter
- A list of our current and upcoming titles and series
- Reading Group Guides and exclusive author spotlights
- Special features with information on the classics and other paperback series
- Excerpts from new releases and other titles
- A list of our e-books and information on where to buy them
- The Modern Library Editorial Board's 100 Best Novels and 100 Best Nonfiction Books of the Twentieth Century written in the English language
- News and announcements

Questions? E-mail us at **modernlibrary@randomhouse.com**
For questions about examination or desk copies, please visit
the Random House Academic Resources site at
www.randomhouse.com/academic

Printed in the United States
by Baker & Taylor Publisher Services